THE SPIRIT BINDS

ELEMENTAL ACADEMY BOOK 5

D.K. HOLMBERG

Copyright © 2019 by D.K. Holmberg

All rights reserved.

No part of this book may be reproduced in any form or by any electronic or mechanical means, including information storage and retrieval systems, without written permission from the author, except for the use of brief quotations in a book review.

If you want to be notified when D.K. Holmberg's next novel is released and get a few free books and occasional other promotions, please sign up for his mailing list by going here. Your email address will never be shared and you can unsubscribe at any time.

www.dkholmberg.com

1

THE LIBRARY WAS SUPPOSED TO BE QUIET AND WAS MEANT to be a place of solitude, a place of scholarship and study. These days, Tolan Ethar found it provided anything but solitude. Part of that had to do with the lack of master librarians around the library, which meant the students were more rambunctious. There were always two librarians at any given time. They took shifts, sitting up on the dais, working diligently on whatever project they were immersed in. In all that time, they managed to remain mostly silent, reserved even, but they kept noise to a minimum.

At least, that had always been Tolan's impression. In the last few weeks, he'd changed that impression. Part of it had to do with the fact he'd been studying with them—and Master Minden in particular. She had been working with him, and it had been detracting him from his scheduled studies, but at the same time, she'd also been adding to his studies and knowledge.

He looked up from the book he was working through, rubbing his eyes. Trying to decipher the ancient language was causing him to grow tired. There were many different works, in many different languages, and Tolan struggled to interpret the ones Master Minden had brought him. Many of them were so old, he struggled to even make out the ink on the page, regardless of the shaping used upon the books to preserve them.

Looking around the library, he realized the source of his agitation. A couple of first-level students sat near the door, talking more loudly than they should have been. He glared at them but doubted his glare did anything to dissuade them. What he needed was one of the master librarians to approach them, but where were they?

The dais was empty today. That wasn't completely uncommon, though it was uncommon when there were this many people in the library. Typically, the librarians preferred to keep visible when they had a considerable number of students in the library. When it was emptier, that was the time the librarians thought it was safer to wander, to roam about and either re-shelve books or occasionally, they'd be found sitting at some of the student desks while reading.

Maybe he was overreacting. He was still only a second-level student, despite the fact he had participated in so many events at the Academy in his time here. What authority did he really have?

None, but that didn't change a certain sense of ownership he had developed when it came to the library. Partly, that stemmed from knowing quite a bit of peace here in the short time he'd been studying at the Academy. Partly that had to do with his growing sense of responsibility when it came to the library itself.

Turning his attention back to Master Minden's books, he tried to focus on the words on the pages, but it was difficult. The voices were boisterous and loud, obnoxious in how they disrupted—and distracted—him.

Swearing to himself, he debated whether or not he should get up and say something. It really wasn't his place, and as he was still only a second-level student, not elevated nearly as highly as he needed to be in order to feel a sense of comfort when it came to disciplining others in the library, he wasn't sure he should be the one to intervene.

Besides, his saying something would only serve to worsen some of the conversation around the Academy about him. Already there was enough. Not only had he come to the Academy as someone with no shaping ability —something that had changed in the time he'd been here —but he'd also been through an Inquisition. Because of that, he had become somewhat notorious, and not for good reasons.

When the voices picked up again, and when there was no sign of either of the librarians who had been here when Tolan had arrived, he got to his feet and made his way toward the table.

Five students sat around the table. He recognized two of them as Velthan's lackeys but didn't know either of their names. There weren't too many of the first-level students he knew by name, which was probably something he should know. Given how often he had to interact with the first-level students, it would be good for him to get to know them a little bit better than he did.

He cleared his throat as he approached. They all looked up at him, and one of Velthan's two lackeys grinned.

He had high cheekbones and his wavy hair was neatly brushed, giving him an almost regal appearance. "Ethar. What are you—"

Tolan leaned close. "There's a protocol in the library. Even if the librarians aren't here, the upper-level students prefer quiet. Most of us here are researching."

"I'm sure you *are* researching," the man said.

Tolan glared at him. "And what's that supposed to mean?"

He grinned at Tolan again. "It's not supposed to mean anything. It means we know you went through an Inquisition. You don't get put through something like that unless you serve the Draasin Lord."

Tolan suppressed the irritation threatening to bubble up within him. He'd been through this enough, usually with people of his own level, but hearing it from a first-level student—and one who was friendly with Velthan—irritated him more than it probably should. Tolan needed to keep control of his emotions and suppress them, along with the urge to rage at him. It would serve no purpose.

"Regardless of my Inquisition—or the fact I was fully cleared—protocol demands you are quiet within the library."

The man stood up. "What are you going to do about it, Ethar?"

"Henry—" One of the other first-level students—a dark-skinned woman with a round face and full lips, reached for Henry's arm, trying to pull him back down.

Henry shook her off. "Don't get in the way of this, Sarah."

Tolan merely stood there. Regardless of how he might have come to the Academy, he had the advantage in that he could shape in the library, something very few others could do. It wasn't something he planned on revealing to Henry or the others, but it was something leaving him feeling far less concerned about this confrontation.

"You might want to take your friend's advice, Henry," Tolan said. "Whereas I may have gone through an Inquisition, I've also passed beyond the first level. How many of you will be able to make the same claim? If you continue to disrupt the quiet of the library, you might find your access to it disappears. And then I seriously doubt you'll be able to progress beyond this level."

Tolan let the words hang in the air. It was what most first-level students feared. Few spoke about it, and fewer still would say anything other than the fact they recognized their position within the Academy was tenuous as a first-level student, but all felt that concern. Tolan had known it himself, and though he didn't have the same abilities as so many others and had come to the Academy without any ability to shape, he had managed to pass beyond the first level.

Getting to the third level was a different story.

Henry glared at Tolan, and for a moment, Tolan thought he might say something. As much as he hated to admit it about himself, Tolan would have welcomed Henry to do so. It would have amused him far more than it should.

Instead, Henry dropped back down into his seat, muttering under his breath.

"What was that?"

Henry looked up. He opened his mouth as if to snap at Tolan before biting it back.

Tolan tapped on the table briefly and spun, returning to his place. He took a moment to clear his mind, breathing in and out slowly and steadily, trying to remove the agitation from himself. It was difficult to do, far more difficult than it should have been. Then again, he should have known better than to allow himself to get caught up in the taunting of students like this. He had gone through more than enough, and certainly knew he attracted the wrong kind of attention. How could he do anything else?

Turning his attention back to the book, he focused on the writing. According to Master Minden, this was in an ancient language called Rens, one he thought he might be able to work through, but processing it, finding the key to it, proved far more difficult than he had expected.

"You were probably a little harsher than you needed to be with them."

Tolan looked up and realized Master Minden stood over him, a stack of books clutched in her hands. "I'm sorry. I should know better."

"There are ways of silencing unruly students that don't involve antagonizing them, but then again, there are ways of studying in the library that don't involve quite as much chaos as many of the earlier-level students seem to think is necessary."

"Not all students think that," Tolan said.

Master Minden smiled at him. "No. Not all, but even the most studious still find ways of being a little unruly at times." She set the books down on the table. "How are you finding this particular volume?"

Tolan glanced down at the book, flipping the pages. "Not as good as I would like."

"No? What about it do you struggle with?"

"It's the language, Master Minden. I'm having a hard time reading ancient Rens."

Master Minden glanced around the library, and her brow furrowed for a moment. As it did, Tolan looked up to see the group of students getting up from the table and heading toward the door. They were a little louder than they had been before, almost as if ignoring there was a master librarian here. He doubted any of them, Henry included, knew just how foolish it was to irritate a master librarian, but then, they likely viewed her as beneath them. Even some of the upper-level students who should have known better often viewed the master librarians in such a way, including Draln.

Taking a seat, she reached for the book, turning to a specific page and tapping on it. "One of the things you will learn about the ancient languages is that many of them have similarities to the one you speak. Languages are like people. They change over time. Many of the terms you use were used back then, though often they had different meanings and purposes. It is much the same with Rens. The advantage you have when trying to understand what you're seeing is that at least they use the same alphabet that we do."

"Some of them are nothing more than symbols."

"Yes, some of the older languages are little more than glyphs, which makes interpreting them difficult."

"It would be a lot easier if we could simply shape the knowledge to each other." There'd been a book like that, though she hadn't brought him any others like it.

"Wouldn't it, though?" She tapped on the book again. "Take a look at this passage, Shaper Ethar."

Tolan looked at where she was pointing. He had pored over that one before. It was the beginning of a new chapter, and there was an image depicted at the top of the page, something like an enormous wolf. For some reason,

Tolan couldn't help but feel as if the shape of it was important. It reminded him somewhat of hyza, though the appearance of the wolflike creature was quite a bit different than the fire and earth elemental he knew.

"I tried looking through this passage, but I haven't been able to uncover anything I can understand, Master Minden."

"Perhaps not yet but give it time. I would start with this section. I suspect you will find it of particular interest."

"Because of the elemental depicted here?"

"What makes you think this is an elemental?"

"The appearance, mostly. I don't know if it really is or not, but something about the shape suggests to me it's an elemental."

She smiled at him. "Perhaps that is all it is. Take your time, see what you can uncover, and when you have an idea, find me and we can talk about what you have discovered."

She got up then, leaving him to his studies once more. Tolan turned his attention back to the book, staring at the page, as he had for the last hour he'd been here. In that time, he had uncovered nothing of any use.

Master Minden wanted him to understand the elementals. It was for that reason she pushed him, encouraging him to continue his studies and his research, trying to get him to find his own answers, much the way she'd encouraged him from the very beginning. She hadn't said so, but he suspected she had always known he'd have some potential to reach the elementals.

Studying the image, he still couldn't shake the sense it reminded him of hyza. It wasn't quite the same. The wolflike creature depicted on the page was considerably larger than the foxlike hyza, and though he knew the elementals were of variable size when they escaped the bond, he still didn't think there were more than a few quite that large. He could only imagine how an elemental like that would be greeted if it were seen having escaped the bond. Already, the elementals were at a disadvantage, striking fear into people—unnecessarily, as far as he was concerned—and yet, very few people really understood what role the elementals had in the world. Tolan included.

"I thought I'd find you here."

He glanced up and smiled at Jonas. His friend was lean and lithe, no different than so many wind shapers. And Jonas was predominantly a wind shaper. The wind had called to him from the very beginning, seducing him and giving him the ability to shape. Tolan had often wondered whether someone's predilection impacted their appearance or whether they were unrelated. It was difficult to think they were completely unrelated. Far too many wind shapers had builds like Jonas, just like far too many water shapers were larger of stature.

"I was just trying to see if there was anything I could uncover as I prepared."

"Prepare? You don't need to prepare for the next test."

Tolan smiled. It was the excuse he had given Jonas ever

since he had begun to spend even more time in the library. Only Ferrah knew the real reason he was here, and in that, he still didn't know how she felt about it. He trusted Ferrah in a way he didn't trust anyone else and didn't think she'd be upset by what motivated him, but at the same time, it was difficult to admit he was drawn to the elementals.

"You never know. One thing they've told us"—*they* being the master shapers who administered the next test—"is the testing will be unpredictable. It's based off of everything they taught us, and in those first few months, I wasn't able to shape at all."

"But you've become so skilled." Jonas threw himself into the chair and leaned forward, resting his elbows on the table. "I wish I had improved as much as you."

"You're a much stronger shaper than you were when you first came."

"That's not really what I'm questioning." Jonas glanced down at the books, pulling one toward him and flipping through the pages. It was one of the books Master Minden had brought, and Tolan had yet to go through it to see why she had brought it over to him. After a moment, Jonas pushed it back, flipping the cover closed. A part of Tolan winced at how rough the other man was being with the book. "I look at you, and I see the things you're working on, the kind of things you're studying, and I don't know. You've grown while you have been at the Academy. I… Well, I just haven't. Not like you."

"I didn't have a whole lot of choice," Tolan said.

"It really makes you wonder, doesn't it?"

"Wonder about what?"

"It makes you wonder about what they're able to see when they perform the testing. What did they know when you went in for a Selection?"

"I wondered the same thing. I don't know that I should have been Selected."

And from what he'd uncovered about himself, and his family, he had a sense his parents had tried to protect him from a Selection. They had wanted him to have the choice and had allowed him to stay in Terndahl so he could decide what he did and who he became, not wanting to force him into serving the Draasin Lord. That was something Tolan actually understood now he had a better sense of the Draasin Lord. He probably wouldn't have understood it had he not experienced it firsthand. And as strange as it was, he appreciated his parents hadn't forced that decision upon him. If they had, he'd have immediately been considered an exile to Terndahl. He would have been hunted, the same way so many others had been hunted.

"I've often wondered whether it had anything to do with somehow using spirit to determine what elements you might have the potential to shape."

"I don't know that spirit shaping works like that."

Jonas shrugged. "Since I don't have any ability with it, I don't know."

Tolan remained silent. His connection to spirit was something he kept to himself. It was for the best. He didn't want his friend to know he had the potential with spirit, much like he didn't want others to know it. As far as he was concerned, it was one element he could keep secret.

The advantage he had was that it allowed him to defend himself from spirit shapers, though from what he'd determined using the other elements, it wasn't only spirit that helped protect his mind. There were other ways of doing so, and they involved the elements he was most familiar with.

"What do you think they're going to do this year?"

"What do you mean?"

"With the Selection. What do you think they're going to do?"

"I guess I haven't given it any thought."

"It was always the Inquisitors who ran the Selection. Now we only have a few Inquisitors, at least few the Grand Master feels remain loyal to the Academy, who will run the Selection?"

Tolan held his friend's gaze for a moment before turning and looking around the library. It was something he should have considered before. Losing the Inquisitors would potentially weaken the Academy. That as much as anything would benefit the person the Inquisitors served.

If Tolan had only been stronger, he might have been able to capture Aela, and then they might've had an opportunity to find out who exactly she served. They hadn't been acting on their own. He was certain of that, but who was the real threat?

"I don't know. I know the Grand Inquisitor remains loyal."

"As far as we know," Jonas said with a hint of a smile.

"I don't know that it's something we should joke about," Tolan said.

"Who's joking? I don't know if the Grand Inquisitor is loyal or not, but what I do know is that she could potentially spirit shape the Grand Master into making him believe she was loyal. For that matter, she could have spirit shaped all of us. What if none of us know who to trust?"

"Well, to begin with, some of the students have potential with spirit, so they wouldn't be able to be spirit shaped." At least, not easily. Tolan had some experience with the power of the spirit shaping and how it could be augmented and recognized that as much as he might try to resist the shaping, it might not even matter. "And then there's the fact the Grand Master can shape spirit."

He didn't feel that was too much of a secret to be sharing, and Jonas needed to know, if he didn't already.

"I know we don't really need to be worried about it," Jonas said. "I just can't help but feel as if the Academy is somehow different. Maybe weaker. I don't really know. Whatever it is, it leaves me uncomfortable."

"I think it's supposed to."

"And now we're supposed to deal with the threat of the Inquisitors. Shapers who can torment us."

"The Academy will keep us safe," Tolan said.

"For how long? Eventually, if we continue to pass, we will be made master shapers, and then we will be expected to go out into the world and face the threat of the Inquisitors."

"You won't be alone," Tolan said.

"I know there will be other shapers who will fight alongside us if it comes down to it, but... I guess I'm just surprised the Inquisitors have been working with the Draasin Lord."

"I don't think they've been working with the Draasin Lord," Tolan said.

"Right. They oppose the Academy. They infiltrated it—successfully. And then they attacked. What is that other than an attempt by the Draasin Lord to grow stronger?"

There wasn't much Tolan could even say to argue. When he had returned to the Academy, he had done so knowing there wouldn't be much he could say when it came to the Draasin Lord. Now he understood who—and what—the Draasin Lord really was, he didn't think he could or should say anything. Eventually, others would have to learn the truth about the Draasin Lord, but given what he'd been through, he didn't know if he was the person who could reveal that.

"If you're worried about passing, maybe you should spend a little more time in the library, too."

Jonas sat up. "I think after talking to you, I might be more content staying a second level. That way, I don't have to worry about facing the Inquisitors."

"You would rather stay a student than continue to progress?"

"Maybe." Jonas grinned. "Besides, some of those first-level students are quite lovely. I think they might be most impressed by my shaping ability."

"Right. And then they won't be impressed when you fail to progress."

Jonas wrinkled his nose. "You know, I hadn't thought about that. Maybe I do need to pass, if only to continue to impress the younger classes. You don't have to worry about that, what with you and Ferrah, but some of us…"

Tolan forced a smile. He often didn't know what to say around Jonas when it came to his relationship with Ferrah. He knew Jonas had been interested in her when they'd first arrived at the Academy, but it wasn't reciprocated. He and Ferrah, on the other hand, had a similar interest in many different things. Theirs was a relationship that had grown naturally over the time he had known her. Despite that, he felt uneasy. He was never sure quite what to say to her when it came to the elementals. So far, she hadn't shared any concern, but eventually, he feared she might. How could she not when his view of the elementals was so different than her experience had been?

"Hey," Jonas said, tapping the table. "I wasn't saying that to upset you."

Tolan shook his head, forcing a smile. "That's not it. I just was thinking about the testing again."

"You really don't need to worry. There aren't too many people in our level that I think are a sure thing for passing, but you've become one of them." Jonas leaned back in the chair, looking around the library. "Why don't we get out of here? We can head out into the city, maybe stop and have a mug of ale in one of the taverns…"

"How about I meet you in a little bit?"

Jonas shrugged, climbing from his seat. "Your choice." With that, he headed out of the library, leaving Tolan alone. It was something he was far too familiar with these days.

2

The city stretched out below him as Tolan sat on the Shapers Path, enjoying the way the city looked at night. From here, the glittering of thousands of candles in windows, the smoke drifting up from an equal number of chimneys, and a faint breeze drifting through the air all connected to him. The longer he sat here, the easier it was to feel a connection to the elements—and the elementals. He had taken to sitting on the Shapers Path at the edge of the city, looking down upon Amitan and simply staring at it, thinking eventually, he might have answers. For whatever reason, answers never really came to him.

"You've been coming here almost as often as you go to the library."

He looked up and smiled. Ferrah approached. With her pale skin, she practically glowed in the darkness. She took a seat next to him, leaning toward him. A shaping built from her, a mixture of wind and fire, and it swirled around him.

"I was just coming up here to look upon the city."

"You've been doing that a lot lately."

"Have I?"

"Most nights."

"How do you know I've been doing it most nights?"

"I don't have to be a spirit shaper to know what's on your mind, Tolan Ethar."

He let out a heavy sigh. "I think back to when the Inquisitors were attacking. There's something more to it, I think. Someone who led Aela, though I don't think the Academy is looking for them."

"You don't need to worry about them anymore."

"Don't I? They're going to return, Ferrah, and when they do, we need to be ready."

"The Academy needs to be ready," she said.

"And we are a part of the Academy."

"Right. A *part*. We aren't the entirety of the Academy. We don't have to take care of this all by ourselves."

He knew that, and she knew he knew, but her reminder was meant as a way of reassuring him, though she couldn't know it wouldn't completely reassure him. He had been through too much with the Inquisitors for that to work.

"We still don't know what they're after." It was some way of pulling the power of the elementals, but different than what he'd experienced. By placing the Keystones, they had created something more—and more dangerous.

"The Grand Master will figure it out."

"Will he?" He looked over at Ferrah. "The Grand Master didn't know how they used the elementals to create the waste."

That was still something troubling him. Not so much the nature of the waste, though that was troubling, but more the fact the Grand Master and others within the Academy didn't understand the reason for it. How could they have not seen it before?

Tolan had drawn for Master Minden what he could remember of the runes used by the Inquisitors to pull the free elementals away, and she'd been researching, but she'd not uncovered anything yet. If anyone would, he knew it would be her.

"Why do you think this is your task?"

At least she no longer questioned what he thought his task to be. Ever since returning to the Academy after facing the Inquisitors, Tolan had known what he needed to do. He needed to better understand the elementals and how he could connect to them, and he had begun to realize they all needed to be freed from the bonds, though he wasn't sure how to go about doing that. It might be tied to the Keystones, though there might be more to it, too.

"I have a connection to them," he said.

It was as simple as that. The connection meant he was the one who could do this, and because of that, he knew he had to do it. Even if he wasn't sure what that would involve.

That connection came from him, but it came from the Draasin Lord—the *real* Draasin Lord, not the one everyone feared. Having ridden the draasin and knowing the power of the elemental, he felt an affinity for it, and he understood more about the elementals and what they'd been through.

They sat in silence for a little while, nothing more than the wind gently blowing around them. There came an occasional sound from down in the city, but this high above it, the city was mostly silent. It was late enough that there wouldn't be much sound even if they were down on the streets, and yet, if he focused, Tolan thought he could uncover some of the chaos within the city.

"Tell me about it again," Ferrah said.

Tolan smiled. He knew what she wanted to know, and even thinking about it, trying to come up with how he'd describe it, was difficult. How could he explain the way the elementals had appeared to him? It was difficult to even know.

"There was power there," he started. "I don't really know how else to describe it, other than to say it existed. There was an incredible sense of each of the elements, but it came not just from the bond, but from all around." He thought about it for a moment. "Close your eyes."

"Why?"

"Just do it."

As he watched her, Ferrah shrugged and closed her eyes as he had asked. She was always so lovely, and he thrilled at the idea she was willing to be with him here, that she would sit with him, and yet, he couldn't shake the feeling it would all end, that she'd eventually decide she didn't want the dangers that came with his connection to the elementals, and eventually she'd decide to pursue someone else. It wasn't as if Ferrah didn't have options.

"What do you feel?" he asked.

"Feel?" She started to open her eyes and he shook his head.

"Sit here and tell me what you feel."

Ferrah took a few breaths, her eyes still closed. "I feel the breeze on my cheeks, pulling at my hair."

"Good. What else do you feel about the breeze?"

"What else should I feel?"

"When I feel the breeze, I feel the currents within it. It stirs, swirling around us, eddies of various currents tugging at my hair and my clothing. If I focus, I can even make out which direction it's trying to shift." It was strange connecting to the wind that way, but it felt right, too. As he focused on the wind, as he listened to its stirrings, he couldn't help but notice the connection to it.

Ferrah was quiet for a moment. "It seems to swirl a little bit."

"Add a hint of shaping to it. Don't actually shape the wind but use it to help you trace it."

As her shaping built, he could feel it. It was steady, gentle, and she had a deft touch with it. Ferrah might be the strongest shaper of their level, and at the same time, she also had the best control of anyone at their level.

"I feel it," she breathed out.

"Now reach beyond the wind." Tolan had closed his eyes, feeling for the wind, doing the same as he'd instructed Ferrah to do. "Feel where you're seated, and beyond that. Reach out around you. Use earth, let your sense of it fill you." From up here, the connection to earth was different than when standing within the forest or even within the city. There, he had a very distinct connection, a more immediate one. Above the city, there was a shifting pattern to what he could detect of earth. Not only was it in the buildings, the sense of the stone having been drawn out from the ground, but it was the nearby forest, the tug of life surrounding the city, the towering trees creating a rim of protection, mingling with the ground, giving their strength to the rest of the world.

As he sat here, connected to earth, he could feel more than just that. He could determine the people within the city, the animals in the forest, and the sense of everything. It was subtle, and took incredible concentration, but he could do it without even shaping.

Ferrah, on the other hand, used a gentle shaping touch. It was much like what she had used when connecting to wind, and hers stretched out from her, far greater than he'd have been able to do. As it did, it radiated toward the ground, washing over it, almost like a rainfall.

"I feel the city. The streets. The cobbles. People walking along them."

"How about beyond the city?" Tolan whispered, not wanting to say anything at this point.

"Beyond the city, there are trees. Small shrubs growing up between the trees. A fox wandering. An owl perched on a branch."

"Now feel the lanterns. The smoke in the chimneys. The dying heat from the day."

She added a fire shaping, and much like she did with earth, she pushed it out from her, letting it stretch, rolling away. She was quiet for a moment, and after a bit, she breathed out. "I feel it. Candles. Crackling flames in the hearth. Coals that no longer burn but are still hot. The smoke."

"Now feel for water. Barrels filled with it. The reservoir beneath the city. Streams feeding it all around us. Blood pumping through the veins of thousands of people." That last was one of the strangest realizations he had when it came to water, but he thought it was one of the most significant. He'd always believed water needed to be around him in order to be used, but it was within him, and within everyone.

Once again, Ferrah shaped, and as before, her shaping stretched out from her, drifting slowly, this one looser, flowing downward before stopping.

"I... I feel it."

"Good. This is how we are connected. All of this is shaping, but it's also all tied to the elementals. Think of fire," he started. "The lanterns sitting in the homes represent something like saa. The heated coals would be chaar. And then the smoke, the power of ifran, all tied to the elementals."

It was something Tolan could feel, and he knew that, but at the same time, there was something of an emptiness all around them. Partly, that came from the fact the elementals weren't found where they once would have—and should have—been found. No longer did the elementals flow the way they should. They were confined, trapped because of man's desire for their power. Despite that, his interaction with the elementals suggested to him they recognized their role in granting that power, and the elementals themselves didn't rebel against it, no longer angry about how men used them. Then again, Tolan wondered if the elementals had ever been angry with the way men used them.

"Why did you want me to feel that?"

Tolan opened his eyes and found Ferrah looking at him. "That's the power of the elementals. Imagine that but multiplied. That's what it was like on the other side."

Ferrah sat silently. "You really know how to impress a lady."

"I wasn't trying to impress you."

"That's disappointing."

"Not that I won't take it as an added benefit," he said, pulling her toward him, wrapping his arms around her and holding her against him. She was warm, and he felt that connection between them, sensing the heat, the awareness of the fire burning within her, the water flowing within her veins. Having been connected as he was to the world, it was easy to detect these things, far easier than it once had been. She rested her head on his shoulder, and they sat like that for a while.

"I worry about you," she whispered.

"Why?"

"Eventually, I fear you'll decide to leave the Academy."

"I chose to return to the Academy."

"This time. What happens when you're given another option? What happens the next time?"

"I don't know there'll be a next time."

"When we're dealing with the Draasin Lord and the Inquisitors, I fear we're headed toward something we haven't seen in Terndahl in quite some time."

"What do you think we're headed toward?"

"War, Tolan."

Could that be what they were dealing with?

Then again, what else could it be? He'd seen what the Inquisitors were willing to do. They had been willing—almost eager—to use the kind of force not seen in Terndahl ever since the fight with the Draasin Lord. And he'd seen the way the disciples had eagerly attacked. The violence had been on both sides.

Tolan sat up.

"What is it?" Ferrah asked.

"I just realized I don't really know anything about the war with the disciples of the Draasin Lord."

"Really?"

"I knew there was a war, but then, everyone knows that, but we also believe the Draasin Lord has studied at the Academy."

"That's what everyone said."

"I just don't really know anything about that time."

Part of that might have come from the fact he hadn't been a shaper before coming to Amitan, but part of it might've come from the fact he'd grown up on the border of Terndahl, far from the capital. Ephra was far enough away that it was difficult for the people there to feel as if they were a part of anything. They didn't have the same connection to the rest of Terndahl, other than the occasional visit from shapers from the Academy. Even those visits were infrequent.

"I don't know what it was like here, but I know in Par, we were targeted."

"Why?"

"It's probably tied to how Par was once a place of power long before even Amitan. I've told you about the archives there and some of the records we have. All of that is a place of considerable power and knowledge. Most who survived the last attack thought the Draasin Lord wanted that ancient knowledge because it would somehow grant him a way to release the elementals more easily."

What kind of knowledge would be there? Would it be any different than what they had at the library in the Academy? It would be surprising for the master librarians to leave that untouched. They would want access to it, if only so they could ensure the Academy had all the knowledge of the elementals.

"That's what you've been trying to research."

"That, and whether there was anything more to the power I suspected—and now know—existed."

"Have you thought about returning?"

"Leaving the Academy?"

"Not leaving the Academy but taking some time away to see if you can uncover anything. Now you know there's a place of Convergence here, have you thought about returning to Par and the seeing if there's something similar there?"

Ferrah shook her head. "I won't be able to return and see what we have until I'm a master shaper."

"Why?"

"Because that type of knowledge is restricted to our master shapers."

"It doesn't *have* to be restricted to your master shapers," Tolan said.

"I know it doesn't, and now I have a better understanding about what to look for, I think I might be more successful in finding it. But…"

"But what?"

"I'm uncertain," she said. "I just don't know whether I should pursue it."

"I worry we'll need to before all of this is over."

"Because you think the Inquisitors intend to use that power?"

Tolan nodded. "I'm sure of it."

Worse, from what he'd been able to determine, they would be successful. Regardless of what he might try to do, and how he might intend to stop them, he had a hard time thinking there would be anything he could actually do that would restrict them from reaching the power of the Convergence.

They sat in silence for a while longer, and after a bit, Ferrah got up. "Are you ready to return?"

"Return to the Academy?"

"No. Return to Ephra. Yes, to the Academy. It's not like we don't have studies we need to be working on."

He took a deep breath, letting it out in a slow sigh. He wasn't sure he wanted to return and deal with his studies. He'd spent so much of the day in the library, and even after leaving, he'd gone with Jonas to a tavern to share a pint of ale, despite having no real interest in doing so. He had done it because he had wanted to be with his friend, and there had been enough strangeness for him and Jonas ever since he had gone through his Inquisition that he wanted to do whatever it would take to restore and maintain that friendship.

"I don't know."

"You might not, but I do. Get up."

He let her pull him up, climbing to his feet at her insistence and following her toward the Academy. Neither of them spoke much as they went, and yet, it remained a comfortable silence. That was something he'd always had with her. There was never any real strangeness between them.

When they reached the main Academy building, they

jumped down from the Shapers Path and made their way back into the Academy.

Ferrah glanced over at him from time to time, watching him as if he might try to run. For his part, Tolan only smiled, making a point of following her but not saying anything.

Inside the Academy, the main hall was empty. There weren't any students meandering through here as they often were, though it was late enough that he hadn't really expected any to have been around. He caught sight of one of the master shapers but made no effort to catch up to them. Tolan wasn't sure what he'd do—or say. The master shapers didn't necessarily interact with the students that often outside of their classes.

By the time they meandered back up to the student dorms, he was beginning to feel tired. He probably should've headed back a while ago, but as Ferrah had said, he'd taken to sitting on the Shapers Path, enjoying the solitude he found there. Perhaps that was a mistake, but it allowed him to collect his thoughts and figure out what he wanted to do, but it also allowed him to connect to the elementals in a way he found more difficult when inside the Academy.

Inside the dorm, they bypassed the excitement often found in the second-level dorm. There were games played, a mixture of some people playing dice while others played a board game, most of them boisterous and loud. There were others who simply sat in a corner, talking. There came the distant sense of shaping, power bursting from various people as they practiced in the area reserved for such things. A few people even tried to study, though Tolan had no idea how anyone would be able to study in a place like this, with as much chaos as there was. He certainly wouldn't be able to, which was why he spent so much of his time in the library and part of the reason he grew so irritated when others didn't honor the solitude that should be found within that space.

Ferrah held onto his hand, pulling him through the door and back to their quarters. Tolan ignored Draln as he made some inappropriate comment about the two of them, as if they would find any quiet or privacy within their dorm. It was one of the problems of being a second-level student. There wasn't any privacy. By the time they reached the third level, at least they were given semiprivate rooms, and there was a hope Tolan would have an opportunity to have more privacy with Ferrah. For now, there wasn't that, which meant they had to find places to sneak off to.

"Just ignore them," Ferrah said.

"It's not as easy as that," Tolan said.

"Considering everything you've gone through I think this would be the easiest thing for you to ignore."

He glanced over at her, grinning. "Are you sure? Maybe I don't want to be associated with you." He grinned as he said it, and she threatened to pull her hand away, but he held onto it, pulling her closer to him. When they got into the room, they found Wallace and Jonas, both of them sitting quietly. It surprised Tolan that Jonas would be here sitting by himself, though Wallace often was alone.

When they entered, Jonas glanced up, setting his book off to the side. "There you two are. Sneak off again?"

"We weren't sneaking anywhere," Tolan said.

"Sure, you weren't. You know, I thought Tolan would want to avoid the rumors about him, but I guess these are a little bit more entertaining than having people talk about his Inquisition."

"Jonas—"

Jonas threw his hands up, leaning back on his bed and away from Ferrah. "Don't threaten me with a shaping just because you ran off with your boyfriend. It's not like we need to be all that creative to come up with what the two of you might have been doing."

She stormed off to her bed and took a seat.

"Thanks for that," Tolan said.

"Why? Are you ashamed of what you're doing?"

"By what we're doing, I presume you mean sitting quietly outside?"

"Quiet? If that's what you're doing, then I think you're doing it wrong."

"Thanks again."

Jonas smiled. "Did you hear?"

"Did I hear what?"

"Oh. I suppose while you were out sitting quietly, you must have missed that we're getting the opportunity to go on a Selection again. From what I understand, since we were brought on the last one, something made it so we were better able to accompany this one."

Tolan breathed out. "When?"

"I don't know. The Grand Master sent out the message."

Jonas reached into his pocket, pulling out a scrap of paper. He handed it over to Tolan who unfolded it. Much like Jonas had said, it was a message that the second-level students would be sent with third-level students and a master shaper to participate in a Selection.

"How are they doing that if they don't have the Inquisitors?" he asked, glancing over at Ferrah. She had looked up, and he could tell there was a troubled expression on her face.

"There's the Grand Master, and from what I understand, there are several other spirit shapers who are going along to participate. Hey. Why do you look so annoyed?"

Tolan folded the paper back up and handed it over to Jonas. "I'm not annoyed."

"You could have fooled me."

He forced a smile. The fact of the matter was that he was annoyed, regardless of how he might say it to Jonas. Going on the Selection would force them to leave the city, which was something Tolan didn't want to do right now. He wanted to have a better understanding of what the Inquisitors were after, and he didn't think he'd be able to do that by leaving the city. They needed to be here, if only so they could uncover what the Inquisitors were planning next—and more importantly, who they served.

"I'm just thinking about the testing," Tolan said.

"Well, you don't have to worry about it. That's the other thing."

"What other thing?"

"All of the second-levels are getting tested before we leave."

3

Once again, Tolan sat in the library, though this time he made no effort of looking down at his book, not bothering to see if there was anything he could uncover from the text he held in front of him. How could he come up with anything now?

His mind twisted, worried about the testing. Soon enough, it would be his turn.

When he had passed the first-level test at the Academy, that had been more accidental than anything. He hadn't known what he was even doing, and it was more a matter of chance. The second testing would be an intentional test, but he worried he wouldn't be able to pass.

The consequences of failing meant he'd remain a second level. He'd be an advanced second level, and because of that, wouldn't be in the same classes as those first levels who were promoted, but it would still be a setback. For him to do what he wanted, to continue to gain an understanding of the Draasin Lord and the Inquisitors, he needed to be permitted to participate, which meant he needed to be as high a level as possible.

"How long do you intend to sit here?"

Tolan glanced up at Master Minden, and he smiled. "We're to be tested."

"Of course, you are. You can't remain a second-level student forever."

"I'm nervous."

"You fear you won't pass?"

"I know I have the necessary knowledge with shaping. It's just..." It was hard to explain to someone who was as skilled a shaper as he knew Master Minden to be. How could she understand what it was like to not have much ability with shaping? She probably had always had incredible shaping ability, something he had only recently begun to acquire. He could imagine she had been someone like Draln, coming to the Academy with the ability to shape multiple element bonds.

"What have you learned about the Selection process?" she asked.

"Why?"

"Humor an old librarian," she said.

"I've learned the Selection seems to be tied to a spirit shaping determined to uncover..."

Tolan wasn't exactly sure what the spirit shaping was designed to uncover. He had thought it was tied to learning about whether or not he'd be able to spirit shape, but then, that wasn't necessarily true, either. And it didn't seem solely based on someone's ability to shape. He wasn't able to shape prior to his Selection, and yet he had somehow passed it. Then again, he had been spirit shaped when he was younger, his mother thinking to conceal from the Academy his ability to shape, trying to prevent him from being brought in and somehow twisted.

Unless that wasn't her intention at all. Could his mother have known about the Inquisitors?

That would make far more sense. He could see her trying to protect him, spirit shaping him so he wouldn't draw their attention, hiding from them his ability to spirit shape. Then again, in doing so, he'd have lost something else. Would she have known that? Would she have even cared?

"Yes. You have seen the Selection is meant to uncover something. What that something is remains to be seen."

"You don't know?"

"The Selection has changed over the years. What I know and what the intent behind it might be have changed along with it. Regardless of my interest, I don't know there is any way to know."

"What happens if I don't pass?"

"There you go again doubting yourself. What have you done in the time you've been here?"

Tolan chuckled. "Probably more than I was supposed to do."

"And who determines what you are supposed to do? You speak as if there is something you were meant to accomplish—or not accomplish, as the case may be. And perhaps that is true. Perhaps you did have something you were meant to accomplish in coming here, or perhaps you get to decide what you are meant to accomplish." She smiled. "Either way, you have proven yourself, Shaper Ethar. It's time you stop doubting yourself."

"You're only saying that because you want me to train with you."

She studied him for a moment. "Do you remember when I took you to the hall of portraits?"

"I remember it." What he remembered even more was that the hall of portraits was some sort of test he had passed. It was much like when he had been tested to pass between the first and second level.

"Do you remember what you saw there?"

"I saw the elementals. I saw portraits of times long ago."

"You saw things very few people are able to see. It tells me you have a connection to the elemental powers flowing through this world that very few people have."

Tolan looked around the library before turning his attention back to Master Minden. The library was mostly empty, though there were a few other students here. Wallace sat alone. One of these days, Tolan would have to figure out what Wallace was doing, and what sort of things he worked on, but that day wasn't today.

"We're at the Academy. Everyone here has that connection to the elements and the elemental powers."

"Everybody here has a connection to the element bonds, and to shaping in general, but as common as it's become, it still is not quite what I was referring to. What I'm getting at is that you have a different connection. It's that connection you have proven over the time you've been here. You have proven it to the point where you have forced yourself into conversations no student of your level should have been a part of. You have learned things about the Academy and the power existing here that no others of your level have known. And you have become a part of the Academy in a way no other students of your level have managed to do. So, for you to say everyone has that connection, you of all people should know that is not the case."

"Is this all your attempt to convince me I will pass?"

"I don't have to convince you that you will pass, Shaper Ethar. It has to come from within you. I'm merely making an observation."

"What's involved in the testing?"

"Now you would have me defy tradition and share with you the secrets of the testing?"

"I don't want to defy anything. I just was—"

Master Minden chuckled. "Sometimes, convention can be unnecessary. Knowing a thing and being able to do a thing are very different. In this case, you knowing the nature of the test doesn't mean you will successfully complete it."

"I thought you've been trying to tell me I'd be able to do so."

"Was I?"

Tolan met her gaze. "Weren't you?"

Master Minden smiled at him for another moment. "You ask about the nature of the testing, and here's what I can tell you. You will be asked to prove yourself in a way you have already done. In doing so, you will find either you have the necessary strength and knowledge or you do not."

"That's pretty vague."

"And yet, I've told you everything you need to know."

She reached across the table to pat his hand. As she did, shaping built from her, and he recognized the nature of it. It was spirit, and it was designed to put him at ease. As it washed over him, he noticed a wave of relaxation, and he smiled at her. That relaxation was meant to help calm him, and he was thankful she was willing to do that for him. Still, since he was also a spirit shaper, the shaping didn't do nearly as much for him as it would to someone else.

Maybe that was the point. It was another way of reminding him of the fact he didn't necessarily need for her to reassure him. He had abilities of his own, and he had developed them in the time he'd been here, learning not only how to shape, but also discovering his connection to spirit.

As she left him, he was by himself once again. He sat there for a long time, staring mindlessly, his mind beginning to work through the various possibilities, thinking through the shaping he'd be asked to perform, trying to come up with everything that might be asked of him. He went through all of the shapings he'd been taught, thinking through them, planning how he might approach them when tested. As Master Minden had said, he didn't know how to shape when he'd arrived at the Academy. And he'd practiced with these shapings, working with them to the point where he was comfortable—and even confident—he'd be able to do them when asked.

Lessons flashed in his mind, many of them provided by the master shapers. Within each of those lessons was something he was to try to recall. He remembered Master Shorav talking about the types of shapings he'd need to know to pass the test, and he remembered him saying specifically which things they would be asked to do. Many of those shapings were not complicated, not the way they once would have been.

After a while, the door opened and Ferrah entered. She made her way toward his table, taking a seat, and glanced down, frowning. "You're not reading anything?"

"I was just trying to come up with a way to steady myself," he said.

"I'm sure you will. The rest of us have seen what you've managed to do over the last few months. You've proven you're a skilled shaper."

"This is different. Passing to the third level means…" It meant he was a skilled shaper. Very few were able to progress to that point. It would mean he was well on his way to becoming a master shaper. "I think I'll feel better when this is all over."

"Well…" She looked up, meeting his eyes.

"Well what?"

"It's time."

"That's why you're here?"

"They came for both of us."

"Who did?"

"The Grand Master."

"The Grand Master is performing the testing?"

Ferrah nodded.

He didn't know if he should be reassured or troubled. He had enough experience with the Grand Master to know he'd be given a fair testing, but at the same time, the Grand Master was an incredibly skilled shaper. More than that, the Grand Master wouldn't have reason to hold him as a second level.

Tolan looked around before getting to his feet. Master Minden was gone, or else she'd disappeared to a hidden section of the library.

"Are you ready?" Ferrah asked.

"I guess I don't have a choice."

She took his hand and squeezed, and together they made their way from the library. They reached the front door of the Academy, and when they stepped outside, sunlight streamed down. As soon as she turned, Tolan knew where she was leading him. There was a park near the Academy, a place students often went to find solitude, but it was also a place powerful with shaping energy.

"It's out here?" Tolan asked.

Ferrah nodded, and he realized she was twisting the fabric of her jacket between her fingers. "They created some sort of seal around the park. Apparently, they do that during testing times, and it prevents others from knowing what's taking place."

"There have to have been testings since we've been here," he said.

"I'm sure there were, but unless we were out here, we wouldn't have known about them."

It was strange, and yet it made a certain sort of sense. There was power in being out among the natural aspects of the elemental energies. Even if it didn't have anything to do with the elementals, the power came from the fact they were here, surrounded by that energy, and in doing so, they became closer to it. It was the same thing he'd been trying to show Ferrah the other night.

"How many people fail testing?"

She glanced over at him. "I don't know if that's the question you should be asking. I think the better question is how many people pass testing."

As he thought about it, Tolan realized he didn't really have much of an idea about how many people passed testing. It wasn't something spoken about, and in that way, it was something like the Selection.

"If you fail, it's not as if you're banished from the Academy, not the way you would be if you didn't reach the spirit tower. Once you reach this point, they hold onto you to see whether or not you can progress."

"Even if we do, we're still separate. If we don't pass, then…"

She nodded at him. "If we don't pass, then others who do will know."

It would be bad enough if he failed, but Tolan thought it might be even worse if someone like Draln passed but he didn't.

There was another possibility equally worrisome. What if she passed and he didn't?

They reached the outside of the park. As she had suggested, there was a shaping around it. It had a shimmery sort of quality to it, and he could detect the energy from the shaping creating a barricade, a separation between the rest of the city and the park.

"What are we supposed to do?" he asked.

She shrugged. "I don't really know. We were just told to meet here."

"Both of us?"

"I have the sense they test more than one shaper at a time."

It was different than the testing to the second level. Tolan looked around. Who else would be here with them? If it was just him and Ferrah, he worried only one of them could be selected.

He didn't see anyone else and began to grow even more nervous about that, but then heard an irritated laugh.

"Ethar. Changen. Why am I not surprised to see the two of you here."

Tolan turned to see Draln approaching. He was a large man, muscular with the kind of build Tolan once had envied. He seemed to exude earth energy, but Draln was equally skilled with all shaping elements, not just earth.

He had grown even more skilled in the time they had been at the Academy, to the point where Draln was already proving himself the most likely—other than Ferrah—to become a master shaper.

"Just you?" Ferrah asked, stepping toward Draln.

"What do you mean just me?"

"They sent the missive for both Tolan and me to come."

"Perhaps they wanted me to show how much more skilled I am than either of you."

Tolan shook his head, turning away from Draln. Engaging with him would do nothing other than irritate himself. Instead, he focused on the shaping in front of him, looking to see if there was anything he could discover about it. From what he could tell, it was a complicated shaping, which left him wondering if perhaps this was part of the test. What if they had placed the shaping as the first layer, a way of determining who had the potential necessary to move on?

Tolan stretched his hand out in front of the shaping, approaching slowly, keeping his hands out in front of him as he did. He searched through the shaping, using a combination of the elements in order to try to unravel what he could detect. It seemed there had to be something about it he could uncover, and yet the longer he stood there, the less certain he was that he could do so.

"What is it?" Ferrah asked.

"This shaping," he started, keeping his focus on the barrier. "It's almost as if I can feel something about it."

"What are you able to feel?"

"I don't know. I think that's part of the test."

Ferrah started shaping, pushing outward with her energy. Tolan was accustomed to detecting her shapings, having been around her often enough to recognize the way she shaped. There was a particular signature to it, an energy distinctly hers. With anyone else, he wasn't sure he'd recognize it quite the same way, but with Ferrah, he was acutely aware of how the shaping built from her.

"I'm not picking up on anything," she said.

"You can tell the barrier is there?" he asked.

"I can. But detecting a thing and being able to push through it are different."

"What are the two of you going on about?" Draln asked.

"You wouldn't want to know. You don't need our help," Ferrah snapped at him.

"What makes you think I need help? I was just trying to figure out what the two of you were blathering on about while you were standing here. Maybe you want me to leave you alone? I hear the two of you have been wandering out after dark to get some time to yourselves."

Tolan glanced over at Ferrah, feeling the seething energy starting to emanate from her. "Ignore him," he whispered.

"I'm trying but ignoring him is easier said than done."

"Then focus on the shaping. See if you can unravel it."

That seemed to be the key. It wasn't so much he had to force his way through it. He wasn't sure he could even do so if he were to try. A shaping like that would be likely powered by multiple master shapers, and possibly even augmented with the energy coming from the runes situated around the various towers. If that were the case, then it would be unlikely he or Ferrah would be able to push through it.

And it was possible that pushing through it was not even necessary. Why would he need to push through it if he could simply find a way to step between it?

He focused on it and opened himself up to the power he could detect here. It was the same way he opened himself up to the various elemental energies when sitting above the city, using that as an opportunity to feel for the various powers flowing around them. As he did, Tolan started with the element he had the easiest time with—fire.

As he suspected, there was heat within this shaping. It was woven through it, a twisting sort of sense. Interestingly enough, it was a shaping he recognized. Not just that he recognized, but it was one Master Sartan had wanted them to know how to use.

Frowning to himself, he shifted the focus of what he could detect. Now he had a sense of fire within this shaping, he moved on to earth. Reaching for earth required a little different touch, and it was considerably different than what he had known when he had still been in Ephra. When he had been there, the connection to the element had left him with some ability to detect earth, but never with much strength, certainly not as strong as many. His time at the Academy had taught him much about reaching for earth—and the earth elementals.

He focused on his connection to the ground, to the earth itself, to the energy all around him. He used that no differently than he did when he was sitting above the city, looking out at it while focusing on what he could uncover while there. He used the same sort of sensing he had used when he had been with Ferrah. It came to him slowly, but there was a power within it.

And he was able to detect the shaping.

It started from deep within the ground, drawn upward, something like a wall that stretched, mixing with the fire shaping, though the two elements were often not complementary.

With that knowledge in mind, he shifted to wind, but hesitated.

The earth shaping had a certain familiarity to it, as well. It was one they had been taught, and as he focused on it, he realized this was one Master Shorav had taught them, much like the shaping that had gone into holding fire.

Was that the key?

He could run through the various shapings Master Rorn and Master Wassa had taught, but it seemed there wasn't the same need, not with the way he picked up on shapings. He focused on wind, letting his awareness of it work through him.

It started with his lungs, the swirling energy he detected with each breath, and he added to that his understanding and awareness of the air swirling around him, small currents within it reminding him of the elementals themselves. From there, he moved on to the shaping, reaching through what he could sense, searching for whether there was anything there he might be able to uncover about the nature of the shaping. As soon as he felt wind within the shaping, he recognized what it was. It was another shaping he'd learned, one Master Rorn had taught.

That left only water, and he focused on his connection to water, the way he could detect it, starting within himself. There was the pulsating of his heart, the contraction each time blood flowed through him. He could feel water within the ground, within the air itself. It was all around. Connected as he was, Tolan was able to reach from there to the shaping, and he used that to draw that power outward and detected the shaping they had created.

Four elements all woven together. Was spirit a part of this? He focused on spirit, searching to see whether or not it was there, but unsurprisingly, it was not.

As he had learned from not only the Inquisitors but from even Master Minden, spirit was different than the other elements. It seemed to bind them in a certain way, but it also sat apart from them. In doing so, it made reaching for spirit more difficult, and those who could do so far more select.

Tolan focused on the various elements, the shapings used to bind them together, and started to pull them apart. It was slow work, but as he went, he found he didn't need to use considerable strength, not as he'd have to if he were to try to destroy the shaping altogether.

A bubble formed within the shaping. He had no other way of describing it other than that. It created an opening, something of a doorway, and Tolan stepped into it. As soon as he did, he realized he should have checked on Ferrah, but once he was inside the shaping, the opening began to close. He turned, trying to separate it, but found he could not.

The bubble started to collapse around him.

Tolan pushed against it, straining to maintain his position and his focus, but turning around as he had looked for Ferrah had made him disoriented. And now, he was no longer certain where he was within the shaping.

The longer he stood here, the more he could feel the shaping collapse around him. As it did, he realized something. If he weren't able to step out of it, he was going to be crushed under the weight of it.

4

The shaping continued to squeeze around him and Tolan stood in place, focusing on it, knowing he needed to be ready for the possibility he'd have to try to force his way beyond it. The only way he'd managed to open up any sort of pathway into the shaping was because he had unwound the shaping slightly, creating a doorway. Now he'd begun to turn, the doorway he'd unwound began to reform, sealing itself once more—and him within it.

Tolan took a steadying breath, focusing on the various shapings he'd detected. He recognized them, and now he knew what they were, he could use those shapings, continuing to work through them, and he was certain he could find some way to unravel them long enough to make his way somewhere.

The challenge was that he no longer knew which direction he needed to go. When he had been standing on the other side of the shaping, he knew he had to head straight through it, but now he was within it, it was evident the shaping was incredibly wide, enough that he'd find it difficult to determine which way he needed to open in order to work his way through it. If he went the wrong way, he could continue to spin around the barrier, winding through the outer edge, perpetually stuck within the shaping.

And yet, he needed to hold on, to use his focus, to hold the unraveled shaping open for as long as possible. As he stood there, he strained.

There had to be some way to detect where he had come in.

It would be more than just stepping through the shaping. He'd have to use sensing—all of the elements—and would have to be quick about it. With every passing moment, the shaping threatened to collapse around him even more.

It took not strength but considerable effort to shift his focus. He didn't need to shape in order to figure out where he wanted to go next but separating from what he could sense was difficult.

Pushing outward, he strained, thinking about what he could detect of earth and wind and water and fire and trying to determine what he could uncover to guide him. The inside of the park was different than the outside, and if he could figure out what was there that might draw him, he thought he just might be able to find a way through.

There came a flicker of energy, little more than that,

and he spun. That flicker seemed to guide him, though he didn't know which element he was following. He strained, using what he could remember of the various shapings, unraveling them as quickly as he could as he tried to push through them, and managed to open up another pathway through the shaping.

The bubble formed again, though this time not nearly as large as it had been the last time. He suspected it had something to do with his growing weakness. The longer he remained here, the more likely it was he'd grow weaker and weaker to the point where eventually the shaping would crush him completely.

He found himself needing to duck, crouching down as the bubble narrowed, and yet, Tolan continued to work his way through it, unraveling it as quickly as he could, scrambling forward. By the time he found himself on his knees, crawling forward, he no longer knew if he was heading in the right direction. It was possible whatever surge of energy he'd detected had guided him in the wrong direction. If that were the case, then he'd end up squeezed, crushed under the shaping. Would the master shapers have any idea what had happened to him? Would they realize he was potentially injured and come for him? He might fail the testing, but at least he'd still be alive.

The unraveling squeezed down to no larger than his body. He was crawling forward on his belly, and he dragged himself forward. Tolan continued to focus on what he was able to do, continuing to unravel that shaping, squeezing forward.

He had to be close. How thick could they have made this shaping?

There was no farther he could go.

The shaping pressed down on him, squeezing.

Tolan strained, taking a deep breath, and he surged against it, creating a little bit of a buffer against the shaping pressing down upon him.

Was there any way he could add spirit and strengthen himself?

It was the only element not present in this shaping, and while he didn't know if that mattered or not, he had found adding spirit to shapings changed them in certain ways, though they were often unpredictable ways. In this case, he could use a little unpredictability.

Drawing upon spirit in this manner, with this sense of urgency, was difficult. Spirit always came from a different place within him. Whereas fire he could feel from the warmth around him and connect to it that way, and wind came from his breathing and the air around him, earth from the ground and everything he could connect to, water from his blood and the moisture he could detect, spirit was something else. It came from a deep place within him, almost buried within him. As he reached for it, his shaping began to fail.

With a surge, he grasped for his spirit shaping, using that to add to the other shapings, solidifying it. He resisted, pushing outward yet again.

The shaping took hold.

He held out, waiting, fearing he wasn't going to be

enough, that the strength he could find wasn't going to be enough.

The shaping held.

Tolan quickly began to work, unraveling more, reaching through what he could detect, separating fire from wind and earth and water, and he created an opening, allowing him to drag himself a little farther forward. With each passing moment, he could feel a little bit more of the shaping beginning to open up, and he pushed upward. Spirit seemed to give him the most strength, and he used that to unravel more and more as he dragged himself forward, the element allowing him to connect in a way he wouldn't otherwise.

Eventually, even spirit wasn't enough. Tolan's strength began to wane even more and he continued to collapse, the shaping squeezing down upon him.

He crawled forward again, barely more than the length of his arm, and the shaping pressed down upon him, forcing him to the ground.

There was one final way to reach for power, but he wasn't sure he should try it. Was it worth it to try to connect to the elementals in order to pass the testing within the Academy?

If he did, and if that power unleashed in a dangerous way, it could potentially not only harm him, but it could harm others around him, and he had no interest in doing that.

Then again, what choice did he have? He feared what might happen here.

Hyza.

He reached for that elemental first, knowing his connection to hyza was strongest. If he could find a way to stretch across the distance, if he could uncover some way of connecting to hyza, he might be able to use that power to separate himself from what had happened.

Ever since he had been near the waste with the Inquisitors, his connection to hyza had changed. In some ways, that connection was like what he had with the draasin, the way he had heard the elemental almost as if speaking within his mind.

"I need your help. Just a hint of strength."

Tolan had no idea if hyza would be there, and even if he was, would he be able to answer and offer any help? It would be unlikely for the elemental to be able to do anything. More likely than not, Tolan was going to be trapped within this shaping, all because he had made a mistake and turned to check on Ferrah when he should have checked on her before he had even stepped into the shaping.

There came another fluttering. As he felt it, power surged with it, a familiar sense he'd grown accustomed to.

It was the power of hyza, the power of the elemental, and it was surprisingly the power he recognized. Hyza was there, lending power to him, granting him strength.

Tolan borrowed it. Even though hyza was an elemental of earth and fire, the strength granted him a connection to power that augmented him, filling him and making it so he could reach each of the elements much more easily.

Tolan scrambled, using that borrowed power to unravel what he could. As he did, he created more of a bubble, enough that he could drag himself forward again. He continued to hold onto that sense of power, letting it flow from him. He continued to unravel the shaping, dragging it free, creating enough of a bubble that he could get to his knees. It was more strength than he had managed even when he had added spirit. Borrowing power from an elemental *would* grant him more strength than he had by himself.

Tolan continued to crawl forward, moving as quickly as he could, scrambling until even that strength began to fade, slowly sapping from him.

"No…"

Tolan sank to his belly. The shaping continued to squeeze down upon him and he tried to crawl, dragging himself maybe the width of a finger, before even that was no longer possible. The shaping pressed down and down, forcing him into the ground. The power of it forced his face against the earth, and he tried to keep his mouth tilted off to the side so he could breathe, but even that began to squeeze, crushing him as it squeezed around him.

He took a breath, and as he let it out, the shaping pressed down on him, squeezing him so he couldn't take another.

Was he going to suffocate here?

He couldn't imagine what kind of shaping the master shapers would use that would kill him for failing.

And his failure was his own fault. Had he not gotten distracted, he should have been able to work his way free, but because he had allowed himself to get distracted, he was no longer able to do that. This was his fault, and now this would be his failing.

"No!"

The word came out with the last of his breath, and the shaping crushed him.

Tolan lay there, waiting for death to claim him.

Moments passed.

Then the weight of the shaping lifted.

Hands grabbed him, pulling him from the ground, and he looked up.

The Grand Master was there, studying him. Tolan blinked, finding it difficult to clear spots from his vision, and he looked around to see he was in the middle of the park, the small pond nearby. How had he crawled so far?

"Grand Master?"

"Rest, Shaper Ethar."

He wanted to sit, but…

The Grand Master guided him toward a bench, and Tolan took a seat on it, looking over at the Grand Master. With each passing moment, his breathing began to ease, his vision began to clear, and his thoughts started to surge back into focus.

He had failed. He was going to remain a second level.

Why did that trouble him so much?

Even Master Minden had made it clear remaining a second level wasn't the worst thing in the world. It gave him an opportunity to continue studying, to continue to find his way through the Academy, and in doing so, eventually he'd be able to test again.

Then again, Tolan didn't know how he could do any better than what he had done this time. He doubted he'd ever have the necessary strength to blast his way through a shaping like that. With as much as it had pressed down upon him, crushing him, he had been forced to borrow not only spirit, but power from one of the elementals.

It didn't seem likely he'd be able to shape any better than that the next time.

Then again, the next time would probably be some other type of test. More likely than not, it would be another test he'd fail. And then what? How many tries would they let him have before telling him he could progress no further in the Academy?

He already knew there was no shame in not progressing further within the Academy. He'd seen plenty of shapers in the world, including in his home city, who never made it beyond second level. He'd still be called master, and eventually, would continue to focus on one of the elements, to use that in a way that would enhance the Academy, and then…

Tolan didn't know what would happen then. Since coming to the Academy, he hadn't given a whole lot of thought to what he wanted to do when he was done. Most of the time, shapers trained at the Academy in order to return to their homeland, but Tolan had no interest in returning to his homeland to offer additional help. There was nothing for him there. There wasn't family. There weren't even all that many in the way of friends. His one friend had been offended by Tolan getting Selected. If he returned, he'd run the risk of Velthan returning, and then he'd have to deal with him for the entirety of his life.

Eventually, Ferrah was there. She sat next to him, looking over. Her eyes had a glazed appearance to them.

He reached over, grabbing her hand and squeezing. "Ferrah?" he whispered.

"Tolan? I... I failed."

Tolan nodded but realized Ferrah couldn't see it. "I failed, too. The shaping crushed me."

"I saw you go in and I realized what you were doing."

"I'm sorry. I think what I did was wrong. It wasn't about unraveling the shaping."

Someone was coughing near them, and Tolan looked over to see Draln joining them on the bench. The other man was ashen, sweat dripping from his brow, and he had much the same glassy-eyed expression Ferrah did—and as Tolan suspected he had.

"At least we all failed," Tolan said.

It was a terrible thing to feel, and yet he'd have hated it had Draln passed but he had not.

The Grand Master appeared in front of them. He looked at each of them in turn, his gaze lingering on Tolan the longest. As he did, a shaping washed over him. He was too tired and weak to be able to resist it, even though he suspected that was what he should be trying to do.

"The three of you have been tested," the Grand Master

began. "This was a test of knowledge and strength. This is a test designed to challenge you, and to determine whether you recalled the various teachings you've received throughout your time here."

Tolan breathed out. He waited for the Grand Master to tell them the next part.

"What was the test?" Draln asked.

"A basic one."

Tolan grunted. Basic. He couldn't even pass a basic test, so what did that say about him and his ability to shape?

"Basic, but powerful. This was designed to test your ability to shape each of the elements simultaneously. A true master shaper, a true master of the Academy, must have control. The first element of control is being able to handle more than one element at a time. You have been working on that in your classes, and all of you have proven that ability during your first testing."

Had he? Tolan didn't recall having proven he could shape more than one element during his first testing, but he didn't recall much about that first testing. Then again, shaping more than one element was something he was capable of doing. It just wasn't something he realized he had proven prior to his testing.

"In order to pass the next level, all shapers must be able to access each of the elements without bondars. You have been taught the approach in your classes, so by the time you reach your testing, the nature of the test is not foreign to you."

The Grand Master fell silent for a moment. "You three were selected to go last. You were identified by your various instructors as the most promising, but even the most promising don't always succeed."

Tolan looked up at the Grand Master, surprised by his last statement.

"In this case, you were tested on how far you could make it through a powerful shaping. This was not a test you could cheat. This is not a test you could complete with a bondar, though perhaps a bondar would allow you to make it a little bit farther. This was a test requiring you to be able to reach the elements, use them in a way displaying your control, and make it as far as possible. I am happy to say all three of you have proven yourself worthy of your instructors' confidence."

Tolan blinked and looked over at Ferrah before turning his attention back to the Grand Master. "We passed?"

The Grand Master smiled tightly. "This is but the first step in many, but today you were successful. You will continue to progress in your training, and you will move a little further. Today, each of you have become a third-level student."

Tolan's breath caught. He had passed?

Then again, the Grand Master had said they weren't expected to make it all the way through the shaping. The expectation was only to see how far they could go.

Somehow, he had gone far enough that he had proven himself.

That should please him, but he couldn't help but wonder if he *had* cheated, despite the Grand Master saying such a thing wasn't possible. While he didn't have a bondar—other than his spirit bondar, and Tolan hadn't even thought about using that—he had used his connection to the elementals, and hyza in particular. What was that if not cheating?

"From this point on, each of you will be referred to as a third-level. You may occupy the third-level dorms, and you will have an increased access throughout the Academy in accordance with your level. You may return."

Tolan started to stand, still feeling stunned. He turned to Ferrah, reaching out to help her to her feet, and when she was standing, they looked at each other.

"Third level," he whispered, smiling.

"Third level," she said.

"Shaper Ethar."

Tolan turned to the Grand Master.

"If you wouldn't mind, I would like to have a word with you."

He swallowed, his mouth suddenly going dry. "I'll catch up with you," he said to Ferrah.

She started off, moving slowly, though Draln was moving equally slowly, something making Tolan far more pleased than it probably should.

When she was gone, the Grand Master drew his attention. "That was an impressive display."

"It was?"

"As I said to the others, the test was a determination of

how far you could unravel the shaping, a test of distance and endurance, if you will."

There it was. Tolan waited, knowing there was going to be a question. "I didn't have a bondar."

The Grand Master smiled again, this time just as tightly as before. "We would have known if you utilized a bondar. This test is designed in such a way that even with a bondar, it wouldn't be as beneficial as in other settings. While you might have been able to go a reasonable distance with one, the fact you were able to go any distance suggests you didn't have a bondar. Like I said, it is a difficult test to cheat."

He nodded, waiting for the Grand Master to say something, to comment on how he knew he was somehow able to reach the elementals, and to question his loyalty to the Academy. That was what was going to come, wasn't it? He'd wanted Tolan to infiltrate the Draasin Lord, and instead, Tolan had returned feeling connected to them, and in some ways, he was now infiltrating the Academy on behalf of the Draasin Lord.

"What is impressive is the distance you were able to go, Shaper Ethar."

"How far did I go?"

"Shaper Sar was able to reach the trees," the Grand Master said, motioning toward the trees in the distance. "That would be far enough for him to have passed. Shaper Changen went a little bit further than him, though not much. That is not surprising, as we have long known she'd be a powerful shaper."

Tolan would have smiled were the situation any different. He had known Ferrah was a powerful shaper, too, and he was certain she'd appreciate hearing the Grand Master had said it, even considering the situation.

"And then there was you, Shaper Ethar. You made it nearly to the pond." He pointed to where Tolan had remembered opening his eyes. "I have done these testings many times over the years, and we have had plenty of students who have passed, making it through to the third level. It is always a time of celebration, a time where the Academy grows stronger because of their willingness to continue to serve. In the case of you, that is no different, but…"

Tolan stood frozen in place, unsure what the Grand Master might say. He couldn't help but think through all the various awful possibilities. Once again, his mouth was dry, a cold sweat washing over him.

"You, Shaper Ethar, a young man who came to us with no shaping ability, have gone farther than any in my recollection."

5

Wind whistled around the city, the kind of heavy breeze they hadn't had for quite some time. Tolan felt the way it caressed him, swirling around him, and closed his eyes while standing on the Shapers Path, enjoying the swirls of wind. There was something peaceful about it, something comforting, and he found it was far easier to connect to the elements than it ever had been before. Perhaps that was little more than the fact he spent so much time doing so, or perhaps there was something more to it.

"Are you ready to return?"

Tolan glanced up and met Ferrah's eyes. There was worry written in them, and he wondered why she would be troubled. She enjoyed returning to Par, not like him and his return to Ephra. "There are other places I think I would prefer to go, but if this is where the Grand Master wants me to go, then so be it."

"At least you can see if there's anything new you can uncover about the waste."

There was that. He wasn't sure there would be anything to uncover about the waste, or even if there would be time to do so. They were going to perform a Selection, and other than that, there wasn't going to be anything for him to do. A part of him dreaded the idea of going, worried that while there, he'd encounter Tanner, and if he did, what he might say to his friend. The last time he'd seen him, Tanner had been resentful of the fact Tolan had been Selected.

"I'm sure the Grand Master has others investigating it."

"I'm sure he does, too, but I know how you feel about your connection to that place."

"My connection?"

"That's my way of being careful—"

"Master Ethar. Master Changen. I am reporting to go."

Tolan looked at Jonas, shaking his head. There weren't very many from the second level who had been promoted to the third level. Tolan, Ferrah, and Draln had all passed, as had two others. The rest remained second levels. Apparently, from what Tolan and Ferrah had discovered, that wasn't uncommon. The only thing uncommon about their testing was Tolan. At least no one else knew about what had happened. He wasn't sure what he'd do if the Grand Master reported how different Tolan was.

"Come on, Jonas," Ferrah said.

"I'm just trying to make sure I demonstrate the appropriate level of respect."

"I'll show you the appropriate level of respect," she said, raising her fist and shaking it at him.

"If you think that would be a lesson I need to learn," he said.

Tolan shook his head. He thought Jonas was only joking with them, but at this point, he no longer knew if that was the case or not. With Jonas, it could be difficult to know for certain.

"Are you returning to Velminth?" Tolan asked.

"Apparently they are taking both of us. They like to have an upper-level student along with the lower-level student."

Tolan's breath caught. He knew what that meant for Jonas, just as he knew how much that would anger him. With Draln having passed and Jonas not yet, it meant there was a natural division between the two.

At least Velthan wasn't coming with them; as a first level student, he wasn't permitted to come along on the journey out of the city.

"Aw, Jonas, I'm so sorry—"

Jonas shook his head, raising his hand. "You don't have to be sorry. I didn't pass."

"It's not a matter of not passing. You will," he said.

"Will I? I didn't even realize the test was for me to burrow into the barrier. I stood outside it like an idiot, waiting for them to come to me."

Apparently, many shapers who didn't pass were like that. As far as Tolan could tell, most of the students waited to see if the master shapers would come out to them, thinking that was the requirement. And why wouldn't they? It made more sense than trying to burrow through a shaping the master shapers had placed.

"I hear they offer a second testing shortly after," Ferrah said. She kept her voice low, almost as if she were giving him some forbidden information.

"Yeah? Well, any additional testing will have to come after we return, which means I'm going to have to return to Velminth as a second-level student and not a third-level student like Draln. Not only is he going to make sure I don't forget about it, but I'm sure he's going to do something to embarrass or anger me while I'm gone."

Tolan suspected Jonas was right. He had a hard time imagining Draln would do anything other than take the opportunity to embarrass Jonas. "You can tell him both Ferrah and I went farther than him."

Ferrah started to smile, but Jonas shook his head. "Do you think I'm going to do that? I have enough trouble with him as it is; I'm not going to make it worse by taunting him. Besides, you weren't supposed to tell me what the testing was."

"I have a feeling the testing will be different next time," Tolan said.

"Are you sure? It sounds like the Grand Master made it seem like the testing is the same."

Would it matter that they knew? As Master Minden said, he supposed it probably didn't. Knowing the nature of the testing and being able to do well with it were very different things. Even if he had known about the testing,

Tolan wasn't sure it would have given him any advantage. He still would've had to find some way of getting through the shaping, and without knowing the specific shapings involved, and being able to hold onto a shaping of each of the elements, he might not have been able to do that.

"I didn't get the sense we weren't supposed to share," Tolan said.

Before anyone had a chance to say anything more, a whistle sounded. Tolan perked up, looking around, curious who might be going with them. They were paired up with a master shaper, much like they had been the last time. Unlike the last time, there was no Inquisitor traveling with them.

The Grand Inquisitor approached, making her way along the Shapers Path and toward Tolan and the others. She stopped in front of him. "Are you ready to go, Shaper Ethar?"

Tolan nodded, resisting the urge to glance at the others. "I didn't think we had any of the Inquisitors coming along."

"The others do not, but as Ephra is far enough out, I will start there, and then I will begin making my way to the other locations throughout Terndahl. Which means the two of us are going."

"Just the two of us? There won't be a master shaper?"

"Not this time."

Tolan glanced at Ferrah and then Jonas. It left him feeling a little bit uncomfortable he'd be traveling with the

Grand Inquisitor, more so after what he had recently encountered.

"You don't need to worry I will attack you. The Grand Master has tested me, and he has ensured I remain dedicated to the Academy."

That was news to him. "How did he test you?" He probably shouldn't ask that in front of the others, but the question came so quickly he didn't have much of a choice.

"I allowed him access to my thoughts."

Ferrah's eyes widened, and Tolan understood the reason for her surprise. He shared in it. Allowing someone access to a spirit shaping, intentionally doing so, was not just invasive, but it was the sort of personal thing Tolan couldn't imagine the Grand Inquisitor willingly offering of herself. Then again, given what they had gone through, she probably felt compelled to do so. Had the Grand Master done the same for her?

"It's time," the Grand Inquisitor said.

Tolan hugged Ferrah, unmindful of the fact the Grand Inquisitor and Jonas were watching him. "Travel safe," he whispered.

"You too."

He released the hug, and as he made his way along the Shapers Path, he glanced back at Ferrah, watching her.

"You will see her again soon enough," the Grand Inquisitor said.

"That's not—"

"That is what it is, and there's no shame in admitting your affection for the girl."

Tolan smiled to himself, wondering what Ferrah might say to being called a girl. She was certainly much more than that, though he had a sneaking suspicion she'd probably not argue when it came to the Grand Inquisitor.

"You volunteered to go to Ephra first for a reason."

The Grand Inquisitor glanced over at him. She had a heavily lined face, and as she frowned, wrinkles deepened along the corners of her mouth and eyes. A shaping built from her, and it swept toward him quickly. Without thinking, he reacted, wrapping his mind in the shaping of fire and wind, rebuffing any attempt she might make at using spirit on him.

Her shaping slipped over him. As it did, a hint of a smile twisted the corners of her mouth.

"You have certainly improved, Shaper Ethar."

"Are we going to do this the entire journey?" They reached the edge of the city. The Shapers Path continued northward from here, and other parties had begun to break away from the central portion of the city, making their way out of the city limits, and from here, he knew it would be only a short journey before reaching Ephra. Tolan had made that journey enough times now that he thought he could do so quickly and easily, and he wondered if perhaps others knew how often he had journeyed this way.

"You mean am I going to test you?" The Grand Inquisitor shrugged. "I haven't decided. I think it might be intriguing to test how quickly you can shape, but then again, I also suspect you've developed enough resistance to spirit shaping that you will be difficult for me to impose my will upon."

Tolan didn't know if that was a compliment or not but thought it sounded almost as if it weren't. "Is this about the waste?"

The Grand Inquisitor nodded. "What you shared with the Grand Master troubled me. I wonder if perhaps there is more to the waste than we realize."

"You think we'll be able to figure out who the other Inquisitors are serving?"

Her jaw clenched. "It is unfortunate they serve anyone other than the Academy."

"Why don't you use spirit on them the same way you and the Grand Master used spirit on each other?"

"There's never been the need, but perhaps we're finding we aren't nearly as safe as we once believed." She fell silent, and they continued along the Shapers Path. Each step took them several miles at a time, the landscape blurring past them far below. As it did, the sense of the land changed. Not only was it in the scents that came along with the wind, but it was in the sense he had from the earth, the shifting nature of the heat all around him. Even that of water began to shift.

"What does it mean, the waste was formed by an absence of the elementals?"

"What it means is we have made a mistake," she said. She didn't look over at him. "It seems as if our master librarians might've been right about the elementals all along."

She didn't elaborate, though Tolan was surprised Master Minden and the other librarians had shared anything about the elementals. He had the sense from her that she preferred to keep that to herself. As they continued along the Shapers Path, they did so in silence. They paused at one point, taking a break to eat, but even in that, the Grand Inquisitor said nothing. Every so often, she attempted to shape him. He began to realize it was a test, though there was some benefit to it. In doing so, she forced him to react, to protect his mind quickly, and it got to the point where he simply held protections around his mind, maintaining a steady shaping.

Near afternoon, she glanced over at him. "It took you long enough to do so."

"To do what?"

"To hold on to the protection."

"You wanted me to do that?"

"We face the threat of Inquisitors who can use spirit shaping, so all must be prepared, especially outside of the city. You more than anyone else, I suspect. Since you have already confronted them and faced the type of shaping they might throw at us, I fear they might use that as an opportunity to try to attack you again."

"Why would they come after me?"

"Perhaps they won't, or perhaps they will see you as the reason they failed."

It seemed almost as if she were threatening him, but that didn't seem quite right. "I only did what was necessary."

"And it was necessary," the Grand Inquisitor said. "Yet someone like Aela is not accustomed to failing. When it comes to using spirit, I suspect she has rarely failed. In fact, she very nearly overpowered me."

It was the first time he'd heard the Grand Inquisitor talking about what had occurred with her and her experience with Aela, though Tolan knew she had nearly been overpowered by the other woman. With Aela gone, they didn't have to worry about her—though they did have to worry about whoever Aela served. He still didn't know who that might be.

"What do you expect to find when we reach Ephra?" Tolan asked.

"Hopefully, nothing other than the city as it was."

They fell into a silence, and Tolan focused instead on hurrying along the Shapers Path, keeping up with the Grand Inquisitor. She moved quickly despite her age, and it seemed as if she added a hint of shaping to it, much like he had done when he'd traveled this way. He raced after her, forced not only to shape protections around his mind, but also to shape a hint of wind and fire to give him the speed necessary to keep up with her.

It was nearly evening when they reached Ephra.

Something about the city pulled on his senses. It was a familiarity, similar to how Ferrah felt familiar to him. With Ephra, it was more a matter of having been here for so much of his life, and each time he returned, it might not feel quite like home, not as it would if the events of his childhood had not taken place, but it certainly felt familiar. He was aware of how the earth felt within the city. The way the wind swirled around it, carrying specific energies. He was aware of the heat, the sun different here than it was in Amitan. He was aware of water. All of it gave a certain distinct energy to the place, and all of it was a way to recognize Ephra.

Other cities would likely be the same, and he wondered if he'd be able to pick up on that if he were to travel to them. Would Ferrah recognize it if she went to Par? What about Jonas and Velminth? How would his home feel to him?

"What is it, Shaper Ethar?"

"I was just realizing there is a specific texture to the city."

"A texture?"

"The way it feels. The various element bonds have a distinct energy here that is different than it is in Amitan." Now he thought about it, he realized even in Amitan, while he was aware of the energy of the city, it was so distinct he could track it, almost as if were he to stretch out his senses, he'd be able to find it using that alone.

"Very good. Rarely do we have anyone not a fourth level or higher who recognizes the distinct energies of each city within Terndahl. It would be the same other places but seeing as how I have rarely been beyond Terndahl, I can't say with any certainty. Each city is tied to the element bonds in a different way. They are anchored, which allows the Shapers Path to give us a certain amount of guidance, as well. We can use the sense of the cities in order to guide us between places."

Tolan hadn't considered that. "How were the Shapers Paths made?"

"Have you not taken the time to understand the shaping?"

"It's complex," he said.

"It is complex, but it's useful, too, especially if you find yourself needing to travel with another who cannot shape, or a great distance where you fear you might not have the strength necessary to return. Forming a path is less energy consuming, and it gives you an opportunity to rest as you go."

Tolan focused on the Shapers Path beneath him. He'd never tried to understand the nature of the shaping that had gone into its creation, but perhaps it would be useful to know. "Which element bonds are used?"

"Why, all of them."

Why would he be surprised by that? It reminded him somewhat of the barrier he'd tried to work his way through during the testing. Much like that, could he find a way to understand the shapings? He didn't necessarily need to understand each of the various element bonds as they had been pushed into the shaping in order to find his own way. His connection to that was different enough that he thought simply sensing it, recognizing the flow of the element, focusing on what he could detect from that, might be enough to get an understanding of what went into the shaping.

He focused on fire, feeling the heat within it. It was there, though it was subtle. It was nothing like the thick band of fire used in the testing. This was a simmering sort of energy, an undercurrent of power flowing deep within the rest of the shapings. Holding onto that connection, he searched for the other elements. If they all were used, then it was possible he might be able to recreate it. The simmering heat of the shaping was not a particularly challenging one, and it certainly didn't require much power, much as she said.

What about earth? There was an aspect of earth he thought he could reach, and as he focused on it, he realized it was tied to the land below. Interesting. It was almost as if the shaping resonated in a particular way, determined to tie into earth.

If that were the case, was there any way to use that?

He had the ability to detect the way a shaping was tied into the land. There was something he'd discovered on his own: Nights sitting outside on the Shapers Path, connecting to everything all around him, had given him that insight.

Wind was next in, but it was a strange undercurrent helping to loft the Shapers Path into the air. He'd always wondered how it remained suspended in the air but hadn't given much thought to it, but now, feeling it as he did, he had that understanding. And then water tied it all together, sealing the various shapings.

This was something he could do.

Focusing on earth—it seemed to him that tying it to

the landscape below was first—Tolan began that shaping, adding wind, then fire, and finally water, sealing it all together. As he did, he sent the shaping angled off to the side, attached to the existing Shapers Path but stretching out a dozen feet. He wasn't sure what to expect, but the path formed, solidifying, and he hesitantly took a step onto it.

Letting out a quiet laugh, he looked down.

He had created this. He'd formed a Shapers Path. It seemed impossible he'd have been able to do so, but what surprised him just as much was that he'd been able to peel apart the nature of the shaping, and in doing so, he'd been able to re-create it.

"That is an impressive talent you have," the Grand Inquisitor said.

He looked up. "Talent?"

"There aren't many who can analyze a shaping and then recreate it."

"It's what I did when I was at my testing."

"You would be alone in that approach. Most try a different tactic, using their connection to the element bonds to attempt a shaping of each one to see which resonates with it."

That would be so much more time consuming. Tolan couldn't imagine trying it in that way.

"I'm just surprised I was able to make a Shapers Path."

"Were you? I was not surprised at all."

Tolan looked at the heart of the Shapers Path he'd created, and as he did, he couldn't help but feel as if there was something more he needed to do with it. Tentatively, he walked out onto it, making his way along the newly formed pathway, and tested it. The connection was there. It wasn't so much that it was difficult to shape. The process of making the Shapers Path hadn't taken all that much energy out of him. It was more it had taken a degree of knowledge he hadn't possessed previously. Now he had a better understanding of what was involved. Having focused on the shapings used in its creation, he thought he could recreate it again.

"How long did it take to create the Shapers Path all throughout Terndahl?" he asked, turning his attention back to the Grand Inquisitor.

"There are leagues of Shapers Paths all throughout Terndahl. You could easily imagine just how long that would have taken to create."

And here he had shaped ten feet and been pleased with it. Creating leagues of Shapers Path would be a considerably different challenge. It wasn't just the journey between here and Amitan. It was the journey between Amitan and all of the other nearby cities, along with those that weren't quite so nearby. Everything involved was incredibly impressive. But then, Tolan had known it was incredibly impressive. He didn't need to know how to shape it to recognize the difficulty that had gone into its creation.

"It is time, Shaper Ethar."

Tolan retreated back along the path he'd made. When he rejoined her she studied him. Another shaping washed away from her, hitting his barricade, the protections he'd placed around his mind, and she nodded.

"I hope you are ready."

"What is it you think we'll find?"

"Unfortunately, I don't know. It's possible whatever we find will be dangerous."

"In Ephra?"

"When did you think this was only about Ephra?"

"It isn't?"

She glanced over her shoulder at him as they made their way toward the city, the outline of buildings within Ephra growing ever closer. As they did, Tolan couldn't help but feel the same sense of unease he'd felt when he'd come for his last Selection. There was no reason for it. He had progressed far beyond that person who had lived here, and yet, there remained a part of him that still felt as if he was the same person.

When they reached the edge of Ephra, the end of the Shapers Path, the Grand Inquisitor paused, glancing over at him. "Are you ready?"

"Do I have much of a choice?"

"With this?" She smiled, straightening her hands over her jacket. A shaping began to build, incredible power flowing through her with it. "Unfortunately, no."

6

The city of Ephra was not large, at least not when compared to many of the other cities within Terndahl. Unlike Amitan, where there was evidence of shapings all throughout the city, buildings that had been simply shaped into existence, the Shapers Path crisscrossing above the city, making it not an unusual sight to find shapers making their way along it, Ephra had nothing like that. It was a place of energy and power, but it was also remote. On the outskirts of Terndahl, not only did they find it quieter, with fewer merchants making their way to and from the city, there was less shaping energy used throughout the city overall.

When he'd been here previously, Tolan hadn't been nearly as aware of that fact. Even now, it was a strange sensation, one that came to him initially as something not quite as he expected it, but the longer he was here and looking around, it became clearer just what troubled him. It was the lack of shapings.

Whereas in Amitan at any given time, Tolan might detect a shaping used around him, in Ephra there was only the rare sense of shaping. Perhaps some of that had to do with the time of day. It was late enough, the sun already starting to set, the breeze gusting in and out of the north still warm but already starting to turn cooler, and a sense of quiet emanating from his earth sensing. All of that seemed to trigger a warning, an alert that things were different.

Despite that, Tolan maintained his own shaping. The journey with the Grand Inquisitor had trained him to hold onto it, to ensure he had protections wrapped around himself, protections ensuring no one would be able to sneak in and spirit shape his mind. He doubted they would be successful anyway, but on the off chance they would, he wanted to be ready. With a shaping held like this, it was even less likely someone would surprise him.

"You're tense," the Grand Inquisitor said, watching him.

"Am I?"

"Your shoulders, mostly. The rest of you seems coiled, as if you're prepared for an attack at any given time."

Tolan took a deep breath, trying to relax. Strangely, it was more difficult than he'd expected. This was Ephra, after all, and the only time he had any trouble here was when he'd been attacked by the Inquisitors. "I think what I went through the last time has stuck with me."

"I'm not surprised. I doubt anyone in the city knows what you experienced."

"Isn't that the point?"

"Perhaps it is. It wouldn't do well for the rest of Terndahl to know something has happened with the Inquisitors." She paused. A shaping built from her, and since Tolan was holding onto a shaping of his own, he was able to detect the way she used earth mingled with a bit of water, a twisting of the two that she pushed out in all directions. It was a strange sort of shaping, but he could understand the utility of it. As she pushed, an unexpected element joined with it: spirit.

"What was that shaping for?"

The Grand Inquisitor pressed her lips together as her shaping continued to build. Power flowed from her, sweeping away and into the street, and then beyond. "This is my way of detecting whether we have any need for concern."

"Are you able to detect Inquisitors that way?"

"It's possible, but mostly it allows me to determine how many shapers are near us."

"Ephra doesn't have that many shapers."

"You'd be surprised."

Tolan cocked his head. He focused on how she'd mixed earth and water, repeating the shaping. As he pushed it out, trying to mimic what he'd seen from the Grand Inquisitor, he added spirit much the same way she had.

His control over spirit wasn't nearly as fine-tuned as hers, and he felt as if he overloaded the shaping, adding far more spirit than he intended. It was a burst of power, and in doing so, it fatigued him.

A reverberation of energy bounced back at him. It came strangely, but it echoed within the portion of the shaping in which he had added spirit.

There were dozens of echoes, each of them varying in intensity and strength. Some of them were far closer than he would've expected, and the closest came from the Grand Inquisitor.

Shapers. Dozens of them.

"There are more than I would've expected."

"You will be dangerous one day, Shaper Ethar."

He retreated, withdrawing his connection to his shaping, a flush washing over him. Perhaps he shouldn't be quite so forward with how he shaped. The Grand Inquisitor had tolerated him so far, and she'd made no comment about the fact he'd created a section of Shapers Path, but how long would he be granted the same flexibility? At some point, he could see she'd grow tired of him and the way he pushed.

"I'm sorry. I shouldn't have done that."

"You're mistaken if you think I'm upset with you. I'm merely commenting on the fact you have a talent for observing a shaping and recreating it. There aren't many who have that same talent."

"I think it comes from the fact I wasn't able to shape on my own for so long. I watched, and it increased my ability to sense so I can detect what shapings are used around me."

"Perhaps that's all it is."

He turned away. He didn't think she knew about his connection to the elementals, but when it came to recreating a shaping he was able to detect, as far as he could tell, that didn't seem to come from the elementals. That came from within him. Somehow he was able to uncover the nature of the shaping, though his ability to do so stemmed at least in part from the time he'd spent working with the various elementals, trying to understand as much as he could about them, if only so he could recreate them.

"When we were here the last time, I understood you did not have a place to stay."

"My parents disappeared when I was young," he said quickly. He'd become accustomed to talking about his parents in such a way, and he said it without really even thinking, though when it came to someone like her, she likely knew what had happened to his parents even if he hadn't shared with her everything about them.

"I'm aware of that fact," she said.

"Master Daniels took me in and allowed me to stay with him, but…" He looked along the street. It was strange. He suspected when others returned to their home villages or cities, they felt a sense of homecoming. There were people he knew, and the places were familiar, but finding more than that was beyond him. There wasn't anything in any of the buildings he'd consider his home. And he didn't have any desire to stay in his old home, less so now he had discovered truths about his parents and the way they'd seemed to deceive him. When he'd been here before, he'd been tempted to go to Tanner and see if his old friend would have put him up for the night, and he suspected Tanner would've at least considered it, even if he'd have hesitated to do so.

"Another place it is, then. We have a long couple of days ahead of us."

"Will you walk me through what's required of the Selection?" He didn't remember all that was involved in the Selection process. Though he'd come before, his experience had been such that he'd been on the periphery. Now he was a third-level student, and now there didn't appear to be any other master shapers with them, it meant he'd most likely take a greater role in the Selection process.

"When the time comes, I will ensure you know your responsibility. For now, we'll have other tasks we must accomplish."

"What other tasks?"

"First we should rest."

She guided him along the street, seeming to know exactly where she was going. He wasn't surprised by that. He suspected the Grand Inquisitor had visited Ephra enough times over the years that she did know where she was going. It was only a little surprising he'd never known about those visits, but then why would he? In all of his years in the city, he'd never been a part of the shaping community. There would've been no reason for him to have known about the Grand Inquisitor visiting, and knowing her as he now did, he could imagine she'd have wanted to keep her presence in Ephra quiet.

They made a few turns, every so often passing others on the street, but no one seemed to pay them much mind. At first, he thought it strange. The people in Ephra were generally suspicious of those they viewed as outsiders. It was something coming from sitting so close to the waste, isolated. Though the people of Ephra were a part of Terndahl, the rest of Terndahl rarely made it here, and when they did, it was to a mixture of excitement and concern.

It took Tolan a few moments, passing several different groups of people, to realize the Grand Inquisitor shaped them with spirit.

"You don't want them to remember you came?"

She glanced over at him. "It serves no purpose for others to be aware of our comings and goings. In fact, I would much rather very few people remember our visit."

"Have you always done that?"

"It's a simple matter to touch someone's mind with just a hint of spirit. It doesn't take away their memories, but it does make it so they don't pay attention to us. It's barely more than a touch, and it's something I would caution you against attempting until you have greater control over your own spirit shaping."

"I wasn't—"

She flashed a smile at him. "Eventually you will need to try, Shaper Ethar. All I'm suggesting is you be cautious when you try a shaping like that. Much damage can be done with spirit shaping. You have used it well so far, but your shapings involving spirit have not required you to attempt to shape someone's mind. The moment you do, everything begins to change. Reaching into a person's thoughts, into their mind, is not only an intimate thing, but it is a potentially dangerous thing to someone inexperienced. That is why we teach the Inquisitors slowly. One shaping must be mastered before another is attempted."

"I didn't know."

"You do now."

Tolan nodded. Could this be why the Grand Inquisitor had wanted him to come with her? It made a different sort of sense, especially given his growing connection to spirit, and he could easily imagine she'd had him come with her so he didn't make a mistake and damage someone else using spirit. She was right—he had only attempted to mingle spirit with the other shapings, never having attempted to use it on someone's mind. Others had done the same on him, but they had all been Inquisitors.

"What all is involved in becoming an Inquisitor?"

"You would be interested?"

Tolan shrugged. "I don't really know what I want to do when I'm done with the Academy. I can shape spirit, and I guess that means I have the potential to be an Inquisitor."

She paused, glancing in his direction. "There is more to serving as one of the Inquisitors than simply an ability to shape spirit, Shaper Ethar. There are many within the Academy who have the ability to shape spirit but who do not serve as Inquisitors. That is no failing of theirs. The

Inquisitors have been a selective group over the years for that very purpose. The training is very rigid and challenging."

"Is that all about spirit shaping?"

"Perhaps I will give you a taste of it while we are here. You can decide if it's something that interests you. If not, then when we return to the Academy, you can return to the library. I do believe Master Minden has claimed you."

Another wash of heat started from deep within him, a flush he tried to suppress. "Master Minden has been working with me."

"Of course, she has. She sees in you an interest in scholarship. She has tried to claim all who demonstrate any ability over the years."

It amused him somewhat that she'd make a comment like that. It seemed almost as if there was some jealousy between various factions within the Academy.

"I warn you. I haven't taught a single student in many years. I have always been known to be something of a harsh instructor."

Tolan could easily imagine how harsh she could be, but at the same time, the opportunity to study with her and learn how to shape spirit would be valuable. Even if he never became one of the Inquisitors, understanding spirit shaping in a way that would not result in harming someone had value. The rumors about the Grand Inquisitor were frightening, though he didn't believe those that claimed her last student had died because of the shaping. That was probably nothing more than a rumor.

He wouldn't need to work with the Grand Inquisitor. There would be others he could work with. He suspected Master Minden would be more than willing to try to help him understand how to shape spirit. Perhaps even the Grand Master himself. Even if they were willing, what could he learn from an Inquisitor—and the Grand Inquisitor, at that?

They veered off, stopping in front of a tavern. The sign hanging from the awning named it the Red Draasin, an interesting name for a tavern. It was quiet inside, not the same bawdy sort of noise he often heard from various taverns, and as the Grand Inquisitor paused at the door, her hand resting on it, a shaping washed outward from her. This was similar to the one she'd used earlier in the street, a mixture of earth and water she added a mixture of spirit to. It was her attempt at detecting shapers within, and in doing so, Tolan couldn't help but wonder what she was detecting.

Using a similar shaping as she had, he added spirit once again, but this time he was more careful with how he did it. It was a gentle touch, and he let it wash away from him, pushing outward so he didn't send an overwhelming amount of power. He didn't want to overwhelm any patrons within the tavern, and as the shaping washed away from him, he had a moment of concern. He didn't know if this shaping caused any injury to anyone inside or whether this simply was some detection type of shaping.

There came no echo, no reverberation, as there had when he'd used it out on the street.

Nodding to herself, the Grand Inquisitor pushed the door open and stepped inside.

Tolan hesitated a moment before following her. She wanted to find a place with no shapers? Was that because she didn't want anyone to be able to protect themselves from her spirit shaping, or was it because she wanted to ensure there was no threat to her before stepping inside?

The tavern was small, though typical for Ephra. A cluster of tables filled most of the empty space. Stools situated around the tables went mostly unoccupied. A couple of lanterns hung from hooks on the ceiling, giving a flickering sort of light. Fire danced in the hearth along the far wall, smoke drifting lazily into the room. Tolan suspected if he were to try, he could detect the hint of an elemental in that smoke. There had to be no more than a half dozen people within the tavern, most of them sitting by themselves, leaning over tables and drinking ale or picking at food. The Grand Inquisitor guided him to a table along the back wall. When she took a seat, she focused on the door leading to what Tolan assumed was the kitchen.

"Why here?" he asked.

"Do you object to this place?"

Tolan shook his head. "I'm not familiar with it."

"And yet, you're from Ephra."

"There are thousands of us who live in Ephra. And I suspect there are dozens of taverns." Unlike some, Tolan wasn't the kind of person to spend considerable time in taverns. It wasn't that he didn't enjoy them, it was just that he had focused so much on maintaining his apprenticeship with Master Daniels, wanting to ensure he didn't anger the man and run the risk of losing that apprenticeship. Had he known then what he knew now, he might have taken more time to relax and enjoy himself.

"I've stayed here before," the Grand Inquisitor said. At least that answered the question Tolan had. He suspected she was familiar with this tavern, and it was nice to have that confirmed. "The owner turns a blind eye to various activities taking place here."

"It didn't take you for the kind of person who needed an owner of a tavern to turn a blind eye."

"I don't, but others do." She scanned the inside of the tavern, and as she did, he realized yet again that she used a shaping. This time, he detected it as a subtle sort of touch. It was barely anything. The shaping seemed to be spirit exclusively, and it made sense why no one looked in their direction.

"How do you intend to get served if you prevent everyone from seeing us?"

"It's not so much I'm preventing them from seeing us. It's more a suggestion they forget about us. Besides, I don't need to worry about getting served. If it comes down to it, I merely need to send a request to the tavern owner, and I have little doubt he will send someone over to provide us with everything we need."

As he sat there, Tolan realized he was hungry. His stomach grumbled, reminding him the last time they had eaten had been while stopping on the Shapers Path. The

Grand Inquisitor watched him, seeming to realize his discomfort, and she grinned at him. "If you're hungry, we can order."

Tolan looked over at a nearby table. The food had something of an unappealing appearance to it. The meat looked fatty and tough. The vegetables were wrinkled. There was no bread. The only things seeming to make up for it were the large mugs of ale, and he suspected with enough ale, any food tasted good.

"Does it have to be here?"

She watched him for a moment, her shaping directed toward him but sliding off the protections he'd placed. "You don't have to stay here. You only have to meet me in the morning. Sunrise. At the edge of the waste."

"The waste? Why would you want to go there?"

"Consider it my way of trying to prepare for what we must do." She looked around the inside of the tavern and waved a hand at him. "You may go."

"That's okay. I can—"

"You don't have to stay here," she said again.

Tolan understood. She didn't want him to stay. Whatever she intended to do needed his absence.

Getting up from the table, he made it to the door. As he did, he realized the people within the tavern turned generally in his direction, but only for a moment before they turned their attention back to their plates or their ale.

It was a strange thing to witness. It was a strange use of power.

That wasn't the kind of thing he wanted to do. If that was what the Inquisitors did, then perhaps he didn't want to train with her.

He suspected the Grand Inquisitor had always intended to send him away. Where would he go? The last time he'd come here, he'd spent his time wandering through his old home, along with wandering through Master Daniels' home and his shop. He had no such interest this time, and it didn't feel as if there was the need to do the same thing.

He found himself wandering through the streets. It didn't take long to reach a familiar section of the city. Ephra wasn't large, but it certainly was large enough that he didn't know the entirety of it, and he didn't know everyone within it, either. It was much like the Red Draasin, places he'd never visited—nor heard of. There were many places like that.

While wandering, he found himself near his old home, and rather than pausing and heading in, he turned away. There wasn't anything there for him, but... maybe there was.

When he'd been here before, he hadn't known about his parents' connection to the Draasin Lord. He'd known the rumors of them, the stories chasing him when he was younger, but at the time of his visit, Tolan hadn't believed anything about them. Now he was here, he knew there was something more to those stories.

Veering off, he paused once more in front of the old home. It was small; at least it appeared small now. When he'd been a child, it had seemed so large. There was a section of the home serving as his father's workshop, a place where Tolan had always felt welcome. Now he understood what his father had done there, he couldn't help but wonder if there was anything he could uncover. When he'd attempted to make bondars before, he'd made mistakes. Having visited with his father—however briefly—he had to wonder if perhaps it wasn't something he could do. Why shouldn't *he* be able to create a bondar?

The technique would be difficult. It was the kind of thing he didn't know if he could ever gain the knowledge to do. As much as he might want to delve into the workings of creating a bondar, there was danger in doing so as well. It was a similar type of danger as what the Grand Inquisitor suggested that existed if he were to attempt to spirit shape someone's mind.

Heading toward the house, he paused at the doorway. As before, he found it unlocked. Stepping inside, he summoned a small shaping of fire, a twisting of saa spinning in his hand, giving enough light to clearly make out the details in the home. It was even more picked over than it had been before. The interior was completely empty, devoid of any furniture that had once been here. He was surprised no one had come and claimed the home as their own. His parents had been gone long enough that someone should have taken it upon themselves to claim this place. Perhaps there wasn't a need for housing in the city, or perhaps there was something more practical to it, the simple fact no one wanted to live in a house formerly occupied by those who had been claimed by the Draasin Lord.

Wandering through the rooms, his gaze swept over the parts of the home, looking for anything possibly remaining. There was nothing.

Passing through the kitchen, he found the various pots and pans once hanging from hooks were missing. There was no sign of the pottery his mother had painstakingly collected over the years, nor was there a sign of any of the silverware. All of this was an empty reminder of everything they had abandoned. Much like they had abandoned him.

When he reached their bedroom, he decided to move on. Tolan didn't even pause at his own bedroom, having nothing there to see. When he reached his father's workshop, he stopped once again. The bench remained, and unlike other places within the home, there were some tools here.

It surprised him they wouldn't have picked over the tools, that they would've left those behind when they had taken so many other things, but perhaps the thieves hadn't bothered to make it all the way to the back of the home. Then again, his father's tools were for specific purposes, and now Tolan understood what those purposes were, he thought he had a better understanding of why they were here. Who else would have wanted to make a bondar? They may not have known what it was his father had done, but they would've recognized the fine detail work that had been required was not something they could re-create.

The only bondar he had was the ring he carried on a chain around his neck. It was for spirit, and if only he had a similar type of bondar for the other element bonds he might be better prepared. It would be incredibly useful to have one for fire or wind or water or earth. Something small like a ring would be incredibly beneficial, though he suspected it wasn't just the runes used on the bondar that were important, but it was also the shape. It was something he should have asked his father about when he'd seen him last.

Fatigue began to work through him, and he debated finding a tavern for the night, but why would he need that? He could stay here. Though he had told the Grand Inquisitor he had nothing left in Ephra, this still remained his home, as strange as that might be.

Leaning against the wall, he rested his head, and it wasn't long before sleep claimed him. With it came dreams.

7

Tolan awoke to light all around him. Something was wrong. As he sat in the workshop, clutching the bondar for spirit, he couldn't tell what he detected. Why should he pick up on something not quite right?

The soft murmuring of voices came near him. As he looked around, he found his father bent over his workbench, as he had been so many times when Tolan had been younger.

"Father?"

His words came out higher pitched, and in a voice not his own—or at least, had not been his own for many years.

Turning in his direction, his father smiled at him. His dark hair was as Tolan recalled from his childhood, no longer streaked with gray as it had been when they had seen each other most recently. Sweat streamed down his brow, and there was a hint of ink smeared on his cheek, something he'd often seen in the years his father worked at his creations, taking notes. Now he understood those notes, Tolan thought he recognized the reason for them. They were his way of documenting his trials with the various bondars. In taking those notes, he was able to get a better understanding of what worked and what did not.

"This is a surprise. What are you doing here this morning?"

Tolan got to his feet. Was this a dream? It had to be something like that, especially since when he'd fallen asleep, he'd been sitting in the same workshop, in practically the same location. It didn't seem to be a memory. Tolan had never taken a nap in his father's workshop and awoken like this.

"I don't know," he said, stammering toward the end.

"Your mother might be upset if you're avoiding your chores."

"I'll get to them," he said quickly. It was all too easy to fall back into those old patterns, remembering what his father had demanded of him, the same demand his mother had placed upon him. He was expected to keep up with his chores, and they didn't ask all that much else of him, but they did ask he remain diligent with getting his assignments done.

Approaching the workbench, he had to wonder if he might be able to uncover something in the dream—or vision, whatever this was. Perhaps having come here would give him an opportunity to understand what his father had been working on, to find some way of grasping the nature of his bondars and how to recreate them. Wasn't that what Tolan wanted? He thought if he could understand what his father did, the way he worked, he might be able to do the same.

"What are you making?"

"Oh, nothing but a few small crafts."

Tolan glanced down at the workbench. At one place, he saw a slender length of rod reminding him of the furios. Even the symbols marked along the surface reminded him of one. He reached for it, but his father shook his head.

"That isn't done. It takes a little bit more work."

"It's different," he said.

His father nodded, pushing the furios off to the side. "There is delicate work for many of these items, Tolan. Perhaps as you get older, I might be able to teach you this."

"Do you really think I could learn it?"

"I don't know. Not everybody has the talent with this." His father flashed a smile at him. "You will, I'm sure. Your mother seems to think you have many talents, and we need to ensure we give you the opportunity to decide how to use them."

The comment almost threw Tolan out of the vision, practically intruding on everything he was experiencing. He swallowed, hating that he was getting caught up like this, knowing his father wasn't really here and, regardless of whatever vision he might be having, none of this was real.

Despite that, Tolan couldn't shake that it felt so real.

He'd had visions like this before. This wasn't the first time he had anything like this, and certainly wasn't the first time he had one like this at his old home. It was almost as if something about this place dragged him into these memories, forcing him to have them.

Tolan looked down at the table, studying the various bondars there. The furios was the easiest to make out, partly because he'd spent so much time using one. There was what had to be a withering, the strange shape giving it the power of the wind. The golan, the earth bondar, was a little bit more difficult to determine, but he recognized the runes worked on it. It looked something like a stone, though with sharp edges, almost as if designed to slide his gaze across it. Then there was nyamin, the water bondar, and the only reason he recognized it was because of the runes placed on it. Otherwise, Tolan wouldn't have been able to determine what it was. There was nothing about it which fit with anything he'd seen before.

He looked up at his father. The other man was working at his bench again, a small lump of stone in front of him. Was there anything he could find? Even though this might be nothing more than a relic of a memory, and even though this was probably not even real, Tolan couldn't help but wonder if perhaps there was some way to glean information from his father regardless of the fact it wasn't real.

"Do they all have these strange shapes?"

His father continued to work, sliding a slender, pointed object along the length of the stone he worked on.

With each pass, he shaved a hint of stone away, almost as if he were peeling a carrot. "Not all. The shape is important, but sometimes people have specific requests about the design."

"What sort of requests?"

Tolan wasn't sure if he could simply ask whether or not his father could make a ring or something wearable. If it were possible, then the bondar would be so much more useful. It would be easier to disguise as well.

"Your mother requested I make her a ring." He looked up, smiling. "Of course, when it comes to your mother, I'm more than happy to do whatever it is she asks of me."

"Why a ring?"

He nodded toward one of the bondars—the withering, Tolan noted. "If she had something like that, it's harder to carry. Your mother wants to have my work with her. She says it reminds her of me." His father smiled. "I think she's flattering me, but you know me. I'll take a little flattery any day."

Tolan forced a smile. The idea his mother had requested the ring for spirit to be made and his father had figured out a way to do so left him thinking there had to be some way for him to do something similar.

"Could you make one like that in a ring if she asked?" he asked, pointing to the withering.

His father turned his attention to it, his eyes narrowing. "That would be difficult. Perhaps not impossible, but for most of these, the person who owns them doesn't necessarily care about the shape. They simply want what it represents."

"And what does it represent?"

"Oh, Tolan. Now you're asking questions a little bit more difficult for me to answer."

Tolan swallowed, stepping back. In his vision, he was still a child, and the movement took him back barely a step, nothing more than that, and yet, he couldn't take his eyes off the bondars. If there was some way to get a sense for the power within them, he wanted—and needed—to do so.

"I think they're interesting," he said.

"They *are* interesting." His father lifted the withering. It surprised Tolan that his father would go for wind, but then, he didn't really know what sort of shaper his father really was. When he had been around him—however briefly—he had the sense he could use each of the elements, and having seen how he moved stone, Tolan suspected he was a powerful earth shaper. That could have been nothing more than his use of a bondar, but it could have been something else, too. "Some view these as a way to connect to the elements. Others view these as little more than a representation of the power of the elements."

"What do you view them as?" Tolan asked.

"A way to understand the world." His father stared at the withering for another moment before turning his attention back to his workbench, and he began to peel away at the stone.

Tolan shifted closer, looking at the projects his father had made. There would have to be some way for him to recreate a bondar, but perhaps this wasn't the way to discover the secret. His father made most of the bondars no differently than the others Tolan had been around, and though they represented considerable power, they also were not all that different than the ones they had at the Academy.

What about his notebook?

Tolan made his way toward his father's notebook, looking down at the page. It was something of a deception to stare at his father's notes, but he suspected his father would not think him capable of reading it. As he looked down at them, he blinked.

They weren't written in the common language of Terndahl. Surprisingly, he did recognize the writing. Having spent as much time as he had with Master Minden, Tolan recognized writings from many different places, and this one was a series of glyphs, much like the more difficult languages he'd tried to interpret.

Tolan stared at it, searching for a way to understand. His father got to his feet and noticed Tolan was watching.

"Be careful with that," he said, smiling at him. Despite the smile, there was a hint of darkness behind his eyes, enough that Tolan looked away, though he knew this was nothing more than a vision. Why should he be scared in a vision?

His father grabbed the notebook, closed it, and set it on his workbench.

Tolan stood watching him work for a little while longer. There was a steadiness to his movements, a regularity to the way he peeled away the stone, carving at it in such a way he stripped a little bit at a time. It was delicate work, and he marveled at the way his father persisted.

Perhaps he shouldn't, but he'd always known his father was a skilled craftsman and knowing the nature of his craftsmanship did little to change his belief. It was a matter that his father was a craftsman of a different sort, and the nature of his work such that it was a little bit different than he'd believed, but that did nothing to change how skilled he was.

Another voice sounded from inside the main portion of the house. His mother.

His father looked up, smiling, warmth spreading to his eyes. "I wonder if she's going to be disappointed it's not quite ready? Soon, but it may not be soon enough."

"Why?"

"Unfortunately, things are changing, Tolan. And we are going to have to make a choice."

"What sort of choice?"

His father straightened, taking a deep breath. "The hard kind."

The door opened and his mother stepped out into the workshop, glancing briefly at Tolan before turning her attention to his father. As she did, he couldn't help but wonder how much of this came from a memory, and how much of this came from his imagination. He also didn't know how much longer he'd remain in the vision. Eventually, he'd awaken, and when he did, he needed to join the Grand Inquisitor, whom he was supposed to meet in the morning.

Tolan watched as his mother gave his father a kiss on the cheek. She glanced down at the table, frowning slightly. "Is it done?"

"You will know when it's done."

"You understand the urgency."

"I understand." His father glanced over at Tolan and a shaping built, this time coming from his mother.

He felt the steady rising pressure of the shaping, that of spirit, and it washed toward him.

Tolan took a step back without realizing what he was doing and panicked. There was no way to escape from this shaping. He didn't know whether or not he had any ability to protect his mind at this time and doubted he did. Even if he did, what would his mother think of him suddenly shaping?

That was the wrong way to think of it. This was a dream.

Wasn't it?

Strangely, though it was a dream, it felt so real. It was the kind of dream he felt as if he needed to escape from, the kind of dream where he felt as if it tried to draw him through, where if he weren't careful, he'd be sucked up into it.

He needed to awaken.

Tolan closed his eyes, thought about his sleeping self, and pushed.

When he awoke, everything was dark. The air had the same musty smell it'd had when he'd fallen asleep. He was alone, the workshop mostly empty, and he was back within himself.

That *had* been a dream, hadn't it?

If it had been a dream, why had it felt so real?

Maybe it was nothing more than a memory.

He'd already learned there were memories he'd had that his mother had wiped away, using her ability to shape spirit to make it so little remained.

Why that dream, though? Why now?

Tolan got to his feet, curious as to how late—or early—it was. Could he have been here too long? The Grand Inquisitor was waiting for him, and he worried he'd overslept.

As he looked around the workshop, he couldn't help but think there was something here he needed to see, though he didn't know quite what it was. Shaping a little bit of fire, he called saa into existence, giving a little bit of brightness to the workshop. The tools along the wall were familiar from the dream, and perhaps that was all there was to it. Maybe that was why he'd had that particular dream. His father had shown him the use of the tools, the way he'd worked with them, steadily and slowly sliding along the surface of the stone while peeling shapes free. It was a combination of the runes and the element bonds that were important, but there was more to it when it came to creating a bondar. Somehow, Tolan believed there was an aspect of elemental energy that went into it as well.

If he were ever to do something similar, if he were ever to attempt to create a bondar, then he might need his father's tools, and he considered grabbing them from the shelf and slipping them into his pocket, but there were far too many.

A memory drifted back to him from the dream—or vision. It was of his father's notebook.

That couldn't still be here.

Tolan had never really looked for it, and he doubted anyone else would find it valuable. It was mostly valuable to him, and to anyone who might understand how to interpret it. His father would likely have brought it with him.

Sorting through the drawers, he didn't find anything. He continued pulling open other drawers, finding other implements his father had used in his work. With each one, he had another flash of memory, almost as if this was triggering him to recall the way his father had used these various items. He hadn't thought about the workshop for so long, and even when he'd been here before, when he'd begun to question whether his father had made bondars, he hadn't remembered sitting and watching his father, but the longer he was here, the more he remembered the time he'd spent watching, observing.

Surprisingly, as those memories came back, he thought he understood what his father had done. Perhaps with that knowledge, he could recreate some of the same techniques. He might not have the steady hands, and he might not have the skill or knowledge of what aspects of the bondars were used, but if he could find his father's notebook...

It wouldn't be in any of the drawers. Tolan suspected his father would have hidden it. It was valuable to him, and he'd have protected it. Had Tolan seen him hiding it before?

He stood in the center of the workshop, his eyes closed. He released his hold on fire, and instead he focused on spirit. He drew it up from within him, dragging it through him, pulling on the strength of spirit, letting it flow into him.

As it did, power poured through him. He fixed his dream in mind, trying to use that to pull out more memories. It was there.

He found resistance. It was almost as if he had to open himself up.

That seemed to be the real challenge. The answer was there, he was sure of it, but it didn't seem as if it were meant to come to him easily.

And perhaps it was not. If his mother had used a spirit shaping on him, concealing those memories, she'd have wanted to bury everything. If she did, that would include memories of his father's journal.

Tolan would have to relax. He would have to find those answers within him, but in order to do so, he'd need to see if he could uncover anything deep within himself.

He took a deep breath, letting it out slowly. What had

he done to allow himself to have this vision in the first place?

Nothing. He'd simply fallen asleep.

Even that wasn't quite true. When he'd awoken in the vision, in the dream, hadn't he been holding onto the ring—the very ring his father had been working on?

Could that be the key?

Tolan gripped the stone ring, the spirit bondar, and added a hint of spirit to it, shaping through it.

As he did, a flicker of power flowed through him.

It started slowly, building. He was familiar with this power, having recognized it before. It came from someplace deep within him, buried within him.

Intentionally buried.

The spirit bondar was his way of bypassing that.

Had his mother wanted him to have some way of reaching it?

She was the reason he didn't have those memories, but it was possible she'd not intended to hide them forever. Could it be the spirit bondar had been her way of returning access to them when he was ready?

That seemed to be reading too much into it, but at the same time, it made a certain sort of sense.

That power flowed into him, the memory of the day he'd been within his father's workshop, and as it came to him, he focused on the journal.

This time, there was more distance to the vision. Not a vision, he realized. A memory, and it was one that had been masked, much like so many others had been masked, much like his own ability to shape had been hidden.

He kept his focus on the journal, nothing more, and in doing so, he watched as his father lifted it, sliding it up underneath the workbench, and then turning and winking at Tolan before hugging Tolan's mother.

Tolan released his shaping, the power fading from him slowly, almost too slowly. As it did, he took a deep breath, drawing upon saa once again. Light flickered into existence, the shaping more like an elemental than a shaping, spinning to life and hovering in his hand. Tolan stood fixed in place, unwilling to move, unwilling to do anything other than step toward the workbench. If the memory was real, if it was more than just a vision, more than just a dream, he would find his father's notebook. If it was only that, if it was nothing more than his imagination, there would be nothing there.

Sliding his hand along the undersurface of the workbench, he wiped away cobwebs, wincing as he did. Then he reached something.

Tolan ducked down, holding his hand out, using the fire shaping to illuminate the undersurface of the workbench.

At the far back of the workbench, there was a small drawer he wouldn't have seen otherwise. He pulled it open, and inside he fished around until he found what he was looking for.

Tolan pulled his hand out, wiping the dust and cobwebs off, cradling the notebook in his hand.

It was real, which meant the visions were real—and that meant it was much more than a dream. It had been something real, something his mother had taken from him, much like she'd taken so much else from him. And though she had, he didn't know why she'd have taken that from him. What did she worry about him knowing?

As he flipped through the notebook, realizing he could read it now better in real life than he could in his vision, he couldn't help but wonder if perhaps his mother was trying to do something more than just hide that knowledge from him. Maybe she was trying to protect it, to prevent anyone else from forcing him to give up what he knew. It was possible she was using the shaping in order to make sure he was ready to receive the knowledge, sealing it off until such time when he'd be able to access it and do something with it. If that were the case, then could he really be so angry with her?

When—and if, he realized—he saw her again, he would have to ask.

For now, Tolan pushed the notebook down into his pocket. He would have to protect it, keeping it safe, concealing it from anyone who might want to steal its secrets. At least, until he knew how to understand its secrets. There *were* secrets within it. He was certain of that. He'd have to dig into them to grasp the nature of those secrets, and he'd need to master the knowledge within, if only so he could use it to make bondars, and do so in a way allowing him to have that power, were he to need it. Given what he'd gone through, Tolan couldn't help but think he'd need power like that.

Taking a deep breath, he wandered back to the house, pausing at a window and looking out. It was still early. The sun had not yet risen, but there was just a hint of color in the sky, enough that he knew it was time to go and meet with the Grand Inquisitor. It was time to go to the waste—and then participate in the Selection.

8

Watching the sunrise over the waste was actually quite lovely. The sun rose slowly, giving the vast expanse of the barren rock an almost otherworldly appearance, and Tolan stood along the border of the waste, holding onto a shaping he wrapped around his mind to protect himself, watching as the sun continued to climb ever higher into the sky.

Standing next to the Grand Inquisitor, he didn't need to look at her to know she was doing the same thing. He did wonder, however, if she was stretching out her awareness of the various element bonds, using that to help her understand whether there was anything out in the waste. When he had stepped out into it before, there had been a separation from his connection to the element bonds, but it had never troubled him the way it troubled so many others. Before, he'd not been nearly as connected to that power as he was now.

The heat came to him first. It radiated off the waste, a dry sort of heat reflecting from the rising sun but also seeming to come from some innate place buried beneath it. It was strange to be aware of that element, especially as he doubted there were so many other elements accessible within the waste.

Then again, there was earth out there. How could there not be? The barren rock might be different than the nearby landscape of Ephra, but it was still earth. There was air out on the waste; when he'd been there before, he'd managed to breathe, not suffocating immediately. And he might not have sensed any water, but there had to have been something. He probably could have sensed water flowing within himself, that which came from inside his blood, but he'd never taken the chance to do so.

It was strange standing here. There was a distinct separation between what he could detect and what he could imagine. While his connection to the element bonds reached only as far as the border of the waste, in his mind, there was power even beyond there.

"Where has it been shifted?"

At her words, Tolan shook himself, looking over at the Grand Inquisitor. He took a deep breath and stepped back, turning to look toward Ephra. From here, the city wasn't visible, the rolling landscape making it difficult to see anything but the grass and the trees. Surprisingly, after removing the markings causing the expansion of the waste, the landscape had rebounded, quickly restoring itself to what it had been and what it should be.

Tolan walked back, following the path they had taken out here. The Grand Inquisitor had wanted to walk, not wanting to shape their way here, and he thought he understood.

What would happen if he attempted to try to create a Shapers Path above the waste? Part of the Shapers Path required he connect to the landscape, and in this case, he wasn't sure it would be possible to do so. From here, there might not be anything other than an empty void. There certainly wasn't much in the way of wind, and that was required to help keep the Shapers Path aloft. There was heat, and as heat was a part of the Shapers Path, he didn't worry about that, but it was water that would probably be the most difficult. Since water bound together the other shapings, he suspected it would be the one that would prevent the creation of the Shapers Path.

"It's somewhere back here," Tolan said, motioning.

He followed along and, as he went, he connected to earth, letting his awareness of it flow from beneath his boots, rolling up through him, until he could detect where things had changed. It was a strange awareness. The longer he went, the clearer it was there was something different here. Though he didn't know quite what that difference was, he was aware the landscape had changed recently.

He held onto that difference, using that to help guide him. When he reached a point where it shifted, things once again back the way they had been—and should be—he paused. This was the edge.

From here, he could almost make out Ephra. He could feel it, the sense of earth and wind and fire and water radiating from the city, giving it the distinct signature he'd noted when they first came close, but it was at least distant enough that the shifting edge of the waste would not have been visible.

"Here?" the Grand Inquisitor asked.

Tolan nodded. "It runs along here."

He motioned toward where the edge had been. He wandered along it, looking for any of the markings, but they had all been destroyed by him or the disciples of the Draasin Lord. When they had been there, confronting the Inquisitors, he'd feared the disciples would try to pull him back to their land since he'd escaped.

And he was surprised they hadn't. Tolan still didn't know if his father had come intentionally to help or if he'd wanted to drag Tolan back with them. He knew their secret, and it was one they would like to keep hidden. Knowing how to find them—and reach them—put them in danger.

More than that, if someone discovered that land, it would put the free elementals in danger. He had no interest in harming them. All Tolan wanted was to protect the elementals. That and understand them.

Taking a deep breath, he continued to trace along the strange remnant of what had shifted. Surprisingly, a vibrancy within the area had been changed, almost as if it rebelled against what had been done to it, demanding it to normalize again. Could that be just his imagination, or was there anything to it?

The longer he stood there, the more certain he was there was something here.

If nothing else, that he could still detect it was helpful, as was the fact the land felt restored. Both were important, though for very different reasons.

Tracking along here, he didn't come up with anything able to remind him of where the runes had been placed. The disciples had removed every bit of them, ensuring no damage remained. That was good and he should be thankful for it, but at the same time, he couldn't help but wonder if there was any way to find something similar near the edge of what was the current waste.

He started back toward it, ignoring the Grand Inquisitor, who was calling after him. When he reached the border, Tolan wandered along the edge. It was a distinct line, cut off from grass to rock. As he trailed along it, he didn't find anything unusual, at least anything more unusual than the reality of the waste. He probed the ground, thinking if there was anything similar to what had been done before, he should be able to find those runes. If he could, then maybe they could remove them.

"We have searched along here and have uncovered nothing," the Grand Inquisitor said, finally catching up to him.

Tolan paused, looking over at her. "If it's the same—"

She shook her head. "I doubt it's the same. There aren't

any runes here, not like what you described experiencing when you were attacked by the others."

Tolan let out a frustrated sigh. There had to be some explanation, and yet, why would *he* be the one to uncover it? It wasn't as if he'd have some new insight the others of the Academy would not have come up with.

On a whim, he stepped across the border and into the waste.

As soon as he did, everything within him was silenced. The shaping protecting his mind vanished. The sense of the ground and of the wind and of the heat burning overhead all disappeared. It was a stark and startling change, and it was one he didn't remember being quite so distressing. This time, he wanted nothing more than to step back across the border, to return to the normal lands, to get away from the absence of everything.

"What are you doing, Shaper Ethar?"

He took a deep breath, steeling himself. "Perhaps the runes are on this side."

"Do you think we haven't looked there?"

"It's possible it wasn't evaluated nearly as closely as the other side of the border. Think about it, Grand Inquisitor. Who wants to spend much time on this side of the waste?"

He continued making his way along the border, focused on the ground, searching for anything out of the ordinary, but it was possible they were hidden. Runes and whatever had been used to form the waste could have been placed on any of these rocks, and they could have been buried in such a way Tolan wouldn't be able to uncover them. Without any way of connecting to the elements or the elementals, he wouldn't know whether there was anything within the waste.

What if he went deeper?

Tolan turned his attention toward the vast expanse of the waste, staring outward. The idea of going deeper into the waste filled him with dread, much like it filled all shapers with that same emotion. He wondered what was out there though from what he understood, anyone who'd tried had never discovered anything.

"Maybe we're looking at this wrong," he said.

"Shaper Ethar?"

Tolan turned back and realized the Grand Inquisitor stood on this side of the border of the waste. Had he been connected to shaping and his abilities, he would have recognized her presence, but separated as he was, there was no awareness of her. It was a strange sensation, and it revealed to him just how much he'd come to rely on his connection to shaping over the last few months. More than anything, that told him how far he'd come.

"What if the waste extends out here because of something done out there," he said, pointing toward the center of the waste.

"We've tried looking."

"How far?"

"Farther than you can imagine."

Tolan turned toward the center of the waste, smiling at it. "I can imagine quite a way."

"And then imagine even farther," she said. "We have

records of shapers who have loaded themselves up with supplies, and they have wandered for days. Weeks. They went until they nearly ran out of water. In all that time, they never uncovered anything. It's nothing more than this. Emptiness. A vast nothingness. The waste is what it is, and though we don't understand it, and we don't really understand why it exists, it is here."

Tolan couldn't imagine spending weeks wandering across the waste. "How did they tolerate it?"

"Most who went had little ability to shape. It would be too hard sending someone who was connected to one of the elements out across it. Some went and were lost." Her voice trailed off slightly. "And yet, we had to balance that with the possible need of finding a place where they could once again shape, thinking if nothing else, if they uncovered some key, some way to reach an aspect of the waste where they could once again shape, they would be able to remove whatever had been done here."

"Before I was able to shape, I ventured out the farthest of my level."

"Now?"

"Now I don't know," Tolan said.

"Rest assured, Shaper Ethar, you still have gone farther than most master shapers are willing to go."

He turned, looking toward the edge of the waste. It was a hundred paces away, perhaps a little farther, and despite that, it still seemed as if it was so far from him. "Only because I know this is temporary."

"Knowing a thing and being able to do a thing are not

always compatible. There are many people who recognize rationally that stepping across the waste, having their connection to the bonds severed, is only temporary, but still struggle to remain out here. Then there is you."

"And you. And the Grand Master." And there had been others, though not all of the master shapers at the Academy had come. It was designed for those who were first-level students, a way of proving themselves, of demonstrating they had the necessary fortitude to venture here.

"Again, there is a difference between knowing a thing and doing that thing."

Tolan breathed out. "I thought we might find something here that would help explain what had happened, and perhaps we might be able to uncover what it is the Inquisitors did to cause the waste to retreat."

"No, Shaper Ethar. You came out here thinking you would find a way to remove the waste."

"I..."

She joined him, standing alongside him. Unlike when she'd joined him on the other side of the border, there was no sense of warmth from her, and there was no connection to her through the earth. He couldn't even detect her breathing, and there was no sense of the blood pumping through her veins. All of that was absent.

And yet, it couldn't be absent, could it?

There was heat in the air. There was earth beneath him. He was breathing. And he could feel his own heart beating when he checked the big artery in his neck, the blood pulsing through it.

Despite the fact he was here, he wasn't separated from the elements.

He was separated from the element bonds.

He had a way of shaping, but his wasn't always the same as others. He could reach for shaping when there was no access to the bonds, and places like the library.

Could he do so now?

"It's time for us to return and to begin the Selection," the Grand Inquisitor said.

She turned and Tolan debated hesitating, wondering whether he could uncover anything here, but despite knowing his abilities would return, he still didn't like lingering here.

He raced after the Grand Inquisitor, catching her, and when they stepped across the border, the power of the elements poured back into him, almost overwhelming him. Tolan froze, staggering under the weight of the sudden awareness of the various element bonds.

"It does not get any easier," the Grand Inquisitor said.

"It's just so much."

"When you go from nothing to everything, it is so much."

"How many times have you done it?"

"Hundreds," she said softly.

Tolan glanced over at her quickly. "Hundreds?" That was far more than he would've expected her to have said. If the first-level students came out even once a year, there would be no reason for her to have come hundreds of times. "Were you one of the people who tried to cross the waste?"

She shook her head. "I know myself better than that. I don't think I would have been able to tolerate going across the waste. No. I step across the border, stay as long as I can tolerate it, and then cross back over so I can feel the surge of elemental energies."

"Why?"

"For many reasons." She stared over the expanse of emptiness in the distance. "I suppose it's my way of being appreciative of the powers I'm given. Feeling that connection to them, feeling that surge, gives me a sense of peace." She smiled, and as she did, it made her seem almost friendly rather than the cold and calculating woman he usually knew her to be. "It helps me remember why I do the things I do. And now, I think it's helped me to be ready for what must come next."

"The Selection."

"Perhaps."

He thought she might explain more, but she shaped herself into the air with wind and fire, streaking toward Ephra. Tolan followed, his shaping far more controlled than it once had been, and he trailed right behind her. When they reached the edge of the city, she remained in the air, so Tolan did the same. She guided herself toward the Ephra Academy of Shaping and landed in the street in front of it. There was no other shaping from her, which suggested she wanted to be seen.

Tolan kept a shaping wrapped around his mind, protecting himself, but he trailed after her.

She strode forward, pushing open the door. She stood there for a moment, looking around the interior. Shaping exploded toward them, a stuttering frequency, and it struck a shaping formed by the Grand Inquisitor.

When it ended, she continued forward.

"Is that how you would greet the Grand Inquisitor?" she asked.

"Why are you here?"

This came from a deep voice. Tolan glanced in his direction and found an older man with gray hair. He was thin. Likely a wind shaper, then, though that wasn't always predictable.

"You would challenge the Grand Inquisitor?" A sudden surge of spirit shaping erupted from her, washing away and striking the man. He was thrown back under the weight of the shaping, and it even startled Tolan, enough so he threw up another barrier, using fire and wind, wrapping it around his mind, prepared for the possibility of an attack.

There was nothing.

The man got to his feet, blinking slowly. "Grand... Grand Inquisitor?"

She nodded. "That is better." She glanced over at Tolan. "See where the other shapers are."

"You expected this?"

"Not at first, but when we reached the city, I detected

something not quite right. I thought it was prudent to ensure we came prepared."

"Then why did we go to the waste?" It seemed to Tolan that had been a misuse of time they needed, especially if they had lost access to the Academy of Shaping in Ephra.

"How do you feel about your connection to your shapings?" she asked, her voice pitched low and sent on a shaping of wind meant only for his ears.

"Stronger, I guess."

She nodded. "There is something about the absence that makes its return stronger."

"You used that?"

"Partly."

Another figure appeared on the stairs in front of them, and the Grand Inquisitor pointed. "Hold them."

Tolan reacted, wrapping wind around them, anchoring it with earth. The shaper tried to fight, but Tolan had enough experience with battling with the various element bond energies that he was able to withstand the resistance, and he continued to hold on to it, keeping the shaper from moving away. This was a younger woman with deep black hair, dark skin, and brown eyes. He had never seen her here before, though it was possible she'd been here when he had visited for the last Selection and he had not known it.

The Grand Inquisitor made her way toward the woman, a shaping of spirit building. This time, Tolan focused on the nature of the spirit shaping, watching the way the Grand Inquisitor used it. She slipped it across the woman's mind. It was a strange sense, almost as if she was trying to swipe it, and then the woman gasped.

The attempts at fighting, struggling against the barrier Tolan held, faded.

"Grand Inquisitor," she said.

The Grand Inquisitor nodded. "Did you see what I did?"

The question was for Tolan rather than for the woman she had just shaped, and he frowned, thinking about the nature of the shaping. He did know what she had done, though he wasn't sure if he could recreate it if it were necessary. "I saw it, but it was too fast."

"Pay attention to the next one."

"I thought you said it was dangerous."

"So too is getting attacked by shapers who have been touched by the Inquisitors."

Was that what had happened here?

"Why didn't you know that sooner?"

The Grand Inquisitor looked over at him, frowning. "It's not as if I am all-knowing, Shaper Ethar. When it comes to what the Inquisitors were doing, it was a mystery."

"What if they did this at all of the other academies of shaping?"

The Grand Inquisitor froze. "Great Mother," she breathed out.

"Could they have?"

"It's possible, which means—"

"Others have encountered the same sort of thing."

The Grand Inquisitor nodded. "That is, unfortunately, what it means. We need to hurry."

She used a shaping of earth and water, the same shaping she'd used the night before, sending it out from her, adding a touch of spirit with it.

Tolan followed her shaping. When he did, he felt the reverberation of dozens of different shapers, some of them quiet nearby. She turned to the closest of them, heading through a doorway leading into a larger, open room. Tolan recognized it. It was the same room he'd gone into during his Selection, and he paused, looking around. There was no one here.

Pushing out with earth and water, adding a hint of spirit, he spun.

There was a shaper masked behind him.

Tolan reached for earth, focusing on it, and as he did, he shifted the shaping the other person was using to hide their presence.

The shaping disappeared with a rumble nearly throwing him off his feet, almost as if earth itself was angry at the fact he was disrupting what the other shaper was doing.

It was a younger man, probably only in his early twenties, and he lunged at Tolan.

Pushing outward with wind, Tolan slammed him back, pinning him against the wall.

He glanced over, but the Grand Inquisitor was gone.

Could he use the same spirit shaping she'd used?

Tolan reached for spirit. The sense of it came to him

slowly, building. As it did, he pulled upon it, using that to push toward the earth shaper. He sent it into the man's mind, sweeping across, using a light touch, feeling for anything that might be…

There.

It was a shaping. The effect was not subtle, and he suspected that wasn't the intention. Spirit had altered something about this man, and now he knew what it was, and now he could feel it, he thought he might be able to remove it.

A shaping built near him. Fire and wind.

He needed to act quickly. If he didn't, then the shaper who was coming toward him might attack, and he wasn't sure he'd be able to be quick enough to withstand it.

Swiping with spirit, he tried to use it the same way the Grand Inquisitor had, and as it did, he suddenly worried he might have been more aggressive.

The shaper collapsed.

Tolan swiped with spirit again, this time a gentler touch, trying to determine whether he'd damaged this person permanently, but wasn't able to detect whether or not he had.

The fire and wind shaping continued to build, and Tolan spun.

Another shaper was on the far side of the room, but he couldn't make them out. Wrapping earth around them, pushing on water to quench the flames, he sent a surge of spirit across their mind. This time, when he met the resistance, he recognized the need to withdraw, to not be quite as aggressive, and he swiped more gently, peeling across the person's mind and stripping free the shaping.

They gasped but didn't collapse as the other had.

He hesitated, pausing for a moment before using a shaping of spirit again, teasing across the person's mind, still fearing he might have been too aggressive with his last shaping. As he did, his breath caught.

"Tanner?"

9

It took the better part of an hour to make their way through the entire Academy. Tolan came across the Grand Master, and they worked together. He found his connection to spirit improved the longer he worked like this, sweeping across shapers' minds, peeling back what the Inquisitors had done.

Each time they did, there was a surge of relief from the trapped shaper. When this was all over, Tolan would have to find out whether or not the person who had been shaped was aware of what they were doing but helpless to do anything different, or whether or not it was more like what had happened to him, a shaping that had changed him, concealing his memories but of which he was completely unaware. It seemed to him the shapings were blunted, not meant at all to be hidden, which meant whatever had happened to the shapers was painful.

"How many more do we have?" he asked, glancing over at the Grand Master.

"Not many, but I worry there are others out in the city we have yet to uncover. And here I thought I was being clever hiding from shapers, not wanting to reveal we were here for a Selection before we wanted it known." She shook her head. "Unfortunately, I might've been more clever than necessary."

They were on the top floor of the Academy, and there were doors lining the hallway. Behind each one, Tolan could feel a shaper, and he'd come to realize they could reach through the door and peel apart the shaping without even needing to see the shaper, and so both he and the Grand Master worked their way along the hallway, quietly stripping free the spirit shaping worked upon everyone here. By this point, most of the people they encountered were young, likely students who stayed and trained here.

When they reached the end of the hall, Tolan focused on earth and wind, pushing it out, adding a hint of spirit to it. He was tired, the effort of shaping his way along the hallway getting to the point where he wasn't sure he'd be able to go any farther but he wanted to know if there was anyone else they needed to be concerned about.

The Grand Inquisitor did the same thing, adding her own shaping, though hers had quite a bit more strength than his did.

"I think that's everyone," she said.

"Does this mean there will be no Selection?"

She glanced over at him. "Unfortunately, that will be pushed back."

"Because we need to see if anyplace else has been attacked."

"My intention had always been to perform a Selection and move on to another city to attempt another, but unfortunately, it seems as if I need to make my way to the next location a little bit sooner than I had expected."

Tolan leaned on the wall, looking down the hallway. He didn't see anyone else, though connected as he was to earth and wind, he was able to detect them. Most of the shapers they'd restored remained far below, almost as if they were unwilling to come with them. The Grand Inquisitor had encouraged that with the shapers she'd restored, suggesting, likely through a shaping, they stay on the main levels.

"What more do you think we will find?" he asked.

"It depends on what the Inquisitors were after. If it was simply about control and sowing discord, we should have solved it by doing this. If it was about something else…"

Tolan frowned. "What else would there be?"

"We still don't know who they were serving."

It was the same concern Master Minden and the Grand Master had. When he'd mentioned it to the Grand Inquisitor before, she'd been dismissive, but that was before seeing this. There was no questioning something had happened here—just as there was now no questioning the Inquisitors were after something.

"Is there any way of detecting it from their shaping?"

"The shaping was never meant to be anything significant. It was meant to cloud their minds and perhaps cause problems, but they weren't shaped into trying to serve."

"What I mean is would it be possible for you to determine what the Inquisitors were doing when they came here?"

"Other than shaping them, it's possible they weren't doing anything."

Tolan wasn't sure it was true. There had to have been something the Inquisitors intended. They would have come through here, and in order for them to have impacted so many, they would've had to have been at a central place where they could have gained access.

Unless they had done something differently.

"How many of these have come for Selection before?"

"Why?"

"How many do you think we've encountered have presented themselves for Selection?"

"Perhaps all of them."

All of them.

And after a Selection, what was consistent? Everyone was shaped in such a way they would not remember the Selection, their memories wiped so they would not recall having presented themselves, thereby opening themselves up to the possibility they could undergo another Selection in the future, though Tolan wondered how many people eventually passed. He had been made to believe someone could present multiple times before passing, and he had seen with Velthan that seemed to be true—but many of these people would never have passed the Selection.

"They all had a spirit shaping, and in order for the Inquisitors to have used the spirit shaping like that, they would've had to have had access to their minds. What if they used the spirit shaping placed following Selection in order to do so?"

"It shouldn't have been possible."

"From what we've seen, there's a lot of things that shouldn't have been possible."

And in doing so, removing the shaping, would they suddenly have memories of their Selection?

"We need to find out if they now remember their Selection."

"Shaper Ethar—"

"Humor me. We don't know if this is the case or not, but I have to wonder if perhaps there is something more to this. It seems to me the shaping of spirit would be far too difficult to use on all of these people." While he didn't know the nature of the shaping used following a Selection, he doubted it was quite like what they had encountered. Then again, it didn't need to be subtle. Once they had a shaping in place, how hard would it be to twist it?

It was his ignorance about spirit shaping that drove him. Perhaps none of this was possible. If that were the case, then everything he was suggesting would not matter.

There was one person he could go to find out.

Tolan headed down the stairs, reaching the main hallway. He searched through the shapers until he came across the one he was looking for.

"Tanner," he said, nodding to his friend. "Can I talk with you?"

Tanner blinked. "Tolan? What are you doing here?" He looked at Tolan, eyeing him up and down. "And why are you dressed like that?"

"I was Selected for the Academy. That's what I want to talk to you about."

"*You* were? Tolan, you couldn't shape."

"Perhaps not, but do you remember when I came for the Selection?"

"Why should I?"

Perhaps it didn't matter that Tanner didn't remember, and perhaps it didn't matter that the only reason he'd gone through everything he had was because he'd tried to support his friend. Were it not for that, were it not for wanting to offer support for Tanner, he never would've uncovered his connection to the elements—and the elementals.

"Do you remember anything about having a spirit shaping placed on you?"

"A *what?*"

Tolan nodded. "Do you remember Inquisitors coming to the Academy here?"

Tanner started shaking his head, looking along the hallway. There were a dozen other shapers, all of different ages, and they still had something of a stunned expression about them. Not that Tolan could blame them. What they had gone through was enough that it would stun anyone. Every so often, he detected a hint of shaping, though there wasn't much power to it.

When a particularly strong shaping surged, he glanced over his shoulder, thinking it had to be one of the instructors, but realized it came from a younger girl, probably no more than mid-teens, and she was shaping fire.

She had considerable potential. He didn't even need to put her through a Selection to know that, and he didn't need to probe her with spirit to be able to detect her connection to shaping was strong, perhaps stronger than some of the instructors working with her.

Was that part of the Selection? Was it all designed to find people like her? She was young, though. She would have been far too young to go to the Academy, where most of the time they preferred older students, given the rigors of the training and the fact they were so far from home.

Tolan shook his head. "I need to know what you can recall."

"I can't recall anything. I still can't believe it's you."

"We've seen each other since I left," he said.

"We have?"

There was so much he needed to tell his friend, and there was something about the way Tanner looked at him that suggested he could tell him. Taking a deep breath, Tolan focused on spirit. He was tired, but maybe he wasn't too tired for this.

Reaching deep within him, he pushed outward, using the touch of spirit, barely more than that, and sent it across Tanner's mind. In doing so, he searched for another shaping. He wasn't going to remove it. If it was nothing more than the spirit shapings used on him following each of the attempts at the Selection, then Tolan wasn't going to be responsible for taking them away, but at the same time, if there was something he could uncover, if there was no evidence of a spirit shaping, there was value in that, too.

As he probed, he found nothing.

There were Tanner's memories, and there was a sense from his friend's mind that his thoughts were jumbled, probably more jumbled than they should be, but that was probably as much from the fact he'd been subjected to the Inquisitor attack as anything.

Tolan released his shaping and forced a smile. "It really is good to see you, Tanner."

"How were you Selected?"

"There is a way of detecting a latent shaping," he said. "The Selection has a way of digging into it and uncovering it. In my case, apparently I can shape."

Tanner's gaze darted to Tolan's jacket and the pin there. "You can't just shape. You're a master shaper."

Tolan smiled. "I'm not quite a master, but a third-level student. If you ever reach the Academy, you'll understand."

"How? Why?"

"I think there is too much for me to explain right now.

We'd come here anticipating a Selection, but I don't know we will do so."

"Shaper Ethar?"

Tolan turned to see the Grand Inquisitor looking at him.

"It is time for us to depart."

He looked around at the other shapers. There was confusion throughout, though he didn't need to be a shaper to know that. "Just like that? There's nothing else we're going to do?"

"There isn't anything more for us to do. We have done everything we can, and unfortunately, because of what has taken place, we need to prepare for the possibility of more like this."

Tolan glanced over at Tanner. His friend still looked at him, the bewildered expression on his face almost hard for Tolan to his stomach. "There isn't a shaping on his mind anymore," Tolan said softly, pitching his words so they were only for the Grand Inquisitor. "I used spirit, and I don't detect anything."

"You might not," she said.

"A shaping would be so subtle I wouldn't even be able to detect it?"

"It could be."

Tolan glanced at Tanner. "He has presented himself for at least two Selections. He doesn't remember my coming the last time when I was here for the most recent Selection, and he doesn't recall me presenting myself in the first place, though I know he was present at both.

Despite that, I can't find any evidence of a shaping in his mind."

"As I said—"

"I know what you're saying, but just check."

Her shaping started slowly and built. As it did, it washed over Tanner. It was a gentle touch, even more gentle than what Tolan had done. As it worked through him, Tanner continued to stare, unmindful of the fact anything was even happening to him.

The Grand Inquisitor continued to push, her shaping washing out from her, and she began to frown.

"Is there a spirit shaping there?"

"No."

"There should have been, though."

"There should have been, but… You were the one to remove his shaping?"

"I removed it, but only because he was preparing to attack me." Tanner had used wind, but also fire. That was progress, though Tolan didn't know how skilled his friend would've been with fire. It was possible even with the ability to shape fire, Tanner wouldn't have done anything to harm him. Tolan's own ability with fire was significant enough that he didn't know if someone like Tanner would be able to do anything harmful. He didn't consider himself immune to fire, but he certainly had gained a certain resilience.

"Perhaps that's all it is," the Grand Inquisitor said.

"You think I just removed his shaping?"

"I think it's possible."

"Not intentionally," Tolan said.

The Grand Inquisitor focused on him for a moment. "As I said, you will need to learn more control. Spirit shaping can be dangerous, especially if used without an understanding of the dangers."

"I'm well aware of the dangers involved with spirit shaping," Tolan said, letting too much of his irritation with his parents surge into his words. The Grand Inquisitor didn't deserve that from him, and she wasn't the one responsible for what had happened to him, though she was responsible for his Inquisition. "I was careful."

"As careful as you were with the first one?"

Tolan glanced over to the man who had attacked him, the one whose shaping he'd first peeled away. He'd been more aggressive than he needed to be and had stripped away with far more force than was likely required. Despite that, the man sat on a chair, awake. When Tolan had probed his mind, testing to see if there was any permanent damage, he hadn't uncovered anything.

Then again, it was possible he wouldn't be able to uncover anything from him. As much as he might try, his own control over shaping and his understanding of spirit was not so much that he'd be able to do so.

"I didn't have much choice."

"No, but now you do, you begin to understand."

"What if the Inquisitors wanted us to peel away those memories?"

"What makes you say that?"

"Only that the shaping used on them was blunt. What if they intended for us to peel that away, for us to find some way of realizing what they'd done so we'd be forced to act and strip away the shaping that might've been used on them?"

The Grand Inquisitor frowned. "I would say that's unlikely. Aela in particular would be far more subtle than that."

From Tolan's experience with Aela, he knew it was true. She was devious, and she likely would've been far subtler than to pull away those shapings, but there seemed to be some reason the shapings had been changed like this. Regardless of what the Grand Inquisitor said, Tolan was convinced the shapings were tied to the ones placed following the Selection.

What was it about the Selection they needed to conceal?

Better yet, what was it about the Selection they wanted to reveal?

"How long would it take for us to perform a Selection?" he asked.

"Longer than I feel comfortable giving us."

"Even if we left now, what are the chances we would reach any of these other cities in time?"

They had delayed once they reached Ephra. Not only had they rested overnight, but they had gone to the waste.

The other parties would likely have already reached their cities. Traveling on a Shapers Path didn't take them long to do so, and it would have given him the opportunity to explore, but then again…

"They were going to wait for you, weren't they?" Tolan asked.

The Grand Inquisitor watched him, frowning. "They were."

"Perhaps they won't run into the difficulty."

"When you came for the last Selection, what do you remember?" the Grand Inquisitor asked.

"We met with several of the master shapers, preparing for the Selection."

"Exactly. And what do you think the others will have done?"

"The same thing," Tolan said slowly.

"Again, exactly. If the other master shapers have been influenced in such a way…"

"What if the master shapers weren't influenced?"

"What we have seen here suggests otherwise."

"Only at the academy, but we haven't gone and spoken to any of the master shapers. There are at least three in Ephra, and none of them teach at the academy." He had often wondered about that, but still didn't have a good answer as to why Master Daniels hadn't taught at the Academy. There was likely some reason tied to how they served following their time at the Academy. If he could find Master Salman, then perhaps they might be able to know.

"I suppose we have enough gathered here that we could attempt a Selection," she said carefully.

Tolan looked along the line of people. "You think they are in any shape to succeed?"

"I don't expect any of them to pass, if that's what you believe."

"Then what's the point?"

"The point, Shaper Ethar, is you believe they will."

She turned and strode away, going to whisper softly to someone at the other end of the hallway. Tolan was left standing with Tanner.

"Does that mean there will be a Selection?" Tanner asked.

"It sounds like it."

"I wish I could remember."

"You understand following a Selection, your memories will be removed," Tolan said carefully.

"We always suspected. We don't talk about it all that much. Most of the time, people are reluctant to share anything about the Selection, afraid if they share too much, they won't be given the opportunity to undergo another one. But then, it never seems as if anyone is ever Selected."

He frowned. "Velthan was selected at the last one."

"Velthan?"

Tanner said the other man's name almost as if he didn't recognize it. That couldn't be. How could they have concealed Velthan? Then again, other than his family, why would anyone need to remember him? He could be removed, memories of him wiped, and he could go with them to the Academy without revealing anything.

Tolan couldn't shake the sense there was something to that, something about the fact there were no memories. That was important.

"Good luck," he said, turning away from Tanner. He found the Grand Inquisitor at the other end of the hall, talking with who he suspected was the head of the Ephra academy. The gray-haired man who had greeted them when they first entered had reasonable shaping ability, though as far as Tolan could tell, he'd never taught at the Academy and had never trained there, either.

When she was done, she turned back to him, watching him. "What is it, Shaper Ethar?"

"I'm just trying to understand why people would have their memories of the shapers removed."

"So, they continue to serve."

"That doesn't make any sense."

"It does, but only if you understand why. Think about it, Shaper Ethar. If you were given the opportunity to present yourself and failed time and again, how would you feel about your ability to offer anything of use to Terndahl?"

"Just because I wasn't selected for the Academy doesn't mean I'd suddenly stop trying to serve Terndahl."

"Perhaps not you. From what I understand of the Selection process, there have been previous iterations where there was no attempt to remove those memories. In those cases, the people maintained their recollection of who they were and what they were prior to the Selection. They remembered those who had been chosen while they were not. They realized some who they felt were weaker shapers were Selected while they remained behind. That has created challenges over time, forcing us to reevaluate our approach."

"Why?"

"There is a natural instinct to want to be better than someone else. There is also a natural instinct to think your skill is superior to someone else's. In the case of you in particular, Shaper Ethar, imagine what would have happened had others known you were Selected while they were not? Would they continue to work as hard as they do at shaping?"

"I think so."

"Even if they believed it didn't matter? Even if they believed their attendance at the local academy didn't matter?"

"But it doesn't matter."

"Of course, it does. You and I both know that, as does the Grand Master and everyone else in Terndahl. Having shapers is valuable, regardless of the level of talent they possess. The need is for them to serve, to remain vigilant, and even more so here. Having shapers in Ephra, this close to the waste, has always been beneficial."

Tolan frowned. "I still worry there is something about the shaping placed that the Inquisitors are taking advantage of."

"It's possible, but I haven't been able to determine anything."

"How many of them still have a shaping upon them?"

"None," she said.

"So, it wasn't just me removing that spirit shaping." She looked over at him. "No."

"Don't you think that's significant somehow?"

"The question is how, though. Right now, their minds remain somewhat jumbled, and though they no longer recall what they had before, they might eventually gain those memories back."

Tolan wasn't sure how to feel about that. If Tanner began to remember the conversations they had before, if he remembered Tolan coming to support him, would he suddenly get his friend back?

Did it even matter? Since going to the Academy, his priorities had changed. He had been isolated in Ephra, and though there had been a similar isolation at the Academy, it was nowhere near what he'd experienced while in Ephra. The isolation he experienced at the Academy was more to do with the fact he had undergone an Inquisition, not so much because he was believed to serve the Draasin Lord.

"If they gain those memories back, you fear that will cause problems," he said.

"I do."

"Which is why you've replaced those shapings." He wasn't sure whether or not she had, but it fit.

"It was necessary, Shaper Ethar."

"What if the Inquisitors return and use those shapings against them again?"

"I'm not convinced it's what they were doing."

"You might not be, but I worry about it."

"Then you should not worry, either."

He snorted. "That doesn't help."

"Come, Shaper Ethar. It's time for us to perform the Selection. It's time for you to understand what the role of the spirit shaper in the Selection to be."

"What will I do?"

"Observe. And if you decide you would like to become an Inquisitor, then perhaps you will perform the shaping."

She turned away from him, heading down the hall, leaving him standing alone for a moment. It was a strange sense. Did he want to become an Inquisitor? He didn't think so, but then again, what were the Inquisitors?

Maybe that was what he needed to understand. Once he did, he could decide, though Tolan had a hard time thinking he'd ever choose to serve in such a way. His role was going to be different.

That was what Master Minden had been trying to guide him toward. And wasn't that what he wanted to do? The idea of serving in the library was more appealing to him, but perhaps it was only more appealing because he thought he had more of an affinity for it. If what the Grand Inquisitor was saying was true, perhaps he had an affinity for something else, as well.

Taking a deep breath, he hurried after the Grand Inquisitor. He had a sense of urgency when it came to this, and it was more than just trying to understand what he was supposed to do. It came from not knowing what the other Inquisitors were after, and the belief whatever it was would cause trouble for Terndahl.

Even that might not matter. To Tolan, it wasn't so much the issue with ensuring Terndahl remain safe. It was more about the elementals.

Everything he did, staying away from the Academy, following the Grand Inquisitor, seemed as if it pulled him further and further from his search to try to understand what he could do to better serve the elementals.

Tolan paused, staring at the Grand Inquisitor's back.

The Grand Master trusted her, and she'd supposedly proven herself, but what if she was the one the Inquisitors served?

Tolan had to be careful.

He formed a barrier around his mind, but was that even enough? What if she had some way of overpowering his mental barrier? What if her connection to spirit shaping was such that she could work past everything he might be able to do to protect his mind?

And why had he only now begun to question?

That last thought worried him most of all.

There was nothing to be done but to continue to observe, to be vigilant, and to be ready.

For now, he would participate in this Selection, and he'd do whatever it took to try to understand what was involved, if only so he might know the kind of things the Inquisitors had done.

10

Standing next to the Grand Inquisitor, Tolan wondered whether or not he should be worried about her intentions. He tried to push those thoughts out of his mind, knowing nothing good would be served by doubting her, at least not here, and certainly not so close to her, where she might be able to somehow uncover what exactly he was thinking.

"You will pay attention to the shaping," she said.

Tolan nodded. What other choice did he have but to pay attention to the shaping? The door to the great hall they stood in opened. The room was enormous, lit by lanterns hanging from the walls, and a subtle shaping energy radiated from the Grand Inquisitor, enough that he wondered whether she was doing that for his benefit or for the Selection.

A line of potential candidates approached. There had

to be a dozen, possibly fifteen, and he scanned the two lines forming, looking for any familiar faces other than Tanner. As Tolan had suspected, Tanner submitted himself for testing, though he wondered if that was helpful or not. Tanner had presented himself twice before and failed both times. While Tolan didn't know if his sudden ability to now shape fire would make a difference, he doubted it.

Where was the young girl he'd seen? She might have only been in her mid-teens, but she was strong with her shaping ability, and the kind of person he could easily imagine passing. He glanced over at the Grand Inquisitor, noting the deep concentration wrinkling her brow and the shaping building from her.

He focused on that. If nothing else, he should pay attention to the way she shaped, prepared for the possibility there might be something within her shaping he might be able to uncover.

It was mostly spirit which Tolan wasn't surprised by. He figured she'd be using a considerable amount of spirit in her shaping, and the longer she did, the more likely she would turn that toward the approaching candidates, and when she did, he wanted to be ready for what she did to them.

"There was another candidate I encountered," he said, glancing over at the Grand Inquisitor. "I'm surprised she's not here."

"Not all candidates have presented themselves."

"Isn't that surprising?"

"Should it be? Some realize they won't pass and don't bother to present themselves for Selection, while others who never will pass present themselves each time. They are no different from each other."

The idea there would be some who might be able to do well at the Academy but did not offer themselves troubled him. Perhaps that was just as well, though wasn't the point of the Academy to train those who might best be able to serve Terndahl? If they didn't come, and if there was no opportunity to uncover what those shapers might be able to do, it seemed to him the Academy would be lessened in some ways.

The door closed and the Grand Inquisitor stepped forward. Her shaping continued to build, sweeping away from her, power radiating with it. Tolan focused on the nature of her shaping, searching for anything within it to help him understand what she was doing. It was powerful and seemed to be simply a burst of spirit, but the longer he focused on it, the more he found other elements buried within. It seemed almost as if she were using spirit as a way to try to mask what else she was doing.

He doubted it was coincidental.

She claimed the Grand Master had tested her himself.

The shaping continued to build, and rather than thinking he needed to question her motives, he focused instead on the nature of her shaping and the way she used it. If he could uncover anything, it would be far more valuable than trying to determine whether or not she was trying to conceal something from him. Perhaps this was little more than another test. She'd already told him she would show him various shapings, and she'd been the one to have demonstrated the shaping used to remove the damage to the rest. It wasn't as if she intended to keep that from him.

"You have all presented yourself for a Selection. There will be several aspects to the Selection, but you should know it will be difficult. In coming before us, you have presented yourself as interested in training at the Academy. As those who have trained before you can attest, the Academy is not for any who do not have the necessary fortitude."

The words were different than she'd used before, and with each sentence, another shaping rolled away from her, slowly sweeping out, washing over them. Through it all came the sense of spirit, a surge of power almost designed to force others away.

That wasn't quite right.

As Tolan focused on what she was doing, he realized there was something within the shaping, the way earth and wind mingled, fire and water, all of them blending together, probing into each person's mind. As it did, he could feel something deep within him.

Strange. There was something like a reverberation, much like there had been when they had been shaping earth and water out on the street. This time, spirit was not just a complementary element; it was the more significant element. In using the shaping as she did, it pushed deep within each individual, and the other elements were the complements, giving her an opportunity to dig deep into them, to probe and see if there was anything there that might be uncovered.

As it did, he recognized what she was doing. The power fluctuated, pulsating, and bounced back.

But not from all of them.

Only a handful.

Strangely, they all stood blankly, and he wondered what they experienced. What had he experienced when he'd first come to the Selection? Had it been something like this? He recalled something, but perhaps it was this. He'd been so focused on the fact he was here, and even when he'd returned, when he'd been a part of the previous Selection, he hadn't paid as much attention to the various aspects within it. Now he was standing alongside the Grand Inquisitor he was far more a part of it than he had been before.

"Some of you will find your desire to proceed has waned, and some of you will find you aren't able to continue onward."

She nodded toward him.

With a start, Tolan realized what he was supposed to be doing. There were many of the shapers who had not yet come around.

He went to them, guiding them, walking them to the door. It opened, and the gray-haired shaper helped escort each of the students away. Unsurprisingly, Tanner remained, though when he'd been here before, Tanner had persisted through several of the levels. Then again, the shaping at that time seemed different.

"You must be prepared to face your fears, and you must be strong in order to overcome them. The Academy trains only the best, and in doing so, we must ensure we have the best potentials."

The shaping shifted. Rather than holding on to the other elements, now she pressed only spirit. The shaping was different, a twisted type she touched upon each of the individuals. Tolan missed what she did the first few times, but by the time she got to the fifth person—Tanner, he realized—he was able to detect the nature of what she was doing.

It was layer upon layer of spirit, and it pressed upon a specific part of his mind, deep and distantly buried within him. It spiraled, twisting through his mind, almost as if trying to burrow within it.

What was she trying to accomplish, using the shaping like that?

Perhaps nothing other than reaching deep within him, but then, Tolan remembered the nature of the shaping he'd experienced. It had been a test. That shaping had forced him to confront an elemental, and though he'd been terrified of it, what had he done?

Nothing other than chase that power. It was the same as what he'd done ever since heading to the Academy. He'd not been nearly as afraid of the elementals as he should have been, and now, confronting it again, but this time from the other side, he still didn't know if he'd done the right thing.

One of the potential candidates fell. It was a young man, only a few years younger than Tolan. He was muscular, with a build suggesting a predilection toward earth. He began to convulse, and the Grand Inquisitor turned her shaping. Tolan had no other way to describe what she did other than that. In turning it, she eased back on spirit, and the convulsing began to abate before ending altogether. She frowned, shaking her head. Tolan went over to him, lifting him—forced to use a bit of earth in doing so—and escorted him to the door with the others. That left four shapers, and the Grand Inquisitor continued to hold onto her shaping.

As he paid attention to what she was doing, Tolan began to realize why the sequence worked the way it did. If she would've gone with this shaping first, it would have required far more concentration than he suspected she had, forcing her to split her spirit focus. The very first shaping was generalized with the wash of spirit used in it. That was what she utilized in order to prevent anyone from recalling the nature of their shaping.

This one was nearly entirely spirit.

Another of the candidates fell. This was a young woman with deep chestnut hair, and she collapsed, lying motionless. As he made his way over to her, he noted the slight twist the Grand Inquisitor used was similar to what she'd done with the last person. That twist was what he suspected concealed the nature of the shaping, keeping her from recognizing what had been done and from recognizing she'd presented for Selection.

When another fell—still not Tanner, Tolan was somewhat relieved to note—he focused more on the Grand Inquisitor rather than the fallen. As she twisted her shaping, he recognized what she was doing. The shaping itself was not complicated. It was the nature of the twist, the way she turned toward the end, inverting in a certain way, reminding him of what he did when he created the shaping around his own mind.

Hurrying this person over to the door, he scrambled back, curious as to whether he'd uncover the same thing when the next person fell.

He waited, but neither Tanner nor the other—a woman nearly the same age—did fall.

The Grand Inquisitor continued to hold onto her shaping. She poured more and more strength into it, letting it flow outward, and he waited for her to release that hold. While waiting, he also waited for Tanner and the other woman to collapse, but neither of them did.

Eventually, the Grand Inquisitor released her shaping.

After a few moments, Tanner blinked open his eyes. The other woman did as well, and she and Tanner shared a look before turning their attention back to the Grand Inquisitor.

"The next step will be the most difficult for you," she said.

Tolan wasn't sure what she would do this time. He didn't remember anything beyond the first parts of it, and now he was here, now Tanner had seemingly passed as much as he had, it was possible he'd still fail. Though he didn't want his friend to fail, he wasn't sure it was safe for Tanner to be at the Academy until they figured out what was taking place with the Inquisitors. Maybe it would be best for him to fail, and for him to come to the Academy another time when the business with the Inquisitors was resolved. For now, it might be best—and safest—for them not to bring new students to the Academy.

"Now you must decide whether you want to be a part of the Academy."

Tolan glanced over at the Grand Inquisitor. He didn't recall that being a part of his Selection, and maybe it was because it hadn't been part of his. The option of choosing not to join the Academy had not been there. He had been told he needed to be a part of the Academy since he'd presented himself for testing.

"If you choose to join the Academy, you will find your training is difficult. We will push you, and though you will become a far greater shaper than you are at this point, there will be challenges, and you will find it is much more difficult than anything else you have ever attempted."

Tolan couldn't take his gaze off the Grand Inquisitor. The idea she was giving them this flexibility surprised him.

There was a shaping mixed with it, though.

The words were meant to distract, almost as if she intended to keep anyone who might be aware of the spirit shaping from detecting it, but Tolan could feel it. It was subtle, far subtler than anything else she had used, but with that shaping, he recognized the way she layered her touch upon them.

She held the shaping in place. If they chose the wrong way, he recognized what she would do. She'd twist it, inverting the shaping, and they would forget everything that occurred. Their minds would be wiped, and everything they had experienced would disappear.

"I want to train at the Academy," Tanner said.

The Grand Inquisitor pressed her shaping forward, but she didn't invert it. That was odd. Did she leave the shaping in place so she could add to it at any given time?

"I choose to train at the Academy," the woman said.

Once again, the Grand Inquisitor did the same thing with her shaping, turning it ever so slightly, enough that it was twisted, bound to their mind, and all it would take would be a hint of another twist and it would be forgotten.

It was something he would have to ask her about when this was all done, but now was not the time.

"Gather whatever you need, and we will depart."

They headed toward the front of the hall, and Tolan glanced over at the Grand Inquisitor. "I don't remember being offered an opportunity to leave."

"I wanted to prepare them. It was one more test."

"What sort of test was this one?"

"It was a final test, and I added a hint of knowledge of what they might experience. I gave them the opportunity to turn away from the threat of the Draasin Lord"—Tolan cringed at the idea the new members of the Academy had to fear the Draasin Lord—"and they were given the opportunity to choose anything else. In this case, they both chose to join us at the Academy to continue their training."

"Did you think they would choose otherwise?"

The Grand Inquisitor turned her attention to him. "Considering everything they had encountered, I didn't know. That was why I thought it was prudent to give them the alternative. Given what they had experienced, and the danger they had come to know, I thought it was reasonable to offer that option to them."

What would Tolan have done were he given that choice? Having passed the Selection, would he have chosen to return?

It was better not to even think about it.

"What do we do now?"

"Now you will be the one to guide them back to Amitan, and I will be off to Par."

Par meant Ferrah, and if there was anyone who he wanted to make sure was safe, it was her. He didn't like the idea of anything happening to her, but more than that, he wanted to be there if she were to confront any of the spirit-shaped people.

"I can see what you're thinking," the Grand Inquisitor said.

"You can see it?"

"I'm not shaping you, if that's what you think."

"I wasn't thinking it, actually."

"You are concerned about your particular friend. And I can assure you nothing will happen to her."

Tolan cocked his head to the side. "I'm not sure you can assure me of that."

"Nothing will happen to her."

"Other than the fact she might be attacked by people like this."

"We don't know the Inquisitors managed to reach them in other places."

"Considering how long they were gone, I think it's possible they traveled throughout Terndahl, using their influence."

The Grand Inquisitor frowned. "Unfortunately, it's possible."

"Which means you might need my help."

"I think I can manage."

"I didn't mean it like that."

"I'm sure you didn't, but as I said, I am sure I will be able to manage quite well. Now I know to be concerned about this, my preparation will be different. That is my assignment. Your assignment will be to escort them back to Amitan. You will ensure they get settled within the Academy, and from there, you will wait until the rest of us return."

Tolan stared at her for a moment, wishing there was something he could say, some way he could encourage her to allow him to go with her. If she was going to Par, and if there was anything he could do to help Ferrah, he wanted to do it. He didn't want to be left behind and wanted to offer her whatever help he could.

At the same time, that wasn't his place. He was a third-level student. He already had enough difficulty with his position from what had happened, and even if he thought he might be able to risk pushing the issue, he wasn't sure he should.

Tolan just nodded. What other choice did he have?

When Tanner and the other young woman—someone he had apparently met once before by the name of Bryn—returned, he had fallen into some sort of silence. They both carried a bag, Tanner having one he slung over his shoulder while Bryn carried one that was smaller but looked to be packed full.

"Are the two of you ready to make the journey to Amitan?"

He glanced at the Grand Inquisitor, but she said nothing. She only watched him, as if waiting for him to make a mistake, but in this case, Tolan was determined not to make one. He would do what was necessary to fulfill his obligations.

Tanner nodded, as did Bryn.

They made their way out of the Academy building, through the city, none of them speaking. When they reached the outskirts, the distant sense of the Shapers Path, Tolan paused. The Grand Inquisitor hadn't followed them, and it troubled him a little bit that she'd gone off on her own, leaving him to wonder what she was doing and where she was going and whether there was anything he might have been helpful with.

"Do you know about a Shapers Path?" he asked the two of them.

Tanner shook his head, but Bryn nodded. "A Shapers Path leads between most of the places in Terndahl," she said.

"Very good. We're going to take it and follow the Shapers Path back to the Academy."

"How will we reach it?"

Tolan hadn't given it much thought. When he had first reached the Shapers Path, it had been Jory who had brought him to it, and because of Jory, he had been carried up to the Shapers Path. That was now his responsibility.

Could he carry both of them?

He wasn't sure he had the strength to lift two others with him, nor was he sure he had the control.

"I will bring you," he said.

Tanner watched him, and Bryn only nodded. With that, Tolan focused on wind and fire, using the two elements and mingling them together as he lifted them into the air, carrying them to the Shapers Path.

Once there, he paused. In the distance, he had the sense of a shaping emanating from somewhere. It was a powerful sort of shaping suggesting it came from the Grand Inquisitor. If that were the case, then why did it seemed to be coming from farther to the north—a place only near the waste?

Tearing his gaze away, he didn't have time to worry

about what the Grand Inquisitor might or might not be doing. He had a task, and he'd fulfill it. It was because of him they had proceeded with the Selection, and he suddenly realized he was the reason the Grand Inquisitor had assigned him the responsibility of escorting them back to the city.

He would ensure their safety.

"Come along. We have a long way to go," Tolan said.

11

IT WAS LATE IN THE DAY WHEN THE WIND SHIFTED. They had been walking for most of the day, Tolan adding a hint of shaping to their journey to give them a boost of speed. As they went, he'd been focused on the distant sense of Amitan. With every passing moment, he was more and more aware of how they approached the city.

Having that awareness was surprising, something he hadn't expected he would be able to do, but he recognized that sense of Amitan. It seemed to call to him, a beacon drawing them toward it.

Tolan paused, listening to the wind. A sudden change was startling. It had been gusting up from the south, carrying with it a hint of cool air and mixing with the scents of Amitan along with the rest of Terndahl. It was the kind of wind he felt should have elemental energy mixed within it, but as far as he could tell, did not. When it shifted, he focused on it, cocking his head to the side, feeling the way it whistled past him, caressing his cheeks.

"Tolan?" Tanner asked.

He'd been generally quiet throughout the entire journey, almost as if he didn't know what to say to Tolan, though for his part, Tolan wasn't entirely sure what to say to his friend, either. There had been some small talk, but mostly it had been excitement for Tanner and Bryn, the kind of excitement he remembered the other shapers having when he had found them on the journey to Amitan. The only person who hadn't shared in that excitement had been Tolan.

"What is it?" Tolan asked.

"Why did you stop?"

"The wind changed," he said.

He still couldn't tell if there was anything he needed to be concerned about with the changing of the wind. It might be nothing. Changing weather patterns weren't all that uncommon. He had enough experience to know there were shifts to the wind, and when it did change, there was nothing dangerous to it, but the suddenness of it, along with the nature of the shift, left him a little uncertain.

"Why are you concerned about changing wind?"

"The changing wind can mean different things. When you shape the wind—"

Tanner started to grin. "I think I know about shaping the wind, Tolan. If you remember, I've been doing it for longer than you."

Tolan turned back to Tanner. "And in your time studying at the academy in Ephra, has your mastery of the wind helped you understand what is taking place?"

"I doubt anything is taking place. If it's like you said and the wind shifted, there's nothing to worry about."

"Only, there might be."

Tolan turned away from them, ignoring the hushed conversation between Bryn and Tanner, her warning him not to push Tolan. For his part, Tolan didn't want Tanner to say anything more, not wanting to get upset with his friend. Even though he'd been the one pushing for the Selection, Tanner viewed him as the same person who had left Ephra. He didn't see Tolan as the man who now had control over each of the elements—and the elementals, for that matter.

The wind continued to push on him. In this case, it had a distinct nature to it. He had felt wind gusting like this, and…

"Elemental," he whispered.

"What was that?" Tanner asked, pushing up against him.

Tolan looked around. Most of the time when there were elementals, he wasn't concerned about them, but something in this gusting wind left him uncomfortable, and it made him question whether there was something to be concerned about. It could be the elemental had been freed from the bond. If that were the case, there tended to be a certain wildness to the elemental. When that occurred, they had to be calmed.

With Tanner and Bryn here, Tolan wasn't sure he'd be able to calm a wild elemental. Anything he'd do would be observed. At the same time, he had the advantage they wouldn't know exactly what he was doing. He could do whatever he thought was necessary in order to soothe an elemental. Once that was done, he could try to dismiss it rather than forcing it back into the bond.

"The changing of the wind is an elemental. With the way it is pushing on us, I suspect this is ara, though I can't be certain." Tolan focused on the wind, reaching out toward it, using his connection to wind sensing in order to try to gain that understanding, but it didn't come to him as quickly as he needed it to.

"An elemental?" Bryn breathed out a nervous laugh. "We haven't seen any rogue elementals near Ephra for a while."

"No. I doubt you have." The runes the Inquisitors had placed would have ensured any rogue elementals would have been drawn to them, forcing them away from whatever it was that had drawn them out of the bond. Which meant the last rogue elemental they had experienced in Ephra had been the one Tolan had been a part of.

"Are you sure it's an elemental?" Tanner asked. "I mean, it just feels like the wind blowing."

"What can you feel about the wind?"

Tanner chuckled. "Tolan. Like I said—"

"What can you feel about the wind?" he repeated. He glanced at Bryn. "Are you able to shape wind?"

She shook her head quickly. "Not yet. Fire. A little bit of water."

That meant whatever happened, he'd have to convince Tanner, and more than that, Tanner was the one from whom he'd have to mask his actions.

"When you focus on the wind, you can feel the way it's blowing from out of the south. It's not just the nature of the gusting wind, it's the way it is pushing, the power behind it, and it tells me it is not completely natural." That wasn't quite right, but Tanner didn't need to know that in some ways, the elemental energy was even more natural than anything else. "If you focus on it, you can feel the ongoing pressure. It's almost as if it's shaped, but not quite."

Tanner stared at Tolan skeptically. "Why don't we just keep going? I think you were supposed to bring us back to the Academy?"

Tolan nodded. "I was supposed to bring you back the Academy, and I will get you there safely, but I'm not willing to rush onward until I know whether we have anything to be worried about with this elemental."

"Tolan—"

Tolan shook his head. Could he really have to argue with Tanner like this? He hated that it would come to that, but he hated just as much that it seemed Tanner didn't recognize Tolan was different than the person who had left Ephra long ago. Then again, with everything Tanner had been through, his memories were jumbled, and even now, he probably only remembered

Tolan in that way. How could he see him as anything else?

The wind slammed against Tolan and he wrapped a shaping around them, holding them to the Shapers Path.

But too late.

The blast of wind struck Bryn. It forced her to the edge of the Shapers Path, and with a gasp, she started to fall.

Tolan jumped. He exploded downward, using a shaping of fire and wind, driving him toward the ground. He reached Bryn, scooping her up, and as they crashed toward the ground, he shifted his shaping, adding a hint of earth below them, trying to soften the anticipated impact.

When they landed, he released Bryn, glancing up at the Shapers Path. Tanner was there, the wind whistling around him, yanking at him, swirling in ways appearing designed to throw him off.

As Tolan stared, he realized that wasn't quite right.

Tanner wasn't fighting the wind. He was the one shaping it.

What?

Tolan held his gaze up toward the Shapers Path, staring at his friend, and realized he'd missed something. Not only was Tanner shaping, but he was calling to the elemental, dragging it out of the bond. As he realized what was happening, he noticed something about the summons was troubling.

It was laced with a threat.

Was Bryn the same sort of danger?

Tolan glanced over at her. He didn't recognize

anything about her, and because of that, he didn't know whether or not she was involved in this. If she was, he wasn't about to leave her to do something similar.

He didn't detect anything from her. There was no sense of shaping, and there was no sort of summons coming from the shaping.

That left only Tanner. And for whatever reason, Tanner was continuing to draw on the wind, the summons he called angry and violent, the kind of summons leaving Tolan filled with agitation. It was the kind of summons posing a threat to the elementals. Considering everything they had gone through, everything he knew them to have experienced, Tolan wasn't willing to stand aside while Tanner continued to threaten them.

That meant he would need to act.

"You need to stay here," Tolan said to Bryn.

"Where are you going?"

"There's an elemental causing trouble." He frowned for a moment. If he left her here, she might observe what was happening. Was there anything he could do?

A shaping of spirit might be enough.

He pulled from deep within him, dragging up the sense of spirit, and as he did, he sent it washing toward her, letting it flow over her. When it struck, she dropped.

It was nothing more than a slight shaping that should allow her to sleep, and hopefully she could do so long enough that she wouldn't see what he was going to do next, but he didn't know whether that was the case or not.

Either way, he decided it was best for her to be here, sleeping, away from anything else that might occur.

Drawing upon fire and earth, Tolan shaped himself, sending himself streaking into the sky, coming to land on the Shapers Path. Wind battered at him, the power within the elemental familiar.

"It's okay," Tolan whispered.

Tanner frowned at him. "What are you doing?"

"Why did you release the elemental?" Tolan asked.

That wasn't even the real question he wanted answered. It wasn't so much about releasing the elemental; it was more about the threat implied in that release, the threat Tanner had for the elemental, the anger it filled the elemental with. It was easy to control the elementals when it came to threatening to force them back into the bond. They were quick to do whatever it was the shaper attempted, thinking in doing so, they might be granted a certain sustained freedom.

Didn't Tanner even know what he was doing?

His friend shouldn't have had enough power to release an elemental before now. It wasn't the kind of thing he'd ever demonstrated any real ability with. Tanner had reasonable wind shaping strength, but not much more than that.

"Tolan?"

He continued to stare at Tolan, the confused expression on his face making Tolan pause for a moment, concerned perhaps he'd made a mistake. He didn't think he had. The longer he stood here, the longer he held onto his shaping, the more certain he was that he detected exactly what he thought.

Tolan shifted his attention to the elemental. If he didn't calm it, it was going to continue to lash at him.

Using a shaping of earth and water, Tolan created a seal, wrapping it around Tanner, holding him in place. With that done, he focused on the elemental.

It was ara, the gusting coming from it telling him that, and as he focused on the wind, as he felt the continued pressure coming from it, he knew he had to do something quickly.

When he'd worked with the elementals before, it had always been with ones he'd released, and there was something very different about that. With those elementals, there was never a threat of return. He'd never tried to force elementals back into the bond, and he'd always made certain they were unharmed. Partly, that was ignorance. He hadn't known what he was doing, and even if he had, he wouldn't have done anything to the elementals to harm them.

The only times he'd dealt with a rogue elemental agitated like this had been in Ephra when he'd observed it, and when he'd been at the Academy, but that one had been under the control of someone else. Never had he tried to calm a rogue elemental on his own.

Tolan wasn't even sure he could. What would it take to soothe an elemental?

Tanner was trying to say something to him, and he was fighting at the shaping Tolan had used to hold him in place, but Tolan ignored him. There was no point in giving Tanner much attention. Once he dealt with the elemental, he could focus on Tanner, and he could figure out what had happened, how his friend had released an elemental—and why. There had to be some reason behind it.

"You don't have to return," Tolan whispered. He let his voice carry on the wind, trying to shape a soothing sense into it.

That wasn't quite right. Adding a shaping of wind wasn't what was needed; it was spirit.

Drawing upon that, he focused on the elemental. Ara was unique, translucent and difficult to see, but he knew he'd be able to find a specific point he could focus his shaping on. If he could find that, he would be able to offer a soothing touch possibly enough to calm it.

Another push, this time with more force. He sent a shaping away from him, letting power flow outward, and as it did, it struck something. It was almost as if he hit darkness. There was anger within it. Violence. He could feel the rage within the wind, and it was that rage causing the wind to continue to gust, slamming against him, wanting to ensure it remained free. There was the threat, an understanding of violence, that he could tell the elemental feared.

Tolan shifted his shaping of wind, adding spirit to it. As he did, there was a slow release.

Gradually the wind began to calm. The more he pushed on the elemental, the more energy he forced into the shaping, the more the elemental began to ease, finally relaxing. Tolan continued to push, knowing if he could hold on to this, if he could find the necessary strength to do this, he should be able to suppress the agitation within the elemental.

Something pushed against him.

Tolan frowned. There wasn't another shaper nearby who could use a spirit, was there?

Ara began to thrash, fighting wildly.

"No," he whispered.

He infused it with a shaping of spirit, trying to augment it in such a way the elemental knew he wasn't going to harm it, but wasn't sure it was enough. He held onto his shaping, pushing more and more spirit into it. It was taking considerable energy.

Maybe there was something else he could do.

If he could use another elemental, perhaps something complementary, this elemental would recognize Tolan didn't mean any harm and would realize everything he was trying to do was to help.

Pulling on more power, he shifted the focus of his shaping. This time, he sent a summons. It would be easier if he had a bondar. When he'd had the withering, he'd been able to draw upon an elemental much easier, but he'd practiced with this enough times, and had enough experience using that power to draw out the elemental. In doing so, he felt the surge of power, the way the elemental was separated from the bond. He wasn't sure if he could separate it completely, but another gust of wind struck, and this time ara was a little bit more translucent, a creature almost visible and yet not.

"Help me," Tolan whispered.

The wind swirled around itself. It formed a funnel, and within the funnel was the agitated and angry elemental ara Tolan continued to try to help. He needed to help it. If he didn't, the elemental would break free and attack. Not only Tolan, but it would attack throughout Terndahl.

He needed more strength.

Tolan slipped the ring onto his finger, squeezing it. With the bondar his mother had once possessed, Tolan was able to send more power, more shaping energy, through it. With it, his connection to spirit increased.

In doing so, Tolan continued to push outward, letting that flow toward ara. He brushed up against it, sending his connection along to it. In doing so, it began to calm. This time, it was more than just what he was able to do. The added additional elemental, whatever he'd summoned, provided a benefit, and he was able to soothe ara.

Slowly, far more slowly than he wanted, the elemental began to calm. The wind stopped whistling around him. The agitation within ara eased.

Tolan breathed out, pushing once more, drawing through his bondar as he shaped spirit a little bit more, enough that he could provide a hint of peace to the elemental. With that, it finally relaxed and he was able to take a deep breath, releasing his hold on it.

"Go," he whispered. "You don't have to remain bound. You will find other free elementals in the north."

He watched for a moment. With a swirl of wind, it disappeared, leaving him with Tanner.

Tanner was watching him, an unreadable expression on his face, but there was a hint of darkness there as well. Mixed within that darkness was something Tolan had never seen from his friend. Could it be hatred?

"What did you do?" Tolan asked.

"What makes you think I did anything? You're the one who detected the rogue elemental."

Tolan shook his head. "Detected it and released it from whatever it was you did to it. Why?"

Tanner stared at him. "I think your assignment was clear, Tolan."

"What?"

"Didn't the Grand Inquisitor instruct that you were supposed to bring us to the Academy? You wouldn't want to fail in that assignment."

Tolan took a deep breath, approaching Tanner. "What is this? Are you working with them?" The idea seemed laughable, but what other explanation was there? There didn't seem to be anything fitting other than the possibility Tanner was somehow working with the Inquisitors.

If he was, then they had spread their influence far beyond what he'd expected. If that were the case, they might already have been too late. And here he and the Grand Inquisitor thought they had released the shapers at the Academy from the touch of the Inquisitors.

"Working with them? What would give you that idea?"

Tolan ignored him, holding on to the bondar and

pushing into Tanner's mind, using a shaping that swirled through him. He didn't have anything like the Grand Inquisitor's connection or touch with spirit, but in this case, he wasn't sure it was needed. All he wanted to do was find out if there was a shaping there he had overlooked. They had believed their thoughts were a jumble, but what if that was wrong?

Tanner merely stared at him. "If you think you're going to find a shaping, you won't."

Tolan continued to push through him, searching for any evidence of what had happened to him, but came up with nothing. "Why?"

"Why would I have done what?"

Tolan waved his hands around, pointing toward where he'd dealt with the wind elemental. "Why were you responsible for that? *How* were you responsible for that?"

"You don't think I'm skilled enough?" Tanner struggled against the shaping Tolan had used to hold him in place, adding wind it to it, but Tolan had used elements he didn't think his friend had a counter to. In doing so, he had bound him to the Shapers Path, holding him in place in a way that should prevent him from going anywhere. "That's rich, coming from you."

"What's that supposed to mean?"

"You know quite well what that's supposed to mean. When you left Ephra, you had no shaping ability. You were brought to the Academy, Selected, when others who could shape were not. The Academy was supposed to be held up as the ideal, the place where if you trained hard enough, you would eventually be granted an opportunity to go and learn, to serve Terndahl."

"It doesn't work like that," Tolan said.

"Obviously."

"How long have you remembered?"

That had to be the key, didn't it? It wasn't so much that there was a shaping on him—from what Tolan could tell, there was no spirit shaping placed on Tanner. It was more a matter of having the shaping removed. In that, he was acting much like the Grand Inquisitor had warned. There was a danger in those who weren't Selected. Tolan hadn't believed that at the time, thinking perhaps there had to be another way, but it seemed the Grand Inquisitor was right.

"Since I was shown the truth."

"What exactly do you think is the truth?"

"That the Academy is not what we were led to believe. You are the perfect example of that."

"I'm the perfect example of how the Academy finds those who can shape even if they don't show that potential early on," he said. It was easier to phrase it like that than to reveal the truth, that his parents had prevented him from knowing about his ability to shape. Had there not been that spirit shaping in place, had his mother not placed some barrier to him remembering, would Tolan have recalled what he needed to know even sooner? Would he have developed an ability to shape before leaving Ephra?

He had to think he was already starting to show those

abilities, and that was why his parents had used a shaping on him, trying to conceal from him what he could be.

"You're the perfect example of how the Academy is nothing but a falsehood. We have been shown the truth."

"By who?"

"You probably would blame the Draasin Lord and would accuse us of serving like your parents served."

Tolan tensed. It was one thing to hear others within Ephra accusing his parents of serving the Draasin Lord—regardless of knowing the truth—and it was quite another for him to hear someone who had long been his friend, someone who had defended him over the years from those accusations, who had helped him find a way of remaining calm despite the fact others within Ephra continued to accuse him of being a secretive operative for the Draasin Lord.

"I wouldn't accuse you of serving the Draasin Lord," he said.

"You probably think we're somehow betraying Terndahl, but we have been shown the truth. The Academy has become the oppressor. And now we know, now we have been shown that, we will ensure it doesn't continue."

"Who?" All he wanted was for Tanner to admit it came from the Inquisitors. The moment he did, then Tolan could find the Grand Inquisitor and warn her.

There was another reason he delayed. It was possible there was more to this, and maybe he might even find out who they served. If they uncovered that, they could begin to unravel what was taking place, why the Inquisitors had managed to work so long in the shadows.

"If you think I'm going to reveal the name to you, you're mistaken. Unfortunately, you will have to find out on your own. And now, I think it's time for you to continue with your assignment, Tolan."

Tolan laughed bitterly. "If you think I'm going to bring you to the Academy, you're mistaken." He frowned, looking at Tanner. There had to be some way he'd managed to release the elemental, but what was it? What was the secret to what Tanner had done to cause the elemental to attack?

Another thing occurred to him.

Tanner was delaying him.

With a quick surge of wind and fire, Tolan took to the air. As he did, he glanced down. He was looking for Bryn, but there was no sign of her on the ground. Either she had been taken or, more likely, she was in on this, and Tanner had been waiting for her to come back around.

He focused on locating any shaping around him. There had to be some evidence of it, and if he could uncover it, then he might be able to know where she had gone. There was no sense of shaping other than from Tanner. His was a surge of wind, a powerful funnel of wind, and it was surprising he was not attempting to shape himself free. The shaping was focused on something near him.

Tolan darted back, landing on the Shapers Path near Tanner, and he sent a powerful shaping at the other man, wrapping him in a barrier, sealing him inside. As he held it, he approached carefully.

"What do you have?"

Tanner stared at him.

"Your shaping. What were you doing?"

"You will never understand," Tanner said.

"You're right. I thought you were my friend. I won't understand what changed and why you became a part of this. You don't have to be. You should know I've been serving the Academy, and I want nothing more than to ensure the integrity of the Academy. You can help with that."

"Help? Why would I want to help with the integrity of the Academy when they have proven exactly what they will do? Why would we want to be a part of anything that's proven it's nothing more than a farce?"

Tolan grabbed for Tanner, peeling his arms back, and reached inside his jacket. There was something there, the source of whatever it was he was shaping upon. As he pulled it out, his eyes widened. It looked something like a withering, but the shapes were wrong. It was a bondar, but it was like a twisted bondar that seemed as if it called to the elementals and twisted them, tormenting them.

"Where did you get this?"

"Would you like one for yourself? I'm sure we could arrange that. With your newfound shaping ability, you might be useful."

There was something not quite right here. This wasn't Tanner. Tanner wasn't the kind to torment and taunt someone, was he? He didn't remember Tanner ever acting like this. He had always been the one who had protected Tolan, defending him when others had threatened him. This was nothing like the kind of person Tanner was.

And yet… What other explanation was there?

He wasn't sure there was one.

He shoved the strange bondar into his pocket, grabbed for Tanner, released the shaping around him, and felt the surge of a shaping near him.

As he did, he frowned. Where was it coming from?

Better yet, what was it targeting? The sense of the shaping continued to build and Tolan prepared for the possibility of an attack, but it never came. He hesitated, remaining where he was, looking around.

"What's the matter?" Tanner asked. "Did you think I was alone?"

With a sudden understanding, power began to build all around him.

Shapers. Many of them.

And Tolan had expended considerable energy trying to withstand the elemental.

12

THE POWER CONTINUED TO BUILD AROUND HIM, THE STEADY sense of shaping energy, the kind Tolan could feel swirling all about him. He wasn't able to detect what type of shaping was used, or whether there was anything within the shaping he needed to be concerned about. He couldn't even detect the intention of the shaping.

Many times, when he was at the Academy, there were aspects to a shaping that he could uncover, but it was almost as if this were hidden from him, twisted in such a way so he wouldn't be able to determine what caused it. And if that was the case, then whoever was there preparing to attack must have had some idea Tolan had an awareness of shaping.

They had either come for him specifically, or they were prepared for the possibility they would encounter someone like him.

Tolan focused on the wind all around him, focusing on

the heat in the air, the earth and everything coming from within the landscape. He tried to draw on that energy, prepared for the need to shape, wanting to connect to everything here in order to do so. The moment he relaxed, the moment he wasn't prepared, would be the moment the attack would strike in a way he wouldn't be able to counter.

There was something off about the air, though he wasn't sure what it was. It was probably whatever Tanner had wanted him to experience, as if he could somehow use that against Tolan.

And perhaps he could.

"Why are you doing this?" he asked.

Tanner only shook his head. "I'm not doing anything, Tolan. This has been the Academy's doing."

The strange thing about a comment like that was how Tolan actually agreed with parts of it, though he doubted it was the same part Tanner agreed with. While he understood there were things the Academy had done, and ways they had addressed the elementals over the years, thinking them something to fear, he also recognized there was more to it. He didn't fear what the Academy might do. They might be misguided, especially when it came to the elementals, but the Academy itself was not the enemy. There were those within the Academy who might be, but the more he learned, especially from people like Master Minden, the more Tolan felt as if there was a desire for greater understanding.

Only, that desire was mixed with the anger and hatred

targeted at the Draasin Lord. They blamed him for whatever had happened, almost as if he was the one responsible for the events transpiring, but that was not the case.

"Who's coming?"

"I wouldn't want to ruin the surprise."

"I already know you view the Draasin Lord as something to fear."

"Fear? *You* should fear the Draasin Lord," Tanner said.

"Why?"

"With everything you went through, everything your parents did, you would question that?"

"Do you know anything about what my parents did?"

"It's what everybody said, Tolan. I know you like to believe they were innocent. And for the longest time, I went along with you, trying to agree with the idea maybe they weren't guilty of what everyone else claimed, but when you hear the same story over and over again, you begin to realize there's truth to it."

"Maybe," Tolan said. There was no arguing in that. His parents had gone to serve the Draasin Lord, and yet, the truth was far more complicated than just that. The truth often was more complicated.

"I'm not staying here while you continue to delay me. You can warn Bryn she can go wherever she intends to go." And Tolan had no idea what she might be up to or whether she was the one who might be attacking. "And then I think I might bring you to the Academy. There's someone there who I'm sure would love to hear what you have to say."

"Great."

"I don't think you'll be saying that when you get to the Academy."

"How do you know what I want? You've been so focused on what you wanted, on all of the stories about you, on poor Tolan, the boy who lost his parents to the Draasin Lord, that you never paid much attention to what your friend wanted."

"You know that's not true," he said. Everything Tolan had been through had been because of his devotion to his friend. The very fact he was now a shaper was because of that same devotion.

And where had it gotten him?

What did it mean that Tanner had betrayed him? Would it mean Tanner no longer believed him? The one person he'd always counted on, the one person who he'd always believed had his back, apparently had not.

Shaping continued to build, and as it did, Tolan realized he needed to do something.

The direction of the shaping came from the south, almost as if they wanted to force him away from the Academy. If they wanted to force him away, then either he needed to go there or he needed to find another plan.

The other plan would be relatively straightforward. He'd go after the Grand Inquisitor and find her, heading to Par if needed, and once he was there, then he could see whether there was anything he might be able to uncover.

He might be weakened from shaping for as long as he had, but he was not completely spent. He still had the spirit bondar, and he had the strange withering. It was possible he could use that strange withering, somehow add to it, drawing power from it. If he could, maybe he could use it in order to draw the wind elemental. It was possible Tolan could use that energy in a way resulting in freeing the elemental rather than angering it.

He wasn't sure if he had the necessary strength or not, but it was something he thought he very much needed to try.

Grabbing Tanner, he kept him bound in earth and water, using the combination to trap him. He'd seen Tanner using fire, so though it was an element Tolan was stronger in, it wasn't one he felt comfortable using on Tanner, especially not when it came to using it for something like a prison, although he hated the idea he'd have to place his friend in a prison. Regardless of what Tanner had done, he was still his friend, wasn't he?

He raced along the Shapers Path. Rather than running away from the Academy, he ran toward it.

He was forced to push strength, drawing from earth. In doing so, he found he was using more and more energy than he intended. The longer he went, the weaker he'd become. He needed to reach his destination as quickly as possible, otherwise he would find he wouldn't have the necessary strength to go on. And more than that, he feared if he were attacked, if whoever was coming toward him managed to reach him, he wouldn't be able to do anything to withstand it.

Thankfully, Tanner remained quiet, though he didn't

know if that was because he wanted Tolan to head this direction or if there was another reason for it. If it was that he wanted Tolan to go in this direction, maybe he needed to veer off.

They had traveled for the better part of the day, so they were close to the Academy.

A shaping built near him. Tolan pushed against it, forcing through the power of the shaping, ignoring what he was detecting. Another one struck, and then another. With each shaping, Tolan realized there was a concerted effort to prevent him from reaching the Academy. They came from behind him, almost as if the shapings were trying to chase him down, and yet, he still thought he could outrun it.

"How much longer do you think you can go on?" Tanner asked.

"Long enough," Tolan said.

"I'm not sure you can. Look at how you have already begun to sag, your strength fading as you go."

"I'm not going to fail," Tolan said.

"You certainly aren't going to succeed."

Tolan grunted, holding on to Tanner and dragging him.

Tanner began to laugh, his voice carrying into the air, a shrill sort of sound. He attempted to shape, using wind, and there came a hint of drag, trying to slow them down. Tolan pushed against it, breaking through the shaping Tanner used. It was strange to realize, but Tanner wasn't a particularly strong shaper. Somehow, he'd made it through the Selection, which suggested either he did have some strength or some way of cheating the testing. More likely it was the last.

"What were you trying to do?"

"As I said, you wouldn't understand."

"Who are you serving?"

"You're running from them."

"Am I? Seeing as how he hasn't revealed himself so far, I have a hard time thinking he would reveal himself for you."

"No. I doubt they would have revealed themselves for me. I think more likely they came for you."

Tolan slowed for a moment. In that brief spell, he contemplated the possibilities. What if he didn't continue to run? What if he chose to do something else? To turn back? He could risk himself, find out who was chasing him, and if he did, what might he learn?

If he were to do that, he'd need to have the necessary strength to withstand what would come, and he didn't know that he did. Not after everything he'd gone through so far. Now wasn't the time to slow and uncover this.

Still, as he went, he could feel his strength waning. The Academy was not that far off. He could tell it was nearby, if only because he could feel the energy from it. What he needed now was to find some way of drawing off that energy, some way he could drag himself toward it.

The strength required to continue on was more than he could summon. As much as he tried, he was starting to fade more and more with each step. Part of it came from whatever Tanner still did to resist him, as if he were pushing back, trailing after him, using his shaping of wind to do so.

And in doing so, he was forcing Tolan to slow. It would take a different kind of energy, and with it, he would have to either neutralize Tanner—something he wasn't interested in doing—or he would have to continue to combat his shaping.

"I think you're stronger than they were giving you credit for."

"Stop," Tolan said.

"You won't be able to win. You already are starting to fail. I can feel it. You've done well this far, but how much longer do you think you can go? How much more do you think you can do when it comes to combating them?"

"Them now, not you?"

"I won't take all the credit. I will let them have it. Besides, it's far more fun this way."

"We were friends."

"Were. And then you left. You didn't say anything."

"Because they wouldn't let me. That's how the Selection works. They don't give the people Selected an opportunity to say their goodbyes."

"And you went along with that? I thought more of you, Tolan."

"I went along with it because I had no choice."

"You went along with it because you thrilled at the idea you might be able to shape. Admit it. For all your bluster,

Tolan, you want the same thing as everybody. You want power."

"I've never wanted power."

"No? And yet, here you are, look at you. All this power you have, and it's not what you wanted at all, is it?"

"It's not," Tolan said.

"I don't believe you. At least I'm willing to acknowledge the fact if the Academy wasn't willing to teach me, another will."

"Who?"

"All you have to do to find out is turn around."

Tolan couldn't deny the interest he had in turning around, in finding out who Tanner had begun to serve and who was teaching him, but if he turned around, there would be a different sort of danger. He didn't know what would happen to him, and until he did, he didn't think he dared. More than that, he wanted to be prepared for the possibility he might need to fight. He wasn't sure quite how.

Another shaping built, this one just as strong as the last, and when it came, Tanner started to smile. "The endgame begins."

Power burst all around. As it came, Tolan tried to ignore it, focused only on hurrying along the Shapers Path. That was what he needed to do, and if for some reason he were unable to continue, what would happen to him?

He could leave Tanner, but that would be losing the possibility of understanding what was taking place and how his supposed friend had a role in it. He didn't want to do it.

He dragged on strength buried within him, pulling it from somewhere. He added to it strength he could summon through the bondar, and in doing so, he continued to shape, calling forth power. It reminded him of how he'd pressed through the testing.

What more was there to do?

Nothing other than continue to race to the Academy.

He didn't even dare looking behind him, not wanting—or willing—to turn around and see if there was anything coming. He didn't need to turn around to recognize the power flowing from the shapers behind him.

Tanner continued to laugh, the sound of it building, irritatingly so.

And then a shaping struck him.

Tolan staggered forward, barely able to maintain his footing, and he lunged, trying to catch himself, adding a shaping of earth to prevent himself from falling. Another shaping struck him. This time it was earth and fire. He had the opportunity to detect the source of the shaping, nothing more, and as it struck him, he tried to stay on his feet, but the power of the combined shaping—and the tiredness within him—were enough that he could no longer stand.

Through it all, Tanner continued to laugh.

"Would you be quiet?" Tolan snapped.

Tanner cackled. "I would, but this is all too entertaining. I never expected you to be the one they were after."

"Why are you helping them?"

"Because they helped me. Because I have learned. Because—"

Another shaping struck, and this time it crashed into where Tanner had been. Tolan grabbed him, trying to pull him forward, but he wasn't quick enough. The shaping struck him, throwing him off to the side of the Shapers Path. Tolan debated jumping down for his friend but realized he couldn't. There was too much shaping power behind him.

Now free of Tanner, he ran. He no longer had the same resistance he'd had before. He raced forward, using the Shapers Path for speed, and he added to it a shaping of wind, giving him a boost, but even as he went, he wasn't sure it was going to be enough.

The city was in the distance. Amitan loomed toward him, but it was still far enough away that he wondered if he'd make it in time.

There came another burst and he pushed back, trying to fight against the power, and found his own strength faded too much. As much as he wanted to fight, as much as he wanted to resist whatever was coming, he didn't have enough strength to do so.

Tolan focused only on shaping the wind, not anything else. When a shaping struck him, it sent him staggering forward and he tried to ignore it, much like he tried to ignore the pain in his back where he'd been struck. Water would heal him, but he didn't dare take even a moment to try to use water to restore himself, not wanting to risk it.

Another shaping built. Tolan struggled against it, feeling the power of the shaping, knowing as it grew, as that power continued to build, there wouldn't be anything he would be able to do to block it. It would be best if he could outrun it.

Wind started to swirl around him.

That one troubled him more than anything else. If the wind was swirling, it was doing so because of Tanner. It had a distinct signature, the kind of swirling pattern he recognized, the kind Tanner had used when they were younger and he was trying to show off his abilities, looking to impress Tolan. Tanner had never understood that he'd never needed to try to impress Tolan. The mere fact he could shape was enough.

Why had Tanner gone to someone else for training?

Then again, was that what the Grand Inquisitor had expected? Had she known there might be some who would be compelled to go and learn from another source?

It seemed almost as if she had.

Another shaping built, and another.

Tolan pushed, using fire and wind, trying to add a hint of water, thinking he could glide along the Shapers Path if he did, but he didn't have the necessary control and his strength faded.

Spirit.

Tolan had seen how spirit would add to a shaping, and if he could use that, maybe he could give himself enough of a burst.

Twisting spirit and wind together, he tried to use the

two of them, hoping the new shaping would send him faster along the way, and if so, he might be able to reach the city.

Would the attack end when he did? It was possible his pursuers wouldn't abandon their chase when he reached the city. Now he had their twisted bondar, it was possible they would want that, that they would worry about him having it. Another burst, and this time Tolan went staggering, the power from the shaping striking him in the back, sending him falling forward.

He crawled. He was tempted to drop off the Shapers Path and down to the ground below. If he did, he might be able to hide within the trees. He could buy himself some time, give himself the opportunity to regain his strength, and maybe sneak back into the city without anyone being the wiser, but he wasn't sure if that would even work. It was possible the attackers could use earth and chase him with it, tracking him and then trapping him.

He wasn't going to be captured.

Memories of the Inquisition came to him, far too painful, too fresh despite that it had been months since he'd encountered anything like it. It was torment, and he refused to experience it again.

Summoning more strength, trying to dig someplace deep within himself, he pushed outward, a mixture of all of the elements, including spirit.

As he did, he focused on the library. He would reach it. He'd find some way of getting inside, and when he did…

A bolt of lightning streaked from the sky.

Tolan could barely look up. He could feel the energy within the lightning before it reached him, could feel the way the heat began to form, the steady caress of that power as it continued to build, shooting toward him. There was significant energy trapped within it, and it was more than he could withstand.

All he could do was brace for the impact, knowing when it came, he may or may not be ready for it, much like he may or may not be able to survive it. As that energy struck, Tolan held his hands up.

It consumed him.

There was warmth within the shaping, and it seemed almost as if the lightning caressed him, much like wind had caressed him. There was wind within the bolt of lightning. Earth was there, the way the lightning bolt connected to the ground, and there was water, mixed with the storm clouds that had to have originated the lightning in the first place. Spirit held them all together, sort of how water bound together the shapings for the Shapers Path.

He felt lifted. There was no other way to describe it, but he was carried up with the lightning bolt, dragged into the air, the power of the shaping scooping him off the Shapers Path and into the sky. Tolan tried to track where he was going, trying to keep sense of what was happening, but he couldn't. There was nothing but the strange power of the lightning, and nothing more than an emptiness around him.

And then he was carried down.

When the lightning cleared and his vision began to

come back around, he expected to be surrounded by shapers, thinking they had found some new way of attacking him. Instead, he found no one.

He was exhausted, almost too much to go on, and with that exhaustion, he collapsed, his vision fading to black.

13

When Tolan came back around, everything within him hurt. Pain radiated from deep inside him, almost as if he'd expended too much energy in the escape. As far as he could tell, he had. He'd very nearly used the last of his ability.

He sat up, looking around. He was in a small room, resting on a narrow bed. A single lantern sat on a shelf bolted to the wall. It glowed softly, shaped light within it giving barely more than a little bit of illumination. He looked around, thinking he must've been captured. Maybe his belief he'd ended up at the library was nothing more than imagination. If he'd been captured, then where had they brought him?

He attempted to shape, reaching for fire as he often did, and found his connection to that element still there. Power bloomed within him, and the lantern surged a little bit brighter. He focused on earth, pushing outward, sending a connection to the ground and through the walls. He was able to connect to that as well. There was water in a basin nearby, and with a hint of shaping, he swirled that water around, connecting even to that.

He wasn't cut off from his shaping, but where was he?

He hadn't tried to pull on spirit, and didn't know it made much sense to try to do so. Not at this point, and not without knowing whether he was in any danger. Instead, he used a shaping of fire and water, wrapping them around his mind, inverting them to protect himself and the possibility there would be someone here who might mean him harm. He couldn't tell whether there would be or not, and until he knew where he was and what had happened to him, he refused to be unprepared.

Getting to his feet, he found he was dressed in his underclothes. A robe hung on a hook by the door, and Tolan threw it on. It was soft, the style unfamiliar, and he checked around, looking for his clothing, but it was gone.

Which meant the strange bondar was gone.

He had wanted to examine that, if only to understand it. How had they used the bondar? Was there any way to counteract it?

He found the door, testing it. Of course, it was locked.

It was possible he could shape his way out, and he considered pushing on earth, blasting open the door, but decided to save his energy. There might be another way to uncover what he needed. Could he use sensing? Rather than trying to rely on his shaping ability, and bondars...

Bondars.

Tolan grabbed for his neck, checking to see if his necklace and the stone ring were still there, and was relieved to find they were.

Breathing out heavily, he reached for spirit and forced it into his earth shaping, combining it, intending to draw a little bit more strength from it and then send that out into the stone, using that kind of shaping to help know where he was and what might be here.

Pushing outward, he tried to detect whether there was anything else he could uncover. There seemed to be some resistance to attempting sensing, and as much as he tried to push, there wasn't anything he could discover.

Tolan continued to draw on earth power, summoning more strength, pushing out. As he did, he used spirit, linking it to earth, and tried to see if there was anything he might be able to learn, and yet there didn't seem to be.

He withdrew his shaping. It would be better to conserve his energy, not knowing whether there was anything more here that he needed to be afraid of. What he needed to do was figure out where he was. While it might involve blasting open the door using the shaping of earth and spirit, he wasn't sure he wanted to do that just yet.

Instead, he hesitated.

There had to be something he could detect, didn't there?

The longer he lingered, the less certain he was that he'd be able to detect anything here. He held onto the connection of the shaping, using earth and pushing outward, but as he pushed, he realized there was resistance. It was almost as if there was someone here pushing against him.

Which meant he *was* captured.

Not that he should have thought otherwise. Considering how he found himself here in the small room, what else could he have been other than a captive? He relaxed his shaping for a moment, deciding he shouldn't focus so much on it. As he did, he changed the nature of what he was doing, holding onto the shaping wrapped around himself, keeping it swirled around his mind, ready for the possibility someone might come for him. If they did, he was prepared.

It gave him an opportunity to think through what had occurred. He still wasn't entirely sure what had taken place, only that whatever it was had surprised him. There had been pursuers along the path. He had fallen, nearly collapsing. When he had, he'd used a combination of the elements, combining them into one, and he'd added a hint of spirit, whether or not he had meant to do so. Lightning had come for him, drawn toward him. Whatever the attackers had done had somehow used that lightning, and Tolan had been claimed by it.

But he'd been brought to the library. That was where he had focused his image, what he had held in his mind, and when he'd followed the pressure of the shaping, he'd been certain that was where he was going.

Only... That hadn't been the case.

Releasing the shaping, Tolan stepped back, looking around. *Could* he be in the library? The idea seemed impossible, but then again, so did the idea he'd somehow called lightning from the sky.

Pressure began to build, pushing upon his shaping once again. As it did, Tolan took a step back and found himself pressed up against the wall. He held onto his connection to the shapings he'd formed around his mind, protecting himself. Hopefully he was able to use it in a way that could keep his mind safe, sealed off from whoever was coming. A part of him wondered whether or not that was what he needed to do.

The door opened.

"Master Minden?"

"Good. You're awake. Time for you to come with me."

"What happened?"

"Unfortunately, the Selection has gone awry."

"When we were in Ephra, there was an attack," Tolan said.

"That is my understanding as well. I need you to come with me," she said.

Tolan followed her. The master librarian guided him from the small room, and he followed her without saying anything. Now in the hallway, he realized he was in the Academy, though there was nothing else about it he recognized.

There was a sense of familiarity to it. It came from the sense of earth and water and wind and fire, all of them mingling together, giving him an awareness of this place. Every so often, the sense of a shaping built, exploding near him and with enough power that he thought he should know who was shaping, but he came across nothing. Master Minden continued to lead him away from the room where he'd awoken and down a long hallway. He paused at one point, realizing where he was.

It was the hall of portraits. She'd brought him in a different direction than before.

"What is it?" he asked, pausing to look briefly at the portraits.

"While you were out, we received word some of the other Selections have been disrupted."

"How many of them?"

Master Minden paused before answering. "Too many. Others have returned, but they bring word of disruption out in Terndahl."

"And the other students who were sent?"

"Most were not nearly as capable as you. It's why we need to know what you experienced, Shaper Ethar."

"I don't really know what I experienced. I… We came across shapers who seemed to have been spirit shaped and they attacked us. We removed the spirit shaping on them, and when we did, we put them through the Selection."

"You did."

Tolan nodded. "We thought everything was fine. The Grand Inquisitor was going to Par to help with another Selection, but she sent me back to the Academy with the two who were Selected."

"And then what happened?"

"And then I was attacked."

"How?" Master Minden stared at the wall of portraits for a long moment before turning her attention back to him. Something in her milky gaze lingered, almost a spark of recognition, though Tolan didn't think there should be one within her eyes.

"By someone I thought was my friend." That was still hard for him to fathom. Not only had Tanner attacked, but he'd done so using an elemental's power. It was that power Tolan had begun to truly understand and having somebody else use it against him left him troubled—and angry. "He was using some sort of strange bondar."

"What do you mean, it was a strange bondar?"

"It wasn't the same as we have here. There was power in it, and it allowed him to summon an elemental from the bond, but it was angry and violent when it emerged. It took everything in my power to calm the elemental."

She tore her gaze away from the portraits and frowned at him. "To what?"

Tolan didn't know if he'd said too much. "To calm the elemental. I did everything I could to try to settle it, but I'm not sure it was successful."

She tapped on her chin. "Interesting. I wouldn't have expected that to have been the case, but perhaps it's for the best you are the one to have escaped from Ephra."

"I grabbed the strange bondar from him. It would've been with my belongings."

Master Minden nodded. Her milky eyes made it difficult to know what she was thinking, the way it was always difficult to know. And yet, she always seemed like she managed to see everything clearly. It was almost as if she didn't need her eyes in order to do so.

"What's taking place here?"

"The Grand Master has sent shapers to investigate. It seems most of the Selections that went awry were on the outskirts of Terndahl."

"The outskirts? Like Par?"

She nodded. "I'm sure Shaper Changen is well. She is a gifted shaper."

Tolan wasn't quite certain of that. If something had happened to her... "I need to go to Par."

"I'm afraid the Grand Master won't allow you to go to Par. He has instructed the students to remain within the Academy."

"Why?"

Master Minden watched him for a moment, and it seemed almost as if she were tempted to say something, but she restrained herself.

"Master Minden?"

She shook her head. "I know you have been instrumental in helping to protect the Academy, but in this case, you need to remain here. It really is dangerous."

"I saw what happened in Ephra."

"And the Grand Master has sent others to ensure the safety of Terndahl."

"What others?"

"Soldiers." She practically spat the word, and Tolan

found himself frowning. His gaze drifted to the wall of portraits. There were several depictions of shapers who had been soldiers. Many of them carried swords, and they seemed to be leading something into battle.

He had some experience with the Terndahl soldiers, but most of them were shapers as well. They had strength and power, but they were rarely called upon to serve at the Academy's behest.

If the Grand Master had summoned their assistance, it meant he was more concerned about something.

"What's going on?"

"Something dangerous, I suspect."

"Does it have to do with the strange bondar I found?"

"I will look into it, Shaper Ethar."

"I should be involved. You wanted me to be a part of what was happening with the library."

"When you progress. For now, you aren't ready."

"Not ready? I'm the reason that device was even brought here."

She shook her head. "I wish there was something more I could do for you. Return to your dorm, rest, and know the Academy has others out trying to protect the rest who have gone for the Selection."

Master Minden turned her attention back to the hall of portraits, staring at them, and Tolan realized there wasn't much else he was going to be able to do to convince her she should continue to work with him. She'd always provided him with more than most others did, but in this case, it seemed she believed it really was beyond him.

Perhaps it was. With what he'd experienced, knowing there was something else out there, someone else who was still leading the Inquisitors and who likely had been the person Aela served, perhaps this was beyond him.

Still, he couldn't shake the feeling he needed to be involved in it.

He wandered along the hall of portraits, glancing at each one. Not many of them had much color or even a scene depicted within them, but he let his gaze linger along them. The one thing he understood about the hall of portraits was that there were messages within these portraits. Somehow, they were shaped so only specific people would be able to see the images, but as he studied them, he couldn't see anything he hadn't seen the first time he was here.

Letting out a long sigh, he reached the stairs at the end of the hall, heading down. He did so slowly, reluctantly, and when he reached the main hallway, he froze.

Master Minden hadn't shared everything with him. Not only were soldiers sent to investigate the sites of the Selection, there were soldiers stationed throughout the hallway. All of them were armed with swords, and all of them were dressed in dark leathers. They marched along the hall in pairs, studying each shaping student they passed.

Was this going to be the new normal within the Academy?

Perhaps it had been like this when the Draasin Lord had attacked, back in a time when Tolan had believed there was a Draasin Lord who would attack the Academy, but even that seemed too much. The Academy was safe. There should be no reason for anyone to be afraid here.

Tolan started down the hall, heading toward the stairs leading to his dorm. He still hadn't settled into the third-level rooms yet, but it didn't feel right to do so without waiting for Ferrah.

And he wanted answers. More than anything else, going to find those answers seemed to be the most important thing.

He turned, heading back along the hallway. One pair of soldiers watched him, marching behind him, and he tried to ignore them. From what he'd observed, they left the students alone, though maybe they would see him as a threat. If they did, would there be anything he'd even be able to do? It wasn't as if Tolan intended to try to do anything.

When he reached the Grand Master's quarters, he glanced over his shoulder. The soldiers continued patrolling past, but he had a sense they were paying attention to him. There was a sense of shaping coming off them, radiating toward him. Tolan tried to ignore that sense, instead pounding on the door and waiting.

It was possible the Grand Master wouldn't even be there, and even if he was, it was possible he wouldn't answer. Knowing what he did about the other man, it was likely he already knew Tolan was here.

Surprisingly, the door came open and the Grand Master looked out at him.

"Shaper Ethar. You have returned."

"Has Master Minden shared with you anything about my arrival?"

"Only that you appeared on a shaping she was not expecting."

"I'm not really sure about that, but…" He licked his lips, swallowing, and then shared with the Grand Master everything that happened in Ephra. As he did, the Grand Master's face remained neutral.

Tolan wasn't sure what he wanted from the other man, though he'd have liked to see more of a reaction—even outrage, something to show him the Grand Master understood the significance of what Tolan was saying.

Then again, it wasn't as if the Grand Master didn't understand the consequences. It was more likely he didn't have anything he could do about them.

"I have already sent reinforcements."

"That's what Master Minden said, but I could go and—"

"You are a student. You have progressed quite well, and you've proven yourself capable, Shaper Ethar, but you are still just a student. In this case, with what we have experienced, having soldiers who have experience is most beneficial. This was an assault upon Terndahl."

"It's not the Draasin Lord," he said hurriedly.

The Grand Master cocked his head, studying him. "Are you certain of that?"

"Well…" He hadn't shared with the Grand Master everything he knew about the Draasin Lord, though perhaps he needed to. Everything they had believed about the Draasin Lord had been wrong. "It doesn't feel like the type of attack the Draasin Lord would have used."

"I was around during the last attack, Shaper Ethar. I know very well what kind of attack the Draasin Lord has used."

"That's not what I was saying," Tolan said, stepping back. He needed to be careful. While he had a good rapport with the Grand Master, he still was a student, and he needed to remain a student in order to continue to progress. More than anything, he wanted to become a master shaper, and he wasn't going to be able to do that by angering the Grand Master. "I just don't feel this represents the Draasin Lord. It's not the kind of attack he has used before. When the Draasin Lord has attacked, at least recently, the attack has been more focused on the elementals."

Tolan had to be careful. What he had shared with Master Minden implied the elementals were involved, though he didn't think this was the Draasin Lord. Whoever had made this strange bondar and however it had been used was the key, though he didn't really know what it was.

"Regardless of what you think, we are prepared for what must take place, Shaper Ethar."

"What cities were targeted?"

"Only the outer cities."

"Which is why you think the Draasin Lord is involved."

"It fits with the nature of the attack."

"What happened to those who were in some of the other Selections?"

"They returned. Without having any way of performing a Selection effectively, they didn't have any reason to stay."

Which meant Jonas had returned.

If only Ferrah hadn't needed to go to Par, but…

"Return to your quarters, Shaper Ethar. You have been promoted to third level, so I believe you have some settling in to do. Your classes will begin to become even more complicated."

"We'll still have classes?"

The Grand Master cocked his head, looking at him. "Of course, you will still have classes. The Academy will go on. Just because we've had an attack at the outskirts of Terndahl is no reason for us to stop pursuing our studies."

Tolan could only shake his head. What else was there to do?

He nodded blankly, trying to think about what else he needed to do, but even as he did, he could tell the Grand Master wasn't going to tolerate an argument. For that matter, Tolan wasn't sure he had anything to say that would be effective.

Instead, he turned away, heading along the hallway, trying not to look at the soldiers marching through it, and resisting the urge to glance back at the Grand Master.

If Ferrah didn't return, what would he do?

The Academy wasn't the Academy without her.

More than that, he still was troubled. Whatever else was taking place was not the Draasin Lord, regardless of what the Grand Master believed. The only problem was Tolan didn't have any idea who was responsible.

14

The next few days passed in something of a blur. He refused to move to the third-level quarters, and though Jonas tried to encourage him to do so, he wanted to remain around others. It was selfish, mostly. He didn't want to move up to the third-level quarters until he was certain Ferrah was going to be safe.

In the time he'd been back, he'd not had an opportunity to speak with Master Minden again. He had gone looking for her, hoping maybe she'd have something she might have discovered about the strange bondar, but every time he'd gone to the library, she had not been there. That surprised him.

He was tempted to go look down the hallway, searching for her in the hall of portraits or in the hidden section of the Academy where the librarians stayed, but some part of him felt as if going there would be a betrayal.

Instead, he spent his days practicing shaping. He

focused on spirit most of all. Given what he'd experienced, the way he'd been forced to use it during the attack, having a way to use spirit seemed to be the most immediately beneficial. For now, he wasn't entirely sure he was going to be able to use it nearly as effectively as he wanted, but he was determined to keep trying, practicing with it, and eventually gain enough facility where he wouldn't have to worry about harming someone.

That was what the Grand Inquisitor had warned him about, and he knew he needed to be careful, ensuring he didn't destroy someone's mind while trying to master a spirit shaping.

For the most part, he stayed outside within the park, and as he did, he avoided most others. Mostly, he wanted to avoid the soldiers. The longer he remained within the Academy, the more the soldiers troubled him. They patrolled everywhere. It wasn't just that they patrolled through the halls, but they patrolled through the library, and he encountered them near the stairs leading up to the hall of portraits, blocking his access to that space.

When he did venture into one of the classes he had been assigned as a third-level student, he was unsurprised to find there were soldiers even there.

He didn't have the focus needed in those classes, but then again, neither did anybody else. It wasn't just Tolan who had a strange sense of emptiness. Others seemed to share in that, and Tolan was surprised that Draln of all people seemed to struggle with the presence of the soldiers.

His instructors never really changed. Regardless of how much he progressed, he kept the same instructors. The only difference was who was present in the classes.

Once again, he found himself sitting out in the park, ignoring everyone else around him. There were others in the park. He could not only hear them, but he could feel them through his connection to earth. Tolan preferred to avoid them.

What he wanted to hear was word about those who had been lost. It wasn't just Par and the Selection there, but it was places like Holawn, and Idarn, and Olosh. Students who had gone on those Selections had not returned either. He wondered whether they would.

"How long do you intend to keep coming up here?"

Tolan glanced up. Jonas approached and took a seat next to him on the ground. He was shaping as he did, pulling on water, letting it swirl in the small pool in front of them.

"I guess until there is word of Ferrah's return."

"And what happens if she doesn't return?" Jonas shifted, turning toward him, holding his gaze. "I know you don't want to think about that, and I don't really either, but there is the possibility she won't return."

Tolan turned his attention back to the pool and breathed out. He focused on the sense of each of the elements, working through each one before releasing them. As he did, he couldn't help but feel a surge of frustration. "She has to return."

"I don't know. I've heard the rumors about the attacks

in the other places." Jonas shook his head. "I don't want to believe she's not going to return to us, but there's the possibility whatever happened has claimed her. The soldiers still don't have everything under control, and they've been working to try to stabilize everything, but as far as I can tell, they haven't managed to do so yet."

Tolan hadn't spent much time listening to rumors. What he wanted was to find the Grand Master or someone like Master Minden, someone who might be able to provide him with real actionable information, but every time he went looking for them, he wasn't able to learn anything of much use. And because of that, he couldn't help but feel as if there was nothing but stories.

"The soldiers will be able to get everything back under control."

"I like to think that too, but I do wonder about why they have focused so much on the Academy." Jonas looked over his shoulder, and Tolan followed the direction of his gaze. When he did, he realized there was a pair of soldiers patrolling along the street. "They have focused so much on Amitan, and with as many as we have here, I have to wonder if there's a reason for it."

Tolan frowned. He thought about what he'd experienced and what he knew. More than that, he thought about what Ferrah had told him about Par.

Why would the Grand Master focus so much here?

There was only one reason. It was the same reason they had been attacked before, the same reason the Grand

Master worried about another possibility, and it was the reason he wondered whether there was an attack in Par.

Could it be the same reason there were other places under attack?

If that were the case, it would explain much.

Getting to his feet, he glanced over at Jonas. "Thank you."

"What did I do?"

"You gave me an idea."

"That's it? I was hoping you'd be able to help me study for my testing. I have it coming up still, you know. We don't all pass on our first try."

Tolan shook his head. "You don't really need my help. All you have to do is remember everything you've been taught. You will pass it."

Jonas frowned at him. "That's it. Remember *everything* I've been taught?"

"As much as you can."

Tolan hurried back to the Academy, ignoring the soldiers marching along the street, and headed straight toward the library.

When he was there, he looked around. There were a few students in the library, but it was emptier than it usually was. A pair of master librarians remained at the front, sitting on the dais. Neither was Master Minden.

He needed to find her.

If this was all about the Convergence, as he suspected, then he needed to let her know.

Without her here, he hurried back into the hallway, racing toward the stairs.

When he'd come here before, the soldiers had blocked his access. This time, he snuck past a pair of soldiers and waited while they patrolled. When he reached the end of the hallway, there were no further soldiers.

Tolan raced along the stairs, heading up.

At the top of the stairs, he paused again. From here, he knew the hall of portraits would be on the other side of the door, but he didn't know whether she'd even be there.

When he stepped out, he was both surprised and not surprised Master Minden was there.

"Did you know I was coming?"

"I could tell you were searching for me."

"I've searched for you before, but I haven't been able to find you."

"You had a different urgency this time."

"What have you been doing?"

"Trying to understand the device you discovered. Unfortunately…"

"You can't find anything." She shook her head. "I might have. I think it's about the Convergence."

"What was that?"

He paused in front of one of the portraits. This had a dark cave, but that was the only thing he was able to really see. There seemed to be something else he should be able to determine, but as he looked at it, he wasn't able to pick up on anything else. For some reason, it reminded him of the Convergence.

That couldn't be coincidental.

"Ferrah has been convinced there's a Convergence in Par. What if the reason that was attacked—and the other places—was because they each have a Convergence?"

"That may be, Shaper Ethar, but you have to trust the Grand Master will investigate everything that needs to be investigated."

Tolan couldn't help but shake his head. "He thinks this is the Draasin Lord."

"And you don't?"

He looked over, locking eyes with her. "I don't think the Draasin Lord is exactly what we have believed."

She looked past him, cocking her head to the side. A shaping built from her, sweeping down.

"I have to go. I can go to Par. I can see if I can find Ferrah, and —"

"There is no going," Master Minden said. She stopped in front of one of the portraits, nodding to it. "How do you think you could reach Par? It's quite a way away, and even traveling along the Shapers Path will take many days."

Tolan studied the portrait. It depicted a tower rising up above a landscape. Behind the tower circled what could be construed as a bird, but he knew better. A draasin.

Was that what it looked like in Par?

He'd never been there, and though Ferrah had wanted to show him, they hadn't had the opportunity. Now was going to be his opportunity. He would do it for her. To see if there was any way to help her. To rescue her. And if he couldn't, then he would have to wait and see what the soldiers might be able to do. Somehow, they would have to save her.

"I need to go and see if there's anything I can do to help."

"Shaper Ethar, you are a third-level student. You are given more freedom because of that, but…"

Why was she saying this? She understood how important Ferrah was to him, and she knew everything he'd been involved in. More than that, she understood his connection to the elementals—and perhaps even to the Convergence.

He frowned, realizing the shaping building from her was a hint of spirit mixed with wind.

He mimicked the shaping. As he did, he became aware of something else. Words were drifting toward him, her voice. It reminded him somewhat of how he communicated with the elementals when he was able to do so, the way he could hear their voices deep inside his mind.

"It's dangerous for you to be here now," she was saying.

"Master Minden?"

"Listen," she said. "With the attacks, the Council sent not only the soldiers, but Inquisitors who were felt to be loyal were sent."

"What if they aren't loyal?"

"They have all been tested and have passed."

"What if they have somehow slipped through?"

The more he thought about it, the more uncertain he

was. He didn't like the idea the Grand Inquisitor was somehow involved, but at the same time, she'd been the one who had sent him back to Amitan, hadn't she? It was because of her he'd been attacked. Without her, what would he have experienced?

Then she was also in Par.

That might only be a coincidence, but what if it was not?

And given everything the Academy had been through, the role of the Inquisitors, he wondered if the Grand Master would even investigate.

"Let me go and see if I can't figure out what happened."

She turned to him, looking at him with her rheumy eyes. "It's more than you figuring out what happened. You need to do what you can to protect the Academy."

Images suddenly surged into his mind, and as they did, he thought he understood. Within those images, scenes of revolt flashed into his mind. He didn't recognize the cities, at least not with any obvious sense, but they seemed to be all within Terndahl.

Soldiers were there in each of them, putting down the revolt.

"Shapers have begun to revolt. This is more than just the Draasin Lord."

"Let me find my friend. See if it is about the Convergence."

She watched him a moment, and he wondered what she might say.

With a deep breath, she nodded. "The shaping you

used to reach us in the first place. It comes from the ancient warriors. I didn't expect you would know it, but perhaps it came to you in a time of need. When you were failing, I wondered if you discovered it when it was necessary. Either way, it brought you here. Now it must bring you away."

They reached a stair along the back of the hall. It led up, away from the rest of the Academy. Tolan studied it, tracing his way along the staircase, feeling it without the need to walk up. It would bring him back outside, up to the top of the tower, and from there he could reach the Shapers Path.

But if she was right, then it wasn't the Shapers Path he needed to reach. It was another way.

At the top of the stair, Master Minden opened the door, revealing bright daylight. He took a deep breath, breathing in the awareness of the city. Taking the Shapers Path wouldn't work anyway. Soldiers would be aware of his travel, but if this other shaping worked for him, then there would be a way to travel without anyone else knowing.

"Where do I go now? How will I find her?"

"I wish I could tell you where you needed to go to find her, but you must find that on your own. You have a unique perspective. Your understanding and willingness to work with the elementals has proven that. Far too many people see the elementals as a threat, and they fear them, though they should not. They blame the Draasin Lord and fail to realize there is real power in connecting to the elementals. They fail to see attempting to secure the element bonds has damaged the world in other ways."

"I'm not sure I know this shaping."

"There is a particular pattern to it. If you can find it within yourself and grasp the connections between the shaping, you should be able to use it. When you do, you will no longer need the Shapers Path." She looked over at him, and for a moment her eyes seemed to clear again. "You remember how you attached the elements together?"

Tolan thought back to that time. It had been little more than a blur, but he thought he did remember. He'd mixed all of the elements, and then he added spirit. "It's the connection. Spirit."

"Exactly. It grants you something greater."

"And if it doesn't work?"

"Then you have lost nothing. You can try the Shapers Path, but you have to get past the soldiers. If it works, and if you gain control over it, you will begin your way down a road the world has not seen in a long time."

"What is that?"

"Long ago, we had a particular term for such shapers, though I feel as if it were something of a misnomer. The language has changed and evolved, and much like I've said, because of that, there is much that's different."

"You still haven't told me the name."

"I suppose I haven't. Many would refer to them as warriors."

"What sort of warriors? I'm not much of a fighter."

"You don't have to be much of a fighter in order to be

this kind of warrior. The ancient warriors, the kind preceding all of us, used a combination of the elemental energies to help them fight. They used swords, the same way as the soldiers today now use them, though there was something special to those blades. With them, they were able to draw even more strength from the elements and from the elementals."

"Like bondars?"

"Something like that," she said. "It's because of those blades they became more—much more. They knew shapings we did not. They had control over the elements we do not. And you demonstrated a shaping not seen for a long time."

"But you recognized that shaping."

"I did, but I doubt anyone else would have."

She paused, and Tolan looked over at her. "How is it you know these things?"

"Is that really the question you want to be asking?"

"I think it's the question I need to be asking. How is it you know so many things others don't?"

"The service to the archives has taught me many things. Because in my time here, the time I have spent studying, I have come to gain knowledge few others have."

Tolan watched her, wishing for a different answer, but he had a sense that even if there was one, she wouldn't share it with him. "What do I do now?"

"Now you must find a way to recreate that shaping. You must decide if you can be something more—something greater. If you head to Par, and if you confront what is out there, you may be putting yourself down the path toward becoming an ancient warrior."

He'd thought he was heading down the pathway toward becoming a librarian so he could learn from Master Minden, but that wasn't the case. And then he thought the Grand Inquisitor thought he might be able to train with the Inquisitors, but what if he was going to be something else entirely?

When Master Minden stepped back, Tolan focused on the shaping. He remembered it, though it came to him faintly. It was a distant sort of memory, vague. Faded. Mixed with his fatigue from that time and the pain, and everything else he'd experienced.

The power of that shaping filled him, the knowledge of it right there. All Tolan needed to do was disseminate the elements and mix them in a specific pattern. Fire summoned the lightning. Earth was the connection, binding it from place to place. Wind stirred up the power needed, and water in a storm cloud he needed to travel upon. On top of all of that, he needed a mixture of spirit, binding it together.

What had he done the last time?

That came to him easier than anything else. He had fixed the library in mind, and in doing so, he'd transported himself on the lightning. It had swallowed him, engulfing him, and carried him.

Where was he going to go in Par?

The only place he thought he could go. It was a place he'd seen in the hall of portraits.

He focused on it, holding that image in mind, and let the shaping wash over him.

It happened faster than the last time, and he was much more aware of the nature of it and how the lightning streaked down, exploding from the sky. When it did, he tensed, fearful of what would happen when the bolt struck him, but much like the last time, the lightning seemed to wrap around him, swallowing him, lifting him into the sky.

With a flash, followed by a clap of thunder, he was gone.

15

When the lightning cleared, Tolan looked around. He stood on top of an enormous tower. Gray sky swirled around him, darkness mixed within, and thunder rumbled, though he wasn't sure whether that thunder came from what he'd just shaped or from the threat of a new storm. Energy crackled through him, almost as if the shaping refreshed him rather than required his strength. It was a strange sort of shaping requiring each of the elements—including spirit—and yet it had not taken considerable effort on his part.

His vision returned slowly. There had to be some way to create that shaping so it wouldn't destroy his vision, so the brightness wouldn't overwhelm him.

Wind whipped toward him. It had a hint of salt in the air, a strange odor, that of moisture and mustiness, but it was mixed with that of fish far below.

Par.

Somewhere here, he'd find Ferrah.

Not just Ferrah, but he'd find whatever had occurred here. He needed to find her first, though. He also needed to see if the Grand Inquisitor was somehow involved. Tolan hoped she was not, but a part of him worried if she were, what would he do? Would there be anything that could be done?

The city of Par was interesting. It was an old city that had been built upon. There was evidence of age everywhere, even more so than in places like Ephra, where the city itself was considerably old. Unlike Ephra, Par had been maintained, shapings having secured the city in ways they had never taken the time to do in Ephra. The tower here was an example of that. It was incredibly old. Tolan could feel that age, could tell how time had passed, how that filled everything. Despite that, the stone remained solid, bound together by earth shapings and perhaps something more.

He pushed down with a shaping of earth, stretching deep beneath him, using the connection to the stone. As he did, he searched for anything that would trigger understanding. There came a familiar sort of sense reminding him of the Academy. Within the stone was a rune.

Tolan smiled to himself. Did the people of Par know they had a rune in their tower? It would be hard for them not to, but even knowing they did, would they have been able to use it?

Could he?

Tolan pushed, letting his power flow out, heading into

that rune. He could use it if he could find some way to tap into that power. And if he could use it, he had to think there was something more within it that he could do. He wanted to search for shapers, and with the power of a rune like this, Tolan thought he might be able to do so. He could add water, mixing with it, and perhaps a hint of spirit.

The shaping flowed away from him. Standing atop the tower as he was, he detected considerable strength within it. It surged down the tower, roiling along the surface of it, striking the rune, where it gained more strength. Tolan didn't have enough access to water and spirit to complement it, leaving earth as the predominant element in this shaping.

That was a mistake. There needed to be another way to drag that power forward.

Tolan focused on the energy beneath him, thinking about whether he could somehow reach for the power within the earth rune and withdraw some of it, but that wasn't the answer at all. What he needed was to draw upon water and spirit in equal portions.

There was the rune at the Academy, but it was too far away. He hurriedly dragged his foot across the stone, forming a rune for water, and then followed it with a rune for spirit. He pushed through those, wondering whether or not he would be able to use them in the same way. They added a certain bit of strength, and for a moment, Tolan thought he might have made a mistake and the power would bounce back at him, but then he flowed through it, surging. In doing so, he was able to send that shaping outward.

It washed over the city.

Dozens upon dozens of reverberations struck him.

There were hundreds. Possibly a thousand. All of them represented shapers, which meant he needed to be careful. If there were shapers here who wanted to harm him, then he'd need to be cautious, but at the same time, would there be any way to detect the two shapers he wanted to find?

He might not know how to find the shaping academy in Par, but he'd been around Ferrah enough that he should be able to detect her shaping and recognize her unique signature. And the Grand Inquisitor.

Tolan stood at the edge of the tower, looking down at the city. Most of the buildings were incredibly old, though there were many newer, most of those on the fringes, working around the older portion of the city. The older buildings all were made of stone, power radiating from them, either shaped power or somehow trapped within it. As he focused on it, he couldn't help but think something within those buildings had secured them in a certain way. It was almost as if they had runes on them, trapping power, but that didn't seem quite right.

He should have taken the time to study Par. He'd known a little bit about it, but not nearly enough to get a better understanding of what the people of Par found important. Ferrah didn't talk about it, other than telling him about some of the strange languages found here. There *had* to be a place of Convergence here, which was the reason she'd gone to the Academy to study, thinking she could get discover it and use that knowledge to understand the secrets of the past.

In the distance, the slight translucent appearance of Shapers Paths caught his attention. There were several of them, each of them crossing over top of the city, practically glistening in the air. Moisture clung to them, and Tolan was tempted to shape himself up to one of them, but there were others making their way along them, and he didn't want to draw the wrong kind of attention to himself. Until he knew whether the shapers had already arrived or whether there was any danger from the Academy here, he would stay hidden.

What he wanted was to find Ferrah.

If only he had some way of communicating with her. He had spirit. Having been with Master Minden, he wondered if there was a way to connect to spirit with her the same way Master Minden had done with him. It might not be possible. Master Minden had connected to him because they both had shared a connection to spirit, and as far as he knew, Ferrah didn't.

Could he identify her shaping in another way?

He focused on the elements of the city. He listened to the way water surged, crashing along some distant shore, the wind swirling around him, noticing the patterns to it, the feeling of the earth, ancient buildings mixed with a steadfast and powerful rock, and finally the heat, however mild it might be, of this place. Par was a place of ancient power.

Tolan breathed it all in, using that to help him connect to the energy of the city. He'd spent so much time above Amitan doing the same thing, it came to him easily. In doing so, it opened him to recognizing the powers around him, the shaping energy he could detect. As it did, he focused on it.

A shaping built that he recognized.

It was not far away, and Tolan used a burst of fire and wind, throwing himself from the tower, shaping along the street and dropping down to the ground. When he did, he found himself in an alley, hidden away from others. He made his way slowly, carefully, hesitating so he didn't reveal himself too quickly.

As he walked, he focused on the shaping that had drawn him here. It was Ferrah's shaping, and as far as he could tell, there was no danger in it.

It didn't mean there wasn't a danger in the city. With what he'd experienced in Ephra, he didn't know if they'd had a similar attack here. Maybe Par was remote enough that they hadn't managed to reach it yet.

Tolan found himself among a crowd of other people. The streets were busy and people wandered along them, heading into shops, making their way toward some of the wider streets, and there was only so far and so fast he could go before butting up against someone else.

He had detected the sense of Ferrah, but now he was

out here, he no longer knew if that was accurate or merely imagined. At this point, it could have been imagined.

He continued to squeeze through the crowd, looking around, searching for anything to tell him where she might've gone.

He came up with nothing.

He paused at an intersection. Buildings rose up on either side, much taller and closer together than they were in Amitan. Most of them were made of a dark stone, and it seemed as if moisture seeped up along with the stone, leaving it damp.

It was almost unpleasant, and yet, there was a familiarity to it.

Tolan wondered why it would be. When he'd traveled with his parents, he didn't recall coming to Par, though it seemed almost as if there should be some memory of being here.

He turned a corner, and he detected a shaping again.

It was behind him.

How was he supposed to get back there? The crowd continued to push him forward. As he walked, he could feel the pressure of the crowd sending him along the road, as if it intended to guide him, and yet where was it going to take him?

Holding onto the sense of the shaping, that power he suspected came from Ferrah, Tolan let the crowd push him until he reached another intersection. When it did, he turned off, heading along an alley. At the end of the alley, he turned back around, following not only the crowd, but also the sense of the power and shaping he detected.

He paused again, looking around. Once more, it seemed as if Ferrah had moved, as if the shaping had drawn her deeper into the city.

He paused near what had to be a tavern. Loud music and shouts radiated from inside the building, and he thought she might be in there, but there came no further sense of her shaping.

When Tolan was about to turn again, he detected the shaping once more.

It dragged him forward along the street, and he paused at the next intersection. Once more, it seemed as if the shaping had shifted, turning, somehow now behind him.

That couldn't be right. Why would it be behind him?

Heading forward, he turned before finally looking up.

When he did, his gaze drifted toward a much taller building. It had to be five stories tall, and surprisingly, it seemed as if many of the upper levels connected with neighboring buildings.

Could it be what he was picking up on?

Tolan followed the outline of the building, his gaze drifting along it, trailing to see if there was anything he might be able to make out. So far, he wasn't able to see anything, but he intended to follow it.

At one point, he thought he saw a rune on the building, and he began to shape before withdrawing. If he added power to the rune, someone who was attuned to it might know what he was doing. He didn't want to reveal his presence quite yet.

Turning another corner, another shaping struck, and this one made him stop in place. People behind him crashed into his back, sending him staggering forward until he shaped slightly, using earth to maintain his position so he didn't get tossed over.

The Grand Inquisitor.

Tolan was certain that was what he detected, and he wasn't surprised she'd have made it here so quickly. She would've followed the Shapers Path, and as far as he knew, it wouldn't have taken her more than a day, certainly giving her the opportunity to reach the city before him.

Another shaping followed hers, and then another. All of them were rapid, but there was something about the first one—the shaping he'd detected when he first picked up on her—that left him worried something had happened to her.

It wasn't his responsibility to protect the Grand Inquisitor, was it?

And yet, if she was going through anything like what he'd already gone through, what choice did he have?

From what he could tell, Ferrah was safe. She was up in some building, and though she was shaping regularly, she was unharmed.

The same couldn't be said about the Grand Inquisitor. She was shaping regularly, and there was power in each of her shapings, enough power it left him worried perhaps something had happened to her. Tolan trailed after it, wanting to make sure he didn't get lost along the way, wanting to ensure he could still detect where Ferrah had gone.

The other shaping continued to build. Tolan trailed after it. It was nearby and came one after another, all bursts of power, and all strangely familiar.

It was the spirit used within those shapings that struck him as most familiar.

Tolan began to ready his shaping. He grabbed his necklace, holding on to the ring. As he clutched it, he readied himself for the possibility he'd have to use spirit shapings.

Turning a corner, he found an open plaza on the street. Carts lined either side of the street, and another row of them worked through the middle. The crowd continued through those carts, pressing together much more closely than Tolan thought he would be comfortable with. And yet, what choice did he have but to follow the crowd? That was where he detected the sense of the Grand Inquisitor, and that was where her shaping came from.

It was spirit, the same kind of spirit shaping that had swiped at the attackers in Ephra. If she were under attack again, if this was something similar, he needed to help.

There might not be a way to do so without revealing his presence.

Another smattering of shapings occurred: earth, then fire, then water. Each one a blast of power and following each one was a moment of what appeared to be silence, an emptiness coming from the shaping after it faded. He worried what that might mean but continued to follow the sense of the shaping. It was moving along the street, somehow winding through the carts.

What he needed to do was get above it, but could he do so and hide himself?

There was a way to use earth to mask himself, but it might be better if he used wind. With the right kind of shaping, Tolan could take to the air. If he could twist it, inverting the shaping so it focused on him, it might hide him. In doing so, he would be forced to use another shaping to propel himself. It would reveal the shaping—whichever one he used, but he might be able to stay hidden as he traveled.

Regardless of what he did, Tolan had to get out of the crowd. The people were smashing against him. Most of them were dressed in drab clothing, no sense of color or style, as was found in other places like Amitan. It was almost as if the people of Par preferred simpler colors. Every so often, he would come across someone wearing brighter colors seeming almost out of place.

Tolan first focused on wind. As he did, he pressed up against one of the nearby storefronts. He wasn't going to reveal himself too quickly. When he first disappeared, it would draw attention in a different way.

The wind shaping built, steadily, but he was careful to pull it up from the ground rather than swirling it around him. As he did, he twisted it, focused downward. It whistled around him, but as far as he could tell, there was no further wind anywhere else out on the street. He was able to contain it, and he prevented anyone else from recognizing his wind shaping existed.

Did it work?

What he wanted was for the wind shaping to mask him and conceal his presence altogether, but Tolan wasn't sure if he'd been successful. As he stood there, focusing on the wind, someone bounced off his shaping, shaking themselves before continuing along the street.

Perhaps it *had* worked.

Tolan held onto the shaping, keeping it inverted. In doing so, it masked that he was holding onto a shaping at all. There were ways someone would be able to detect it, but they would have to focus on him. They would have to somehow know he was here and search for him.

As he prepared a fire shaping—he'd have more control over that than over many of the other elements—a dark-robed figure moved into view. Through the wind shaping, there was something of a haze. The figure strode forward, power radiating from them, and he detected the energy of their shaping.

A soldier.

The man was large, muscular, and rested one hand on his sword.

If there was a soldier here, it meant he was heading in the right direction, but he would somehow have to get ahead of them.

Tolan breathed out and then hurriedly pushed off with a shaping of fire.

Maintaining the shaping of fire while pushing off on the wind was not quite as easy as he'd hoped. Despite being able to shape effectively, there was something about inverting his wind shaping that made it more difficult.

Lifting into the air, he hovered, staying overhead as he surveyed the street level. He moved along it, shaping quickly, following the sense he had of the Grand Inquisitor. He continued to feel the steady shapings, the ongoing reverberations echoing against him. If he could reach her before something else happened, he thought…

Something slammed into him.

Tolan twisted, focused on whether there was anyone aware of him, but he couldn't tell. His shaping held him in the air, and as far as he knew, the wind masked him. Someone must have recognized he was here.

Tolan raced along the street, staying below the roofline. Another shaping slammed into him, but with the wind wrapped around him, it prevented him from getting injured the way he would have been if unprotected. It was a barrier of sorts, though wasn't intended to be that.

If he could hold onto it, he might be able to make it out of here.

As another blow struck, he wondered if they were aware he was here, or whether the attacker was simply aware there was a shaping moving above the street level. It was possible his wind shaping had simply been detected, and not that they were trying to strike him.

There came another surge of shaping, but this was down below. It was a series of spirit shapings, one after another, blast upon blast. As he turned a corner, he saw her.

The Grand Inquisitor was down on the street, several shapers all around her.

She was striking at them with spirit shapings, but they were bouncing off.

Could he help?

Another blow struck him, this one sending him slamming into the nearby building.

Tolan twisted, holding onto his wind shaping. He added a hint of fire to it, twisting that inward as well. If nothing else, he wanted to have a protection around himself, a barrier and buffer so he didn't end up crashing to the ground below.

He shaped his way closer to the Grand Inquisitor. From here, he could practically feel the shaping she attempted. They were defensive. Each of them was attempting to swipe at the person below them, but none of them were effective.

Was there any other way to do something to help?

They were defending themselves against the Grand Inquisitor, but they didn't know about Tolan.

Drawing upon spirit, he turned toward the person nearest the Grand Inquisitor.

It was an older man, with thin-framed glasses on his face. He was wearing a gray jacket. Tolan sent spirit across his mind, sweeping through. It bounced off a barrier.

He pushed, squeezing his ring, drawing more power through the bondar, and found the shaping. Sliding up underneath it, he unraveled it, twisting it free and releasing his hold on it.

The man stopped attacking the Grand Inquisitor. He turned to the others, and Tolan was preparing for the possibility he might need to drop to the ground to help the Grand Inquisitor when another shaping struck him.

Tolan ignored it, shaping his way closer.

This time, he focused on another of the attackers. There was a spirit shaping on their mind, much like there had been on the last, and he drew through the bondar, summoning power. As he did, it allowed him to free the mind of the attacker. It was much like the last one, and he was able to clear it.

Two were free.

The Grand Inquisitor seemed to realize something was changing, and though she didn't look up, there was a probe of spirit. Tolan reached toward her, connecting with a hint of spirit, much like Master Minden had done when he'd been at the Academy.

"I can help," he said, communicating to her with spirit.

"You shouldn't be here."

"And you shouldn't need my help."

Tolan focused on the next attacker and pushed harder, faster, sweeping free of the mental barrier, moving onto the next one and then the next one and then the next one. There were only a few remaining, and as he turned to help her again, a shaping struck.

It slammed into him and he was thrown into a building.

He spun around, focusing his energy on each of the elements, prepared for the possibility he might have to use the warrior shaping to transport him away, but stopped.

The shaper across from him made his breath catch.

"Ferrah?"

16

Ferrah looked at him with a blank expression, almost as if she wasn't there. Her shaping built, a combination of wind and water, and it swirled together, an attack aimed for him. Tolan doubted he'd be able to withstand many more of those blows. Ferrah was a strong shaper and the emptiness within her eyes suggested she wasn't going to hold back.

"Ferrah. It's me. Tolan."

The shaping unleashed, and Tolan did the only thing he could think of. He dropped to the ground.

It missed, the shaping streaking over his head, and he shot back into the air, hurriedly shaping a combination of elements, drawing them together and adding spirit.

As he did, he grabbed for Ferrah, wrapping his arms around her.

As she struggled, Tolan held onto her, determined to keep her with him. As the lightning bolt connected, the shaping lifted him, carrying him away from Par, and carried her with him back to the Academy.

He stood on the rooftop, stepping back from her. She still had a dazed expression on her face, and he swept toward her with spirit.

As he did, he hesitated.

When he'd used spirit on others, they'd been people he hadn't known. If something had gone wrong—and considering the likelihood, given everything he'd done—he wouldn't have felt quite as much remorse.

This was Ferrah.

If he did something that damaged her…

"Ferrah," he whispered.

A shaping began to build from her. If he didn't do anything, she'd continue to attack. He had ways of subduing her, and now he was back at the Academy, he thought he could use the runes themselves in order to confine her, but what he needed to do was keep her from continuing her aggression.

Her shaping continued to build. Tolan couldn't wait any longer.

He pushed out, surrounding her with spirit, and began to push gently, slowly, down into her mind.

As he did, he held onto the bondar, using the ring to connect him to the power of spirit, mostly so he had greater control. He wanted to ensure he had some way of protecting her safety and didn't want to do anything to lead to her injury.

Her shaping struck the spirit wall he'd created. As it did, he held firm.

There came a flash of light, bright and white, and it was incredibly potent. He held onto it, ignoring everything else around him, focused only on Ferrah and what he could do to help her. It was possible he wouldn't be able to do this without harming her, but he was determined to find some way. There had to be something he could do to clear her mind without damaging her.

As he pushed inward, squeezing with the spirit shaping, he felt the resistance of the shaping placed upon her.

It was far more subtle than the ones he'd detected at the Academy in Ephra. As he noticed that, he realized something. Those shapings had been intentionally obvious. The only reason he was able to detect this shaping was because he knew Ferrah. Anyone else, and he might not have known.

Tolan continued to push, working slowly, steadily, squeezing through her mind, drawing the shaping across her, everything in his being allowing him to do so. The power flowed out from him, and he worried he was doing too much, that he was somehow harming her. Despite everything he did, she remained silent.

In some ways, that bothered him even more.

Shouldn't she cry out? Should there be some sort of reaction from her?

Continuing to squeeze, drawing the shaping across her, he felt it press in on the spirit shaping.

He hesitated. That forced the spirit shaping deeper into her mind.

That wasn't what he needed to do at all. He somehow had to unravel it. In doing so, then he might be able to free her. If he could do this to Ferrah, then maybe there was hope for others. Maybe Tanner *had* actually been spirit shaped, and there would be some way of saving him as well. Tolan hated the idea his friend had attacked him. If there was something to be done, some way of saving him, he'd do it.

And it wasn't only Tanner who needed help. It was anyone else who'd been shaped similarly. There weren't enough spirit shapers remaining, and those who did were potentially compromised. It was possible even the Grand Inquisitor was compromised, though she had been fighting the others.

Tolan shifted the nature of his shaping, sweeping it beneath what he detected, drawing it through her mind. As he did, he pulled. It came slowly, almost as if it were tearing free from her mind, and in doing so, he worried the shaping would be harmful to her.

The longer he waited, the more likely there were going to be ongoing attacks from her. For her sake, she needed him to continue to try.

Trying to sweep the shaping free of her mind didn't seem to be working, and forcing it down didn't seem to be working, but was there something else he could do?

What about the other elements?

Tolan didn't know if the other elements could be used

in the spirit shaping like that, but it had to be possible. If he could mix them, the same way he could mix the shapings for the strange warrior lightning bolt, maybe he could use that to remove and lift the shaping free.

It was potentially dangerous. This was the kind of thing that could damage and destroy her mind. This was the kind of thing the Grand Inquisitor had warned him about.

He started slowly. He mixed each of the elements together, adding them one after another, and used those with his connection to spirit, sending it through the bondar. There came a surge.

The power flowed, building from within him. At first, he worried perhaps he was too aggressive, but the longer he sent that surge, the clearer it became that something was changing.

Hopefully it was what he needed to change.

Ferrah started to thrash, and Tolan almost abandoned the shaping. He didn't want to do anything to cause her pain, and the way she was thrashing suggested this was causing her significant discomfort.

She cried out. "Tolan?"

The word was strangled, twisted, and there was something mixed in with it.

Darkness.

He had recognized that as the same sort of thing used on the wind elemental.

Was it not a shaping of spirit? Could it have been something else?

Whatever he was holding onto now, the shaping he was drawing away, certainly felt to him to be spirit. The more he pulled, the more certain he was of drawing off spirit, and if he could lift it, then she would be free of the taint.

"Why are you doing this?"

There was a sense of her affection for him, but he had to ignore it.

"Don't do this to me," she whispered.

The last came out strangled, and it was almost enough to make him abandon his attempt, but he could not. He knew he could not.

Sending more power into the shaping, he realized maybe there was another approach. Not only did he need to add each of the elements, but what he needed to do was use something similar to what he'd done with the wind elemental. If he could send a soothing sense through the shaping, he might be able to calm her, the same way he'd calmed the wild elemental. If he did, he could lift that shaping off, remove the threat of whatever had been done to her, and restore her. More than anything else, that was what he wanted to do.

"I don't want to hurt you," he whispered.

"But you are."

"I'm helping. I care about you. Regardless of what they did to you, I care about you."

He took a step toward her, wondering if he'd made a mistake before. He'd had her wrapped up near him, his arms encircling her, and he had held her against him. That closeness should have given him a way of maintaining that connection, but for some reason, he'd released the hold.

What he needed to do now was bring her back to him, to wrap his arms around her again, to push out the power of the shaping he used. If he could do that…

He took another step. She thrashed again, and Tolan felt the way she was raging against his shaping. What choice did he have but to continue toward her?

He reached her. As he did, he grabbed her, pulling her to him. He pressed his shaping out, washing it over her, and then he pushed. He started slowly, but the shaping continued to build, rolling through her with increasing intensity.

More pressure.

There was resistance. It was almost an active thing.

Tolan didn't know what to make of it as it squirmed beneath him. As it continued to thrash, he realized there was something else he could try. What he'd been doing before had been trying to either push it out of her or pull it out; instead, now, what he wanted to do was wrap it in spirit. Once he did, he could mix the other elements within it.

The shaping continued to build, and he shifted the way he held onto it, spinning it so it would turn inward. As he did, the shaping focused on her mind, twisting and rolling inward. He swirled it around the strange darkness he detected.

He captured it, sweeping it within his shaping, holding

it in place. Only then did he add the surge of the other elements. Power exploded from him.

She thrashed again, kicking and screaming, reminding him of what had happened to those they'd tested during the Selection. He continued to push, sweeping the strange foreign shaping tighter and tighter inside his bond, constricting it. As he did, he could feel the way it continued to fight, but Tolan ignored it. He squeezed, more and more pressure building. He recognized the pressure was going to overpower whatever strangeness was here.

There came a burst of energy, a flash of light, and the foreign strangeness was gone.

Ferrah dropped to the ground. She kicked, and for a moment, Tolan thought she stopped breathing.

Fighting whatever it was that had happened to her had taken considerable strength on his part, and he found himself weakened and tired. He didn't know if he had enough strength to return to Par, though he knew he needed to. The Grand Inquisitor was there and still needed him.

Crouching down next to Ferrah, Tolan took her hands. He squeezed them before lifting her, scooping her off the ground, carrying her toward the tower. Master Minden would have to understand what he had done. She would have to understand he'd tried to save her.

The door came open before he reached it and Master Minden approached.

"Where is it?"

Tolan looked around the rooftop. The sun hadn't really moved across the horizon since he'd left. He hadn't been gone all that long before needing to return with Ferrah, and as he stood here, studying Master Minden, he frowned.

"Where is what? I found Ferrah in Par, but something had been shaped across her mind."

"Yes. It was shaped across her mind, but where is it?"

"What do you mean?"

For a moment, Master Minden's eyes cleared, as if the milky film always present across them faded. As it did, she looked over at Tolan, irritation flashing within them. "Did you release it?"

"I didn't release anything. I just—"

"You just removed the shaping on her mind."

Tolan looked down at Ferrah. She was still breathing, and it looked as if color had returned to her cheeks. He hadn't realized how much color had been missing until just now. Now he was aware of it, he couldn't help but stare.

"What was it?"

Master Minden continue to shape, looking around. The power building from her was incredible, and as she held on to it, she swept her gaze along the rooftop before settling on Ferrah. She touched two fingers, one from each hand, on either side of Ferrah's forehead. A surge of shaping, a mixture of water with spirit, washed over Ferrah. As it did, the shaping seemed to help her relax and

Ferrah took a deep breath, breathing in and then out again before seeming to fall into a slumber.

"Bring her down with me," Master Minden said.

Tolan followed her downstairs along the hall of portraits, the color in them increasing in intensity since the last time he'd been here. That had to be his imagination. She brought him to a door along the hallway and pushed it open. It was similar to where he'd awoken, and she motioned for him to set Ferrah down.

Tolan did, and Master Minden pressed her fingers on either side of Ferrah's temple again, a wave of shaping washing through her before she motioned for Tolan to follow her back out of the room. When they did, she paused in the hallway, pressing her hand across the door, sending a surge of power flowing into it.

"Is that necessary?"

"I don't really know if it's necessary or not. All I know is a dangerous power has been once more unleashed."

"The shaping across her mind?"

"Yes. Do you have any idea what it was?"

"No, but what you're saying suggests you know what it was."

"Not personally, but there have been stories of that kind of power out in the world. I have heard about it, read about it, and have feared seeing it."

She motioned for him to join her along the wall of portraits, and Tolan did so, standing near the middle. He had been here with her before, and this time, she paused, motioning to one of the paintings. "What do you see?"

Tolan studied the painting. Was it the same one he had seen before? It was difficult to tell; all he knew was something about it seemed strange. It came from the nature of the image. Almost as if there was darkness swirling around it, but it wasn't just the darkness in the image. It was the sense of destruction all around it.

"I don't know. It's unusual."

"It has to be unusual. There aren't very many ways to depict this."

"What is it?"

"We don't have a name for it. The power this represents is something ancient, as ancient as the power of the elements and the element bonds. As ancient *as* the elementals."

"Is it an elemental?"

"Possibly. And yet, if it's an elemental, it's vastly different than any others we've encountered. The nature of it is destruction." She sighed. "You have a better understanding than most about the nature of the elementals. But you also recognize that power is a part of everything. It's a part of life, a part of the world around us, and because of that, because of that elemental and element power, we all exist."

"What are you getting at?"

"When you shaped that thing from her mind, I felt it fighting."

"That was something real?"

"As real as the wind elemental you fought. It's destruction. It thrives on death and decay and chaos. And yet, there are some who seek its power."

"I don't understand."

"No. I didn't imagine you would. The Academy was founded at a time when the memory of that had faded. There were stories, rumors mostly, about a creature and power built from destruction, but I think even then, they didn't know whether to believe it or not. How could you believe it when you never experienced it? And yet, the longer we went, the more we faced whatever it was, the clearer it became that power had to have existed. We find it in things like this painting. We find it in references, small details we uncover during our search of the archives. We find it within the darkness of people's minds."

Tolan shivered. As he stared at the painting, he had a sense of an unpleasant and almost oily sort of power. "When I faced the wind elemental outside the city, it came across as twisted. Angry."

"I suspect whoever summoned it used this chaotic elemental."

"Chaotic?" He glanced over at her and found her staring at the painting. Her jaw was set, clenched in a tight frown, and he had a hard time reading her expression. It seemed to him she was angry, but that couldn't be. What would she have to be angry about?

Maybe it wasn't anger at all. Maybe it was nothing more than fear.

If this creature—this strange and chaotic elemental—

had not been seen in some time, he understood having fear. He shared in it.

"What else could it be but an attempt to bring chaos to order?" She shook her head. "We have been trying to understand who the Inquisitors served, trying to understand what could cause them to turn from serving the Academy. I, along with the Grand Master, had thought perhaps it had something to do with them believing the Academy had turned away from its purpose. It was possible they began to understand how we recognized the nature of the elementals and begun to realize keeping them trapped as we have, holding them within the bond, does nothing more than continue to torment them. I would never have imagined they were responsible for this."

Tolan's mouth was dry. Could that be only because he'd been battling some strange power? Or was it more? Did it have to do with his uncertainty with this… Whatever this was?

He continued to stare at the portrait. He wanted nothing more than to turn away from it, but he felt as if he needed to stare so he could understand, to try to know what it was Ferrah had encountered.

"How would she have come across this?"

"Someone released it. That same someone is the very same person we've been trying to find, Shaper Ethar. Despite our best effort, we haven't been able to uncover who is responsible for everything that's been taking place. In this case, whoever it is has used that power on her."

"Did they use it on her because of me?"

He knew it was ridiculous to ask, but at the same time, he thought he needed to. If it was his fault, if they had used the shaping on her because of him, then he needed to know.

"I wish I could tell you it was otherwise, but the possibility exists they did use that on her because of you. It's equally likely they would have expected you to be unable to remove the shaping."

"So, they attacked her without giving her any way of removing it."

"Unfortunately," Master Minden said.

That angered him. Perhaps that was the point, though. He could imagine the attackers had wanted to anger him, but he also could imagine it was about more than that. He had to wonder if they had not only hoped to use her against him, but they could also have intended to infect him, if such a thing were possible.

"What will happen to her?"

"That's a good question. I don't know. I think we were successful in removing it. And by that, I mean I think *you* were successful in removing it. If you were, then she needs time to recover."

"What about others who might have been attacked in the same way?"

"If there are others, we may not have anything we can do for them."

"There has to be something," Tolan said.

"How many do you think you can work with?" Master

Minden looked over at him, meeting his eyes with her strangely milky ones. "With as much effort as it took on your part to remove what was done to her, do you think you can repeat it?"

Tolan only stared. He wasn't sure, but what choice did he have other than to try?

"There have to be others who are capable of doing it."

"I'm afraid, Shaper Ethar, that this element—or elemental, as I don't know which it is—requires a different approach. It is not simply a matter of shaping strength. If that were the case, then someone like Shaper Changen wouldn't have succumbed to its effect."

"Then what is required?"

"In order to defeat this, one needs to have an understanding of the various powers. Not just the elements, not just the element bonds, and not the elementals. The entirety of it. Unfortunately, considering how we have structured the Academy, there are very few who have the necessary ability to do that."

Tolan glanced back at the door where Ferrah rested. If others had been twisted in the same way, he couldn't simply stand aside, could he?

And yet, there might not be anything he could do. As much as he wanted to help, as much as he might want to fight, it might be beyond him.

"The soldiers were in Par," he said.

"You saw one."

Tolan nodded.

Master Minden turned her attention toward the painting.

"I don't think they were tainted."

"Even if they were, it's possible we wouldn't know."

"Why not?"

"Their training is different. It has always been that way. Despite everything we've tried over the years, the soldiers have separated themselves."

"What if they are responsible for what's taken place?"

"Then we are in far greater trouble."

Tolan went to the other room and crouched next to Ferrah, and when he did, he found something on a chain around her neck. Pulling it out, he held it up, studying it.

A bondar.

That had to be what it was, but more than that, the bondar reminded him of the one he wore.

Could it be coincidence?

"Shaper Ethar?"

He tore his gaze away, holding the ring up for Master Minden. "I think I know who's responsible for these strange bondars."

She leaned close, studying it. "Who?"

"My father."

17

As he had done with the shaping of each element before, he held a place in his mind, a vision of what he wanted to do and where he wanted to go, uncertain whether it would be enough, or whether he'd be enough.

Then again, he didn't feel as if he had any choice but to try.

As the shaping surrounded him, coming for him, he felt lifted, pulled free from the building. There was a brief sense of movement and then he was shot back down toward the ground.

The moment he landed, power swirled around him. It was a strange change. The power he detected in these lands—a place of the Draasin Lord—filled him in a way he rarely felt power.

All around him was elemental energy. When he'd been here last, he'd been dependent upon someone else guiding him and bringing him away. Now he'd discovered this warrior shaping, this burst of lightning that could carry him away in a moment's notice, he felt strangely free.

The energy of shapings continued to build around him, one after another, and Tolan searched for a particular shaping he could track. He needed to find his father. He needed to understand.

He strode along a path. In the distance, the mountain with the pathway through it blocked him, and though he knew there was some way of shaping a doorway through it, that his father had used an earth bondar in order to do so, Tolan no longer needed that path. He no longer needed the Draasin Lord to carry him back to the Academy and to Terndahl.

What he needed was to understand why there seemed to be a connection between these bondars.

As he made his way along the path, he noticed hyza off in the distance. Was it the same elemental that had helped him all those times? He didn't really know without speaking to the elemental, and he wasn't even certain whether something like that was possible. If it was, then perhaps he could get a better understanding of where to find his father. He could ask the elemental to guide him, though he didn't know if hyza would be able to do so or if hyza would even know where to find him.

Instead, Tolan focused on the nature of the shapings he could follow, searching for something to help him. In the distance, he noticed the building where he'd been brought, a temple of sorts. There was power within that building, shaping power unlike anything he could find anywhere else.

There were people out working. Some were farming, pulling in wheat and filling the field, using shapings as they did. Others were using their shaping touch for other things, lifting stone, creating buildings, working with the elementals.

And still others had a singular focus, a tightly-honed shaping, one that was recognizable…

Tolan went toward it.

There was a sense of energy to the buildings and everything around him, something he could almost recognize, though he wasn't entirely sure what it was or why he would be aware of it. That sense filled him, and the more he searched all around him, the more certain he was of what he was detecting.

Though there was elemental energy all around him, there was something more he thought he needed to understand.

Something felt off.

Why should that be the case?

The longer he remained here, the more certain he was that he detected something amiss, though he wasn't entirely sure why that should be. Perhaps it was only his imagination, but he didn't think so. He recognized there was something strange here, some strange energy, and the more he focused on it, the more certain he was of what he detected.

He couldn't linger. That wasn't the reason he'd come

here. He had come looking for answers, and until he had them, he wasn't going to be able to go anywhere.

Tolan took in a deep breath, turning toward the small building nearby.

He stopped at it. It seemed to be made of shaped stone, solid, as if pulled from the ground itself. Grasses grew along the sides almost as if the ground didn't want to give up the building. Strength seemed to radiate from it, a distinct sense Tolan was aware of. Though he didn't know if this was his father's creation, the shaping inside certainly was.

He held his hand above the door, focusing for a moment. As he did, he could detect the shapings on the other side, the power there, and he hesitated.

Hadn't he detected similar shapings in his visions?

They were there, distinct, and he recalled just how much he'd noticed when he'd been there. The memory of them was faint, but when he'd been trapped within the dream, living almost as if it were real, he'd been all too aware of how his father had used a combination of tools and shaping in order to create his bondars. It was a skill set his father was not supposed to have had, but knowing now what he did about his father, he realized he must.

Taking a deep breath, Tolan knocked.

The shaping continued for a moment before stopping. There was a shuffling sound, a rumble he detected through earth, and a stirring of wind. Tolan wasn't sure whether that came from something his father was doing or whether from his ability to sense. Either way, he realized when his father reached the door and pulled it open.

His breath caught.

"Tolan? What are you... How are you here?"

Tolan looked past his father. "I need to talk to you about the bondars."

"Did the Draasin Lord bring you back?"

Tolan shook his head. "I brought myself back."

"How?"

"Now isn't the time. I need to speak to you."

His father hesitated, looking past him, looking into the city, and a series of shapings built.

If his father was responsible for creating the bondars, was he now summoning help? Tolan didn't think his father would harm him after what he'd done to help him when it came to the Inquisitors, but he couldn't help but wonder if perhaps he didn't know the man nearly as well as he thought.

Stepping into the room, it reminded him somewhat of his childhood home. There was a certain sense of warmth, a carpet, and a fire crackling in the hearth, the elemental saa flickering within it. All of that flowed with power, the kind of power that would be unusual otherwise.

A table and chairs occupied one wall, a stove with a pot on it near another. His father motioned for Tolan to come with him, and they took a seat at the table. His father sat with his hands clasped together. He was a solid man, though smaller—and frailer—than he'd been in Tolan's visions. It was a strange contrast, especially as in Tolan's mind, he had just seen his father as the younger person. He had graying hair, and it was thinning as well.

His clothing was a mishmash of styles, nothing like what he'd find in Terndahl, but perhaps that was the point. Everything here was supposed to be different than Terndahl.

His father continued to hold onto a shaping, and it occurred to Tolan he did so because he wasn't sure whether his son had come to harm him.

"What can you tell me about your bondars?"

His father shook his head. "You aren't ready for that."

"No? I traveled here on a warrior shaping." He watched his father, wondering if the man recognized that term and if he did, did he know what it meant?

There was a flicker behind his eyes, a hint of movement, enough that Tolan realized his father did know the term.

"You recognize that?"

"I recognize it as a shaping that's been lost."

"I don't know it's been lost or whether there's not all that many who can use it."

"And you can?"

Tolan nodded. "I've been having visions."

"What sort of visions?"

Tolan almost grunted. It was surprising his father didn't even question the fact he'd been having visions, and he simply moved on to the fact he wanted to know more about them. "The kind that seemed to be more like memories than visions. In them, I was young, watching you at your workbench. You were making bondars."

"I was a craftsman, Tolan. Nothing more."

Tolan held out the ring, showing it to his father. "You were much more than a craftsman. Tell me about them."

His father stared at the ring. "Where did you get that?"

"Why?"

"I made that for—"

"Mother? I know. That's the way it seemed in the vision."

His father stared at the bondar before dragging his gaze up and looking at Tolan. He shook his head. "No. I made that for you."

"For me?"

His father nodded. "There is much you don't understand, Tolan."

"I understand you left me. I guess I can understand it to a certain extent, and I no longer blame you the way I once did."

He wasn't sure whether or not he should still blame his father, but there was no benefit in doing so. His father had done what he thought was necessary and had left him, abandoning him so he could work to help the elementals. If he was a craftsman of bondars, then it was possible everything he'd done had helped the elementals.

"It's more than that. I did go to seek the Draasin Lord, but I did so because of your mother."

"Mother?"

His father closed his eyes and squeezed his hands, his

knuckles going white. "You were young. You had shown potential, but she was concerned about that potential. She knew with your ability to shape, the Academy would come for you. When they did, you would serve Terndahl."

"I ended up serving Terndahl anyway."

His father nodded. "And I don't know that is such a bad thing. You have been so much more than what I think anyone could have expected."

"This is about Mother, remember?"

His father took a deep breath. "Your mother wanted to protect you. She thought by masking your ability to shape, we might be able to keep you from the Academy for a little while, at least long enough for her to complete what she wanted."

"And what did she want?"

His father took a deep breath, shaking his head. "At first, it was nothing more than understanding. She realized there was something about the elementals we didn't fully grasp. I think my creations helped. It allowed us to reach into the bonds deeper than we could otherwise. I didn't realize they were bondars at the time. I only knew them as things my parents had made, and I had created them the same way my father had taught me to create them. In doing so, I thought I was helping, that I was connecting to some greater power, though I don't even know if that's the case anymore."

"They are bondars."

His father nodded. "I understand that now. Bondars are nothing more than a way to reach deeply into the element bonds, and when you reach so deep within the bond, you can connect to the elementals. When I did, I felt their pain."

Tolan frowned. When he'd reached through the bondars, he hadn't felt the pain of the elementals. Then again, he'd mostly been excited about the fact he was able to shape at all and less concerned about finding the elementals. When he had begun to reach them, there had been a sense of fear, a worry he was somehow damaged, and that by reaching as deeply as he did into the bondar, he was potentially freeing elementals. That was one thing the Academy had instilled in him. If he freed the elementals, there was danger. It meant he'd serve the Draasin Lord.

"I can see from your expression you didn't detect the same thing."

"I guess I didn't notice their pain."

"The bondars you must have used at the Academy wouldn't connect you quite the same way."

That was true. They were reflections, little more than that, not nearly as powerful as the bondars his father would be able to make.

"Your mother wanted to understand the elementals. She searched to try to gain knowledge. At first it was a quest for understanding. That quest brought us to the Draasin Lord."

"That's why you left?"

His father shook his head. "We stayed, even then. I continued to make these bondars, and we managed to smuggle them out of the city, getting them to others who served. In doing so, they were able to reach the elementals better than they would otherwise. In that, we were serving. It wasn't enough for your mother."

"I don't understand."

His father took a deep breath. "She wanted to release them, but she wanted to do so in a way that did something else. She wanted the strength of the bondars. She had begun to blame the Academy and their shapers for what had happened." His father looked down at his hands. "She wasn't alone in that. There were others of the disciples who felt the same way. They viewed their mission as more than just freeing the elementals. They viewed it as getting revenge."

That was more in line with what he'd heard about the disciples of the Draasin Lord all along. Could it be his mother had somehow served that way? It seemed impossible she'd have been responsible for some of the attacks, but then, hadn't there been attacks on Terndahl since he had been at the Academy? Those attacks didn't seem to fit with what he understood of the disciples like his father. They were more peace loving, and in that, they wanted nothing more than to help and to free the elementals.

His father breathed out a sigh. "She began to influence you, Tolan."

"What do you mean?"

"She had a subtle touch. She used it on me, and it wasn't until I began to work with my creations that I realized what was happening. She started to place her touch upon your mind, and so I decided it was time to create something to protect you."

Tolan looked down. "The ring?"

"It connects you to spirit, to your spirit."

"I don't really understand."

"A spirit shaping is unique. From what I understand of it, and admittedly, that's not much, the nature of the shaping is such that yours is different than others. While the shaping is such that you might be connected to the spirit bond in a certain way, the shaping itself, a real shaping of spirit, comes from each person individually, connecting them as a unique person."

Tolan fingered the ring, twisting it. "Is that why I started having these visions?"

"Visions or memories, or whatever they are. I suspect you finally coming into possession of the ring has allowed you to regain some of what was lost. You were never meant to lose them. I never wanted that, at least."

"Why?"

"You won't want to hear this, Tolan."

"I think I need to."

"Your mother decided she wanted power. Real power. More than what she could gain by using these bondars. She wanted to have control. And she didn't think she could do so without something more."

"What more?"

His father shook his head. "I don't know. All I know is she's been chasing something. Whatever it is will give her access to even greater power. I don't know whether she should have that access. More than that, I don't know how to stop her from chasing it. You see, she used even me. As I said, her touch is subtle. With it, she had me make other items."

Tolan reached into his pocket, pulling out the other ring they'd found on Ferrah. "Like this?"

His father's breath caught. "Where did you find that?"

"On someone who attacked people I care about."

His father nodded. "That's one of them," he whispered.

Tolan sat back, holding on to the ring. He had been wondering who had led the Inquisitors. He'd wondered who had been responsible, and through it all, he'd never suspected it would be his mother.

How was he going to stop her?

18

Sitting in his father's workshop, Tolan was brought back to a time long ago when he was a child. When he'd been there before, he had felt a sense of awe at watching his father work, and a part of him had always wondered if perhaps he might one day be able to do the same thing as his father and be a part of some family tradition.

Now he understood his father created bondars, and now he knew how those bondars had been used, Tolan wasn't sure he did want anything to do with it.

He breathed out, looking around. The workshop was so similar to the one in their home when he was a child. A series of hooks in the wall held the tools his father had used over the years, the same sort of tools still found in the house in Ephra. Many of them were strange and exotic, the kind of tools with no purpose other than to create these bondars. Tolan had never really known anything about them, other than the fact his father had used them for his creations. Now he'd had the visions, he'd seen the way his father used those tools, peeling away the stone, adding the various runes that granted power.

Beneath the hooks was the workbench. It was so similar to the one his father had in Ephra, right down to the crisscrossing beams supporting it. There were items of various stages of completion resting upon the bench, and then, stacked on shelves on either side of the workshop were other items. All of them had to be bondars, and there had to be dozens of them. Hundreds. It was the type of power and the type of wealth the Academy would want.

Tolan couldn't help but stare at it.

Despite coming here and feeling the sense of awe at what his father had created, he was filled with an emptiness.

His mother had betrayed him.

Worse, it fit with what he'd experienced. As much as he'd like to deny his mother was involved, as much as he'd like to embrace the warm memories, they couldn't be real. Not after everything he'd experienced. The fact his shaping ability had been separated from him, that there had been an active attempt to keep him from knowing about shaping, told him all he needed to know.

What he didn't understand was why.

If his mother was chasing power, and if he had shown potential, why would they have kept him from it?

"I know this must be hard for you," his father said.

"You do? Why didn't you tell me this when I came here before?"

"Because there was no need to tell you before."

Tolan grunted, looking down at his hands. He gripped the stone ring and couldn't help but wonder if perhaps the ring was not at all meant for him, not as he'd been told. What if his father was misleading him?

Then again, it would be strange, and the fact of the matter was that it felt like what he expected. It fit with what he knew.

"I'm sorry this is happening."

Sorry didn't seem to fit. It was more than just needing to be sorry. If his mother was the one responsible for freeing this chaos, then Tolan had to do something, didn't he?

Only... What was there to do?

"We have to stop her."

"I wish I could, but I've been working, trying to remember some of the things I knew when she and I were together. You see, before she left, she stole memories from me. She wiped my mind. It's taken all these years for me to reach a point where I have any idea about what I was creating. It forced me to copy some of the earlier works I've made, but copies are not nearly as effective as the originals."

Tolan nodded. "We've seen that at the Academy. The bondars they allow the students to use aren't as effective as the originals. There's something about them that is weaker."

"They don't connect nearly as well to the bond. In the copying, something is lost. It's the original creation I'm able to use, and because of that original creation, I can focus on it, and I can use that to connect to the bond in a way I couldn't otherwise. Only… When I make a copy, it seems as if I'm losing something. I've been working," he said, sweeping his hand around him. "But even so, I'm not able to do so with as much effectiveness as I would like."

"Why hasn't she come back for you?"

"I think she tried. In this place, surrounded by the elementals and the freedom to use the shaping power, and by the threat of the Draasin Lord—the true Draasin Lord—she's unable to get me."

"That's why you didn't want me to leave."

His father nodded. "I thought when you came, I'd be able to protect you, but I don't know if that's right."

"There are others who have started to fall under the influence of what she's doing, Father. There are others who have begun to experience the power of what she is doing to them. We need to help them."

"I don't know how."

"With this?"

His father stared at the ring he'd taken off Ferrah. "She took the one I made for you and twisted it."

"Did she do it or did someone else do it for her?"

"I don't know."

"Could it be you did this?"

His father frowned. "I wish I could say I wasn't involved, but…"

"You don't know."

His father shook his head. "I don't know. I might have

been. It's possible she used me, the same way she used me before. If she did, it could be she wiped away any memory of that, keeping me from being aware of what she had done."

Tolan got up and went to one of the shelves, lifting a bondar. This one was a furios, and he was drawn to it the way he always seemed to be drawn to the furios. It was a little bit different than the furios he'd used in Amitan. Its shape was a spiral, not quite as straight as the Academy's, but the runes along the surface of it reminded him of those. Since he'd studied it so much at the Academy, he had a better understanding of what the symbols represented, and which elementals were drawn by which symbol.

Pushing a shaping out through the bondar, Tolan focused on it, this time focusing on how it connected him to the element bond. It was a test of the bondar, searching for whether there was some way to understand whether his father was telling him the truth. A spirit shaping might help, but for some reason, he was hesitating to use it.

The sense of the fire bond flowed into him, powerful and surging with a great energy. As it did, Tolan continued to pull on fire, letting it swirl around him. As he pushed deeper and deeper into the fire bond, he realized something. This furios connected him far more strongly than the one he'd used in Amitan.

"This wasn't a copy, was it?"

His father joined him, looking down at the row of shelves. "None of these are copies. I've destroyed all of the copies, as they don't seem to be nearly as effective, and they mask the connection to the element bond—and the role of the elementals within it."

"What role of the elementals?"

"What do you feel when you shape fire into the bondar?"

"I feel a connection to the element bond."

"You need to reach deeper. It's there, though my experience is that it's difficult to reach. Considering the strength you've shown, and that you've reached for a warrior shaping, I have to believe you would be able to do so."

Tolan continued to shape through the bondar, sending power through the furios, and as he did, he didn't shape anything. He simply sensed power through it, reaching toward the element bond, letting fire and awareness of fire come to him.

Deep within it, he felt a strange connection.

The elementals were there.

Not just the elementals, but the ones whose symbols were represented on the surface of the bondar. He could focus on them, could feel their presence within the bond, and with each one, he recognized their touch.

Tolan opened his eyes. "I feel them. I never have before."

"I don't know most people who use the bondars realize what they do. Most see them as a way to reach for the element bond power, but few realize they can also connect you to the elementals within the bonds."

"You've been using these to help free the elementals."

"We have. It's slow work, mostly because it takes considerable strength, and partly because there is danger in freeing the elementals."

"Why?"

"Have you ever wondered why the elementals were placed into the bond?"

"To help shapers reach for power."

"That's what the Academy believes, but I wonder if it might be something else."

"What else?"

"To protect them." His father took a deep breath, lifting one of the other bondars—a withering—off the shelf. He held it carefully between his hands, looking down at it. "As I hold onto this, I have a sense of wind, but I also have a sense of the elementals buried within the wind bond. They don't care for where they are, but at the same time, when you push deeply enough, some recognize they need to remain."

"Why would they need to remain?"

His father glanced over at him. "The same power your mother seeks."

Chaos.

Could it be the elements had been placed into the element bond in order to protect them from this chaos?

If that were the case, then why? How long would they have needed to stay trapped within the bond?

"We need to help those she's influenced."

"If I could, I would offer you any sort of help."

"But you can."

His father shook his head, turning away. "Perhaps if I still had that knowledge, I might have been able to help you. If only. Your mother took that. I think she claimed it for her own, stealing it with a shaping of spirit so I couldn't counter her." His father reached his workbench, leaning forward on it. "I don't know that I would even try to counter her, if I could. I still miss her."

"What if she's been influenced in some way?"

"I don't know that anything could spirit shape her like that. What you're talking about is an incredibly powerful shaping of spirit, and as far as I know, there aren't any shapers who have that kind of power."

Tolan glanced down at the ring his father had set on the desk. What if something had happened to his mother? What if she'd been influenced by this strange chaos? He'd seen how it influenced others, so it was at least possible the same thing had happened to his mother, and if so, he knew how to remove it.

First, he had to remove the shaping done to the others.

His father didn't think he knew enough, but what if there was a way to remind him?

Tolan reached into his pocket. There, hidden where he'd left it, was his father's journal.

He handed it to his father. "Would this help?"

His father blinked, wiping away a tear streaming down his cheek. "Where did you find this?"

"Your workshop."

"There wasn't anything there. Tools. Nothing more."

"There was this. I found it buried. It was in a hidden drawer at the back of the workbench."

His father took the journal, flipping through the pages. As he did, his breath caught. He continued to flip through them with increasing speed, and he glanced over at Tolan. "These are my notes."

"I know. I remembered seeing them in the vision. Dream or memory or whatever it was."

"I don't remember making them."

"You don't?"

His father shook his head. "I don't remember anything about this, Tolan."

"Can you read it?"

His father chuckled. "I can, and that's how I know these are mine. It's an ancient language, but it's one my parents used to use, taking notes when they worked." His father continued to flip through the pages, stopping at one near the back of the journal. He ran his finger along it as he read. "This one depicts the ring I was making for you. It is one of the last entries I must've made."

Why would his mother have stopped right then?

But, of course, she would have. If she realized what his father was doing, she would have realized he was making some way of protecting Tolan, so why wouldn't she have intervened?

If only he had more of his memories.

Then again, why couldn't he reach for them? If the ring was meant to open him up to spirit, then it seemed it was with the ring he would find those memories, that he could call them back, and perhaps he might even be able to regain some sense of himself.

"Can you see if there's anything in there to help you understand what Mother used?"

"I don't know whether there would be, but there might be something in here to help me find a way of countering it."

Tolan watched his father continue to flip through the pages of his journal. It would take a while, he suspected, and while he worked on that, was there anything Tolan could do?

His mother was the one responsible for what had happened to him. If she was the one—and the reason—his memories had been taken, then was there some way to search through his memories, to uncover what had been stolen from him?

If there was, what might he learn about himself?

Maybe nothing. It might be the only thing he learned was that his mother had stolen from him, something he already knew. Even if he knew that, would it change anything? He'd begun to uncover the secrets to his shaping ability. He didn't need to dig any deeper, did he?

The key to his shaping ability was buried within him, though. Might he be even stronger if he uncovered what she'd stolen?

Tolan took a seat on the chair, squeezing the stone ring. As he did, he focused, pulling upon spirit. What had he done when he'd uncovered those visions before? What had been the key?

Whatever it was had been tied to the ring each time. The last time, Tolan had fallen asleep, and the dream had come to him, but this time he wanted to do so intentionally, to see if there was any way to draw out those memories, to force himself into an awareness of what had taken place.

Was it even possible to do so?

Tolan watched his father. He was caught up in flipping through the pages of his journal, and if there was anything he could uncover, Tolan wasn't going to be able to help. Not only did he not understand what was involved in creating bondars, but he also couldn't read the writing on the page within the journal.

Unless he could.

What if that memory was trapped within his mind, too?

It seemed to Tolan that if his father had known what his mother was doing, he'd have tried to protect him, and he also would've tried to prepare him. Regardless of what his father remembered, he suspected there was something within his mind, but he just had to find it, to dig it out, and if he *could*, he would be able to understand the nature of how his father had created bondars, and whether or not he'd be able to do the same thing.

Holding on to the shaping, Tolan focused, summoning spirit, letting his awareness of it fill him. It rolled through him, and he pushed, drawing it up from some place deep within him, sending it out through the stone ring.

And then he pulled the shaping into himself.

Tolan didn't know if that was the key or not, but it seemed if he could shift the nature of the shaping, if he could pull it toward himself, then he might be able to use it. In doing so, he hoped to free his mind, to find what his mother had taken from him.

The shaping washed through him.

Much as he had when he'd been shaping the Inquisitors, Ferrah, and even the other shapers at the Academy in Ephra, Tolan focused on what he could detect as the shaping washed through him. It came to him slowly, building steadily. Then, as it washed over him, he felt the power flowing through him.

Surprisingly, or perhaps, unsurprisingly, there was a resistance.

He should have expected there would be, and with it, he hesitated. Was there a danger in trying to remove the resistance from his own mind? He'd seen how others had fared when they had parts of their mind trapped, and he worried about what would happen to him if he were to suddenly remove that trap. What if he damaged himself? His father wasn't a spirit shaper, and though he had the bondars, and though he might be able to reach for the various element bonds, his father would be unlikely to be able to heal him in any meaningful way.

If that happened, it would leave Tolan injured, perhaps permanently, and then who would be available to stop his mother? No one would even know she needed to be stopped.

If he did nothing, if he refused to overpower this resistance, he worried what might happen as well. He would be lost.

All these years, he'd thought he had known who he was. There had been memories, but they had been faint, and through it all, Tolan had believed the faintness of those memories had come from the fact he was traumatized by losing his parents. And perhaps that was what it was, but there was more.

How had the Inquisitors never noticed the shaping on his mind?

Probably because they didn't have access to the bondar. Without it, Tolan wouldn't have noticed, he didn't think. It took the bondar, and the power from it, for him to know what was buried within his mind.

Continuing to shape, Tolan pulled.

At first, he pushed gently, trying to remove that strange shaping from his mind, and as he met resistance, he pulled with even more force, drawing more and more away, until he found he began to hurt.

He cried out, suppressing it when his father glanced in his direction. Tolan didn't want his father to know what he was trying, uncertain if he'd do anything to stop him, though equally uncertain as to whether there would be anything he could do to stop him.

The spirit shaping began to give. As it did, Tolan knew he could separate it. He felt the way it started to peel apart, the freedom it gave him, and he knew he could drag it off his mind, but though he knew that, he also knew it would be painful—possibly incredibly so.

Drawing with a little bit more force, he decided he would shape one more time.

He prepared for the pain, preparing for what was going to come, the nature of the agony to strike him as he peeled this shaping free of his mind. He braced for it, and surprisingly, it seemed what he'd experienced in the Inquisition gave him the necessary strength. Because of that, he knew he could withstand it. He had tolerated something much worse and come out of it alive.

Heaving the shaping away, he tore it free. It came with a burst, and as it did, the pain overwhelmed him and he collapsed.

Tolan convulsed. He began to shake, and surprisingly, he was aware of the shaking, and was reminded of what he'd seen from the shapers encountered in Ephra during the Selection. They had convulsed in a similar way, and he vaguely knew if he did nothing, if he left the shaping alone, something would happen. He was certain whatever happened would not be for the best.

He needed to help himself.

The thought came distantly, in the back of his mind, as the convulsion continued to work through him. He felt himself growing more distant, his mind beginning to fade, and worried if he did nothing, he would ultimately fall.

Spirit. That was what the Grand Inquisitor had used, wasn't it? She'd used the touch of spirit on those shapers, sweeping across their mind, calling them.

Tolan could do the same thing. He suspected he only had a few moments left before whatever was taking place would overpower him. The pain in his mind made shaping difficult, and he squeezed the stone ring, holding a shaping, and with it, he held onto a memory. It was one of Ferrah, and it came to him easily, a memory of another quiet time they had spent sitting above Amitan on a Shapers Path, feeling the energy of the city. Tolan focused on that, and as he did, he was able to connect to the energy of this place. It was there in the heat all around him. The feeling of the stone beneath him. The wind, that coming from the air in his lungs, the slight breeze from his convulsions. There was water, that from the blood pumping his veins. And spirit. Always spirit.

Tolan sent a surge and pushed it inward, the same way he had when he was trying to blast the sense of chaos free from the Inquisitors' minds.

The shaping washed over him, a steady sort of sense continuing to build. Tolan held onto it, letting that sense fill him. It came to him steadily, slowly, and as it washed through him the pain began to ease.

With the pain easing, images flashed in his mind.

They happened in rapid succession. They were places he'd traveled. He recognized places throughout Terndahl, cities he had visited since heading to the Academy. There was Ephra and Par and Velminth and a dozen or more others. There were places outside of Terndahl. Places like this city, where his father and the others who served the elementals—the real Draasin Lord—had come. There were other places. Places of shadow, darkness. Cold places, snow swirling around him. Hot places, sand and barren rocks stretching around.

Had he really visited all of these places?

It seemed impossible to believe he had, but what other explanation was there? If this was what his mother had done, looking for sources of power, then it made sense she'd have visited some of these locations, as if searching. Within each vision, each snippet of memory, there came a sense of shaping. It washed through him.

It was these times when his mother had shaped him. She'd tried to keep him from knowing where they were going. How many times had they traveled and she had shaped him again?

Far more than he realized.

Was it her way of keeping him from recalling not only the visit, but why she had brought him?

That answer wasn't within those snippets of vision. It might be if he had a way of sorting through them and trying to come up with what had motivated his mother, but he didn't have a way to sort through them. It was possible she'd said nothing, bringing him with her as she traveled, keeping his memories from him. Even now, with those memories returning, Tolan still didn't know what they signified. Perhaps that was the key. She had wanted to keep that from him, and had wanted to keep knowledge, a sense of himself, from him.

Was there anything else he could uncover? It wasn't just places that came to mind. It was other things as well. There was knowledge. Maybe not as much as he had hoped for, since he didn't seem to have any real recollection of the technique of shaping, but there had to be something within it.

Tolan focused on his father. Lying as he did on the ground, he thought he could find something about his father, some way of knowing how involved his father might have been in all of this. Surprisingly, his mother had trapped those memories, too. Even as she did, aspects of them came back, parts of his past he was able to recall, painful parts telling him his father had been used. Every so often, there came a shaping from her, a soothing sort of shaping of spirit. She used it on his father, and then used it on Tolan, making it so neither of them truly knew what was taking place.

How could she have done something like that?

That troubled him most of all. For whatever reason, his mother had used him. She had changed him, and that angered him. Why would she have done that to him?

What if Father had the answer?

Tolan was tempted to shape him with spirit, to see if there was anything he could uncover about his father, and perhaps about his mother, but would that really make him feel better?

What he needed was some way of stopping her.

The answer might not come from his memories. Even if it did, it would be distant and varied and he would need far more time to fully grasp what would be needed. The answer to how to stop her would come from the memories his father had lost. To Tolan, that seemed the most significant. She'd taken away both of their memories intentionally, in order to prevent them from stopping her.

Which was why he had to get those memories back.

The key would be difficult. How would he find what she was trying to keep from them?

The strange language his father had written in his journal. Maybe there was some answer there.

Tolan focused on the journal, on the memory he'd had before and kept that at the forefront of his mind. All he wanted to do was find some way of uncovering that answer.

It had to be there, didn't it? All he had to do was find what was hidden within his mind, and if he could do that, he thought he might be able to know how to interpret the writing.

He tracked back within his mind, holding onto the memory that was there. He let it come to him, remembering what it had been like when he was sleeping, the way the memory had been there, trapped deep within his mind.

And it was a memory he could reach for, one he could grasp if only he could find how and why it was kept from him.

He had seen the journal. When he'd seen it, he had known the answer, hadn't he?

That was the key. He had seen it, and he had known how to interpret it.

And as he returned to that image, as he came back to it, letting the memory of that image return, he saw the words forming in his mind. The notes were there, and his understanding of them was there, too.

Tolan paused. As those memories washed through him, he could see the language forming. It was an ancient language, one his father had taught him from the very first time Tolan had watched him in the workshop. He remembered the way his father had used that language, scrawling it out on the page, and in doing so, he'd shown Tolan. It was a sequence of glyphs, but they weren't foreign glyphs. They were symbols he knew. Symbols he'd always known.

Tolan blinked, looking over at his father who stood, poring over the book. The answer was there, it had to be. There had to be something within that journal Tolan could uncover, some way to learn how to stop his mother, and together, they would find it.

Tolan got to his feet and joined his father.

"I'm sorry. I just can't find anything."

"You don't have to be sorry. You're trying to relearn everything she took from you."

A pained expression crossed his father's face. What must that be like? At least Tolan hadn't known his memories were gone. His father, on the other hand, had known his memories were missing, and because of that, he'd tried to restore some of that knowledge, but because of the way they were trapped, he hadn't been able to do so.

It was possible Tolan would be able to remove the spirit shaping over his father's mind, but it was also possible he'd harm him.

At this point, he didn't dare attempt to do it. He was

worried if he did, there would be some irreparable harm and he'd lose his father—and his father's ability to use these bondars.

"Maybe I can help."

His father looked over at him. "It sounds as if she took away your ability to help me."

"She did," Tolan said. "But… I think I just restored it."

His father studied him for a moment. "How?"

"I don't really know. It is there, hidden in the back of my mind, but…"

He looked down at the book, the glyphs all coming together, the writing he thought he should understand. The knowledge was buried in his mind, and it took him a moment to start to uncover what he saw, to unravel the memories in a useful way. The longer he looked, the more he stared, the easier it was to do so.

And as he looked at the pages, the writing came back to him.

Tolan flipped back to the beginning of the book and he began to turn the pages, flipping one after another. He could do this. He understood what was involved, and he had seen the nature of the shaping used on the others. If he could find something in his father's journal, maybe— just maybe—there would be some way of reversing it.

More than that, they needed to find some way of preventing her from doing it again.

"How about the two of us look together?"

His father looked at him, and another tear rolled from the corner of his eye. "I would like that."

They started going page by page, moving with enough speed that Tolan was able to read through each one. As they went, he was aware of how much time had passed and how little time they had remaining. The attack in Par wouldn't be the only one. He needed to uncover answers. Otherwise, they would fall.

"I don't see anything in here," he said.

"We can keep looking," his father said.

"I just don't know if there's going to be anything here. At least not with any sort of speed." Maybe if he returned to the Academy, it was possible someone who had more experience might able to help. He could easily imagine Master Minden might have some answers, and if she did, there would be some way of uncovering what would help make the necessary bondars that would bring an end to what his mother had done.

Even if they did that, it would take time. Master Minden would need to sort through the journal the same way Tolan and his father had just done, and they had the advantage his father had created it. Though he may not have the same memories, and everything he had done to create the journal was still distant in his mind, the simple fact was that his father was responsible for it. Because of it, he could—and should—come up with some way of breaking through the code, coming up with the key to understanding what his mother had done.

He just had to find the answers.

19

As Tolan sat back, he twisted the stone ring. He'd taken to wearing it, and he felt the surge of spirit from it once again.

"Whatever she did was tied to this ring," Tolan said. "I can't seem to shake that, but the more we study it, the less I am unable to uncover."

"It's similar, but it's not the same," his father said.

"Similar enough," Tolan said.

And because it was similar enough, he felt as if he should be able to understand just what she'd done. That sense of understanding wasn't there.

"What if we attempt to shape through the ring you found?" he asked.

"You already have said such a thing is dangerous."

Tolan nodded. As far as he knew, it was incredibly dangerous to try to shape through the ring. He'd seen the influence that happened when the shaping was done, and if he were to try to do the same thing again, he'd run the same risk of releasing that chaos. It was possible he might even end up assaulted by the chaos. If that happened, there wouldn't be anyone who would be able to help restore him.

Then again, Tolan had an understanding of what to expect.

It wasn't about shaping through the ring, at least not entirely. He wondered what would happen if he tried to shape through both of the rings at the same time.

There was the one his father had made, the stone ring that granted him his access to spirit, to the spirit defining him, but then there was also the ring his mother had created, and that somehow twisted things.

If he focused on both of them, could he gain an understanding of what was involved?

Maybe he could use a shaping of spirit through his ring to help them understand the ring his mother had made.

Focusing on spirit, deciding to do it quickly, he drew power. Power flowed from him, blowing through the ring, and he held onto it. He took a deep breath, focusing the shaping. There was a way of probing with spirit that he'd learned from the Grand Inquisitor. If he could use that now, he might be able to find more information about the ring. If he could treat it as if he were trying to layer a shaping spirit over someone else's mind, then maybe he'd be able to know the same things he needed to know.

Tolan pushed outward, wrapping slowly, sending that

shaping washing away from him. As it did, he pushed it around the ring. He curved it on a whim, sending it inward rather than pushing through it the same way he would if he were trying to unleash the power within it.

It was the same sort of shaping he used when trying to contain the chaos.

That was the key.

He was trying to contain the chaos. It wasn't only spirit. It was all of the elements.

Tolan sent a surge of each of the other elements but realized that wasn't even right. He scrambled to his feet, holding onto the rings, and grabbed for various bondars off the shelf, reaching for one for each of the elements. He set them in his lap, situating himself on the floor, and pushed shaping through all of them. That power flowed, augmented by each of the element bondars, and he sensed power around the ring his mother had generated.

Power flowed through him. It was the kind of power he'd only known when he'd been at the Academy and using the power of the runes worked into the towers. Now he was here, holding onto it, he felt it flowing through him, and he pushed. It swerved around the ring he'd always carried. Tolan held it, and the ring began to glow with a strange, sickly looking color. It was deep black, almost purpleish, like an angry bruise. The ring pushed against him, as if rebelling against the shaping.

Not just rebelling, but it was trying to surge out that same power, sending it away and trying to push into him.

There had to be something he could do.

Tolan continued to push, ignoring the sense flowing from the ring, holding each of the bondars, and power radiated from him. It was incredibly strong, the kind of potency he'd only felt a few times before. The longer he held it, the more the power in the ring started to fight. It was almost as if it fought the way it had when he had shaped the chaos free of Ferrah's mind.

Tolan continued to push.

As he did, the darkness began to fade. It continued to thrash, almost as if it were something alive, separate from the ring.

How could the ring have something alive within it?

As he pulled on the power flowing through him, he overwhelmed the darkness. With a burst of shaping energy, the power exploded.

Tolan twisted at the last second, holding the stone of the ring intact.

And then he relaxed.

The ring was inert. He could feel it. The strangeness about it was gone. The runes were missing. And the energy trapped within it was gone as well.

"What did you do?" his father asked.

"I think I did the same thing I did when I have helped others who were influenced by this shaping. I overpowered it with a combination of each of the elements."

As he stared at the ring, he was left with a sense of emptiness. If it took that much strength to overpower this one ring, what chance did they have of trying to do the same thing again? It seemed almost impossible to believe they'd be able to overpower the likely multiples of bondars existing out in Terndahl.

"Each of the elements?" his father asked.

Tolan nodded. "It took each of them," he said, pointing to the bondars in his lap, along with the one on his finger.

"I wonder if there's a way of creating a single bondar to allow us to use each of the elements."

If he could, it would have to be stronger than the individual ones.

The fact he had drawn upon a single bondar and had taken the time and effort to join multiple bondars together, had taken considerable power. If he had a single bondar he could draw his power through, twisting it all at once, maybe it would be easier to overwhelm this type of shaping.

"There wasn't anything in your journal to suggest that type of bondar."

"I don't know that I ever used anything like that. Maybe it's not even possible, but I think it's worth a try."

"I could help."

His father nodded. "From what I've observed, you have a considerable knowledge of the various runes. That might be necessary. The key then becomes what shape we use. While a ring would be useful, simply because it's wearable, it's also hard to contain each of the symbols upon it. The detail work becomes far too small, and in order to contain the necessary power, I don't know that the ring is going to be effective. The shape..."

Tolan sat back, closing his eyes. As he did, he thought

about what shape would be effective. It had to be something easy to carry, but it also had to be something that would be useful.

For some reason, images of the hall of portraits above the library kept coming to his mind. In them, he saw those shapers, ancient warriors from what Master Minden had said, and saw how they were fighting that chaos.

Was there anything in those portraits that he could use?

What was the defining feature of them?

As he tried to come up with it, it came to mind all too easy.

"A sword," he said.

"A what?"

Tolan smiled to himself. "Not that I know how to use one, but I think a sword would be an effective shape. At the Academy, there are portraits showing some of the ancient shapers, and they all carry swords." And as he thought about it, he couldn't help but wonder if some of those sword bearers also had something else about them that he'd found familiar. There were runes on the swords.

As he focused, he almost saw those runes, could almost make out what was necessary, and in doing so, he wondered if perhaps he might be able to help his father create this sword. A bondar of each of the elements. If that were possible, would it be effective against this chaos?

There was only one way to find out. They had to try it.

If they were going to try using a sword, then they

needed to have a sword. Where were they going to find that?

Tolan looked around his father's workshop. He thought of everything his father had used over the years, the way he had carved along stone and had no recollection of his father ever using metal, anything swordlike.

"You don't have a sword here, do you?"

His father stared at him for a moment before shaking his head. "Unfortunately, I do not. We can test some other shapes, and—"

Tolan shook his head. "Other shapes would all be stone. In this case, I think we need to have something that really is a sword." He didn't know why he felt that strongly other than the fact in every image he'd seen in every portrait hanging along that wall, the warriors carried swords. None of those had been made of stone or anything like that. They were all functional swords, warrior swords.

In this case, the answer meant going back to Amitan.

"Grab your journal," he said to his father.

"Why?"

"We might need it."

"Tolan?" his father asked, calling after him as he headed back out of the building.

When he stepped outside, his father joining him, Tolan shaped the warrior shaping.

It came to him quickly, suddenly, and as he called to it, the lightning streaked down toward him. His father started to back away but Tolan grabbed for him, wrapping him in his arms, and as the lightning bolt claimed him, he said, "Hold on."

And then they were carried.

It happened quickly, little more than a blink of the eye. When they stepped out, they were atop the Academy building, once more in Amitan. Tolan hurried toward the doorway, dragging his father with him. When they headed down the stairs, reaching the hall of portraits, his gaze darted along the pictures, noticing that in all of them, as he had thought, the warriors carried swords. It made him feel even more certain about what they were going to do. On many of them, the shapes were exactly what he suspected they would be. They were symbols, runes, patterns designed to draw upon the strength of the elements—and the element bonds.

He raced down the hall, looking for Ferrah, but the room was empty. He paused, sending out a surge of earth shaping, but all of the rooms along this hallway were empty.

He ran forward, reaching the stairs leading down into the main part of the Academy. His father resisted, pulling back against him.

Tolan glanced back.

"I can't go down there," his father said.

"Because you think they will accuse you of serving the Draasin Lord?"

His father nodded.

"Maybe they will. Is that the worst thing?"

"You know that isn't, but you also know their accusing me of serving the Draasin Lord is dangerous."

"You'll be with me," he said.

"Have you risen so far?" his father asked.

Tolan smiled. "I'm a third level."

His father frowned. "I don't know what that means."

"Me neither. All of this happened before I was able to understand. Unfortunately, what it means now is we need to keep working through this, if only so we can ensure we finish it."

His father stared at him for another moment, then took a deep breath, nodding. "I don't have much choice."

"You can continue to hide."

Regardless of what his father said, that was what he had been doing. He might have been trying to help the elementals, but he'd been hiding, staying away from Tolan's mother, afraid she might come for him, shape him again, and if she did, then it was because he didn't know any way of stopping her.

Tolan was determined not to hide, not any longer. Even if that meant he had to reveal the way the elementals were used, the power they possessed, and their connection to the element bond being different. Even if it meant going to the Convergence...

Could that be it?

He needed to find Master Minden.

There was a sense of power within the Academy building, and Tolan focused on it, pausing at the bottom of the stairs leading into the rest of the Academy. It felt as if it had been so long since he'd been here, long enough that everything that was here had changed, but then, the only thing that had changed had been him.

Racing toward the library, he pulled the door open, glancing inside. Master Jensen sat upon the dais, but there was no other master librarian there.

His father followed after him. "Why here?"

"Because there's someone here who can help."

When he reached the dais, he looked up at Master Jensen. "Where is Master Minden?"

"Shaper Ethar. You have been gone."

"I know, but now I need to find Master Minden."

"I'm afraid I—"

Movement caught his attention and Tolan jerked around. He realized something was amiss that he should've realized before. Maybe because he'd been so focused on Master Minden, or the fact he had focused only on Master Jensen when he'd entered the room.

Soldiers. Two of them.

They were stationed on either side of the library, and they approached with hands reaching for their swords. Tolan glanced up at Master Jensen, who made a point of ignoring Tolan.

The rest of the library was empty. That wasn't terribly surprising considering the fact there were these soldiers here.

What had Master Minden said to him?

The Council had sent the soldiers. They had come to stabilize and establish a sense of peace.

Tolan pushed on them, drawing upon a shaping of spirit, using the bondar to do so. In this place, there weren't many who could shape. It was the only advantage he might have. The library didn't separate others from shaping quite the same way as they were separated at the waste, but the effect was similar.

As he pushed spirit upon them, searching for something that might suggest they were compromised, he didn't come across anything.

He frowned. Their swords.

He needed a sword in order to test whether or not the combined bondar would make any difference.

Taking a deep breath as the soldiers approached, he whispered, "I'm sorry."

Then he pushed out with a shaping of spirit, letting it flow out from him and slam into them. He used it to overwhelm them. When they collapsed, Tolan hurried forward, grabbing one sword before racing over to the other and unsheathing it.

He glanced up at Master Jensen. "I'm sorry about this."

"Master Minden is safe," Master Jensen said.

"Where is she?"

"With the Academy under surveillance, she has decided she would stay isolated."

"If you find her, send word to her that I might need her help."

Tolan took a seat at one of the tables, and as he did, he looked at the sword. It was a plain blade, nothing about it unique or remarkable, and he sent a surge of power through it.

Was there a way to add a rune using one of the elements?

He started with fire, adding that on one aspect of the blade. It was slow and meticulous work, and had he not done the same with his father, he wasn't sure that he would have known how to do it now. Once it was set, he moved on to water, then wind, then earth. He alternated the symbols, staggering them on either side of the blade, the forms appearing with his shaping. It took an agonizingly long time and sweat dripped down his brow with each passing moment, but he didn't dare wipe it away. He needed his focus. If he lost that now, the shaping would fail.

That left one element remaining.

He knew only one shape for spirit. Carefully, he added that to the hilt. It seemed right.

"Did it work?" his father asked.

Tolan took a deep breath, holding onto the sword. He hesitated. It seemed making the bondar—if that's what he had made—like this was unusual, and he wasn't even sure whether or not it would work.

He sent a shaping through it.

When he started, he used fire first. It surged, power flowing through him more strongly than it usually did, and he added each of the other elements quickly in succession afterward, adding spirit last.

"Look at the blade, Tolan."

Tolan's gaze darted down to the sword blade. It glowed with a white light.

A shaper's sword.

Not just that, but a *warrior's* sword.

Tolan hurriedly did the same thing with the other, and he handed it to his father. "Can you use it?"

"I might be able to use it for the other elements, but I can't shape spirit. I never could. If I could have, I would have been able to protect myself from your mother. Unfortunately, that was why and how she was able to use me as she did."

Tolan gripped the two swords, heading into the main part of the Academy building. He stalked down toward the Grand Master's room, and he pounded on the door.

It took a moment, but the door opened. The Grand Master glanced from him to his father.

"Come in."

"I don't have time."

"There is always time, Shaper Ethar."

"You don't understand. There's an attack. I finally understand who's behind it."

The Grand Master nodded. "Come inside."

Tolan frowned and followed the Grand Master into the room. When he did, Tolan nearly dropped the two swords he carried.

His mother stood behind the desk.

20

Tolan stood frozen, unsure what to do or say, and unsure whether or not there was anything he even could say. This was his mother. There was no mistaking her, and as he looked at her, he was certain it was her, and he couldn't help but feel anger flowing through him.

"There he is," his mother said. There was warmth in her voice, and mixed with it was a shaping, a spirit shaping, and it washed over him.

Tolan resisted the spirit, using his own connection, and found as he did, he was forced to push through the ring.

He stared at his mother. She had the same dark hair he remembered as a child, and the same smile he'd seen on her face, but more than that, there was a look of concern, almost as if she actually worried about him.

"What are you doing here?" Tolan asked.

"I thought you would be happy to see me."

"Happy?" He turned to the Grand Master. "Why did you let her in here…"

Tolan hurriedly started shaping, pulling on spirit, and sent it washing over the Grand Master. As he did, he felt the subtle sort of resistance within the Grand Master's mind.

He'd been compromised.

The Grand Master was a powerful shaper. For her to be able to overwhelm him told him just how powerful she was.

"Why don't the three of us have a conversation?" his mother asked.

"Three of us? You don't want the Grand Master to be a part of this?"

She smiled. "Seeing as how he's sleeping?" With that, the Grand Master collapsed and remained unmoving.

Tolan studied him for a moment. The level of control she displayed in her shaping was incredible. There was power to it, too.

What had his father said? She'd been working all these years, training and searching for power.

She knew far more than Tolan did. The only thing he had was the possibility of the swords and the possibility they were an effective bondar, but what if they didn't work?

"I hadn't expected to see you again, Felicity."

His mother smiled at his father. "I thought you would be more excited to see me."

"After everything you did to me?"

"What did I do other than help you find the affection you craved?"

"I didn't crave anything."

"No? I felt it within you." A shaping began to build from her, and Tolan could sense the way spirit was starting to rise up. If he didn't do anything, his mother would use a spirit shaping on his father and that spirit shaping would somehow destroy everything he'd regained.

He jumped forward, pressing himself in between his mother and his father, and pushed out with a spirit shaping of his own. He drew upon the ring his father had made for him and sent a surge of spirit wrapping around his father's mind. If nothing else, he thought he could protect his father. He had no idea whether the shaping would work or not.

"You should know better than to get in between your parents, Tolan."

"Why?" Tolan said.

"You who have begun to taste power would need to question?"

"I've been able to recognize there is power, but I also recognize there is danger to certain kinds of power."

"The only danger is not using the power we've been given," she said.

"I'm not sure that's true," Tolan said.

"You stand there holding a sword of the soldiers, and you would question?"

He frowned. Could she not recognize it was a bondar?

If she didn't, then there was an advantage. It was good she didn't know. The longer she didn't know, the more likely it was they could use that.

First, they needed to know what she planned.

"Why are you here?"

"I came for you."

"I'm not going with you, so why else are you here?"

She flashed a smile. "All this time, and I had never expected my son to be the key. Then again, perhaps that's my own fault."

"You shaped it so I wouldn't remember anything."

"I protected you from him" she said, nodding at Tolan's father.

"Protecting me from him? He's the one who needed protection."

"Don't let him convince you he was so innocent. He was the reason I began to understand there's power in these bondars. As much as he might want to hide from it, and given his fear of it, he would conceal himself from the power existing in the world. I would do otherwise. I would embrace that power, and I would use it. I would use it the way it was meant to be used, and with that, I would see there was control and order established."

Tolan frowned. "And by order and control, you mean chaos." He took a deep breath, focusing on his shaping, readying for the possibility of an attack. Would he even be able to do so? He didn't know if he could attack his mother if it came down to it.

He had to push away that doubt. He realized where

that came from, some deep place within him where his mother had instilled it.

"I mean the power that exists. Where do you think the elements and the power of the element bond comes from? Where do you think the elementals come from?"

"They are the power of this world."

"They are part of the power of this world. Only a part. I have uncovered another part. It's that power I would seek."

Tolan shook his head. Of course, that was what she wanted to pursue. "You know how dangerous that power is?"

"Only if you don't know how to control it."

"And you don't know how to control it. You might think you do, but I've seen how that power rebels when it's stripped away."

"You wouldn't be able to have stripped it away."

"You'd be surprised," Tolan said. "You tried to hide my abilities from me."

"Because you weren't ready for them."

He wanted to move, to shift off to the side and check on his father, but he didn't dare do so. Whatever his mother was planning involved keeping them both in front of her. What he needed to do instead was find some way to incapacitate her. Maybe it was time to stop talking and to act, to use his new sword bondar. Once he did, he had to be prepared for the possibility it wouldn't be enough to overwhelm her. If she had access to all of the bondars his father had made over the years, it was possible she had enough strength to draw from.

"When would I be ready for them?"

"When I could help you understand them."

"And by that, you mean when you could control me?" Tolan thought he understood, then. She'd continued to use spirit shapings on him for a very specific purpose. It was because she hadn't been able to control him. She'd been forced to mask his memories, hiding them from him, and in doing so, she had thought she'd be able to conceal things from him, including his ability to shape.

It still didn't explain why they had abandoned him. He thought he understood why his father had left, but he didn't know why his mother had left, unless it was all part of some plan.

"You wanted me to come to the Academy."

She smiled. "I knew eventually you would be claimed. He thought that would be a mistake, but then, with his growing affinity for the elementals and his attachment to these trinkets he was making, I wasn't surprised. I knew the more I could work with you, the more I could show you. But then, when it became clear he'd be unwilling to ever allow you to come to the Academy, I decided to take matters into my own hands."

"That was the shaping that wiped everything," he said.

"It was. And I even cast a little doubt throughout Ephra, letting the others believe we went off to serve the Draasin Lord."

"That was you?"

She smiled at him. "Don't be sad, Tolan. It was meant to strengthen you. Eventually, I knew you would get drawn into the Academy, though this is a little later than I was expecting. It had taken some prodding."

"I only submitted myself for Selection because of a friend."

As he said it, he realized what she was doing. She was trying to convince him she was somehow responsible for what had happened to him, when in reality, she had nothing to do with it. It was not all about her or what she'd done or any plan she'd made. The fact he had ended up in the Academy was not a part of that.

What was she really after?

She was taking time, and…

Shaping him.

He barely noticed it. The level of control she displayed was incredible. It was spirit shaping, but it was so subtle and so soft, he'd almost not been aware of what she was doing. Had he not focused on it, had he not considered what she might be trying to do, he might not have even noticed. The fact she'd had that level of control was almost enough to make him want to work with her to know whether there was something more he could do. None of the spirit shapers he had been around had demonstrated that kind of control.

Which left him with a different understanding.

"You were an Inquisitor."

She smiled. "Very good, Tolan. I'm surprised it took you this long."

"That's why you used the Inquisitors."

"They were an obvious target, and their passion for unseating the Draasin Lord was easy enough to use."

"And the Grand Inquisitor?"

"You didn't recognize her?"

Tolan frowned, shaking his head. "No. You didn't get to her, though."

"Not yet. She's next on my list."

"But you failed."

His mother cocked her head to the side and the shaping continued to build, but now Tolan was aware of it, he was able to create a subtle buffer against it, sending it sweeping away from him. He drew upon not only the ring his father had made, but also upon the sword, the bondar *he* had made.

Combined together, those two bondars gave him incredible strength, and spirit seem to flood within him, drawn from some store that he could feel. And as it did, Tolan continued to pull upon it, using it to protect himself, though he didn't know how much his mother might be able to do. She was a skilled spirit shaper.

And an Inquisitor.

"If you trained at the Academy, then why do this?"

"It's *because* I trained at the Academy that I have done this. I recognize the way they use those who trained here. Not only those who trained, but especially those who would try to master some of the more challenging connections."

"Spirit."

She tipped her head in a slight nod. "Spirit."

"Spirit isn't necessarily difficult. It's just whether or not you are born to it."

"They refused to teach those who are born to it how to connect. You do realize anyone with a connection to each of the elements has the capacity to reach spirit?"

"But I get the sense from you that you don't want everyone to reach spirit."

"Perhaps not."

"You can stop trying to shape me," Tolan said. He drew himself up and took a deep breath, meeting her gaze. "I know what you're doing. I can feel it."

"If you know what I'm doing, then you would have acted by now."

"What makes you think I'm not?"

The nature of her spirit shaping shifted. Because of how much power he was drawing, he could feel it. It flowed up from her, roiling through her, a burst of power that was overwhelming.

Tolan pushed against what she was doing, ignoring it. "As you see, I must have inherited your talent with spirit. And I also have something else."

She frowned. "What?"

Tolan raised the sword. "This."

She started to laugh. "I'm well aware you are no soldier, Tolan. If you think I haven't been paying attention to your progression throughout the Academy, then you are mistaken."

"I am no soldier, but I am something else." He began to

pull on his shaping, letting it flow. It was a significant burst of energy, a powerful explosion filling him. As he drew it through the sword, it was incredible, overwhelming, and he aimed it at his mother. "I'm a warrior."

The shaping exploded from the end of the sword.

Tolan had not seen what the shaping would look like when he pulled all of his element bonds through the sword, but drawing upon it, he could see it was incredible power.

His mother pushed against him, and as she did, he recognized each of the elements mixed within her shaping. She was carrying bondars, one for each of the elements, but they were separate.

Hadn't his father speculated the various individual bondars weren't nearly as potent as all of them combined? It had been Tolan's experience when using the warrior shaping that the nature of that was more powerful than each individual shaping. He had speculated that because of it, he would be able to draw even more power, and as he pulled on his shaping, as he was aware of it flowing through him, he could feel that power surging. He let it flow, and it exploded into his mother.

She continued to resist, and he realized something else.

While his bondar might be more powerful, her strength was greater than his. She'd been working longer than him, and more than that, she had searched for other sources of power, things Tolan had not yet learned.

Because of that, she knew aspects to shaping that he did not—and did not necessarily want to know.

She took a step toward him. "That is interesting, Tolan. I must admit I didn't think your father had any new bondars in him. He had shown me everything he knew when we were together."

Tolan shook his head. "He didn't show you everything he knew. He protected me from you."

"Perhaps he did, but now you will still join me."

"I won't let you influence me with chaos."

"Do you really think you're strong enough to refuse? I certainly don't. You might believe you have more power than you do, but I know what you possess. I helped instill that power within you. And it's because of me that you will serve."

Her shaping continued to build and Tolan was forced back. His father was there, his hand on his back and his eyes wide. Shaping flowed from his father, and Tolan realized he hadn't been opposing his mother alone. His father had been trying to help, adding his own shaping, and the two of them had been working together, though Tolan hadn't even felt the nature of his father's shaping until now. As he did, he realized that despite the fact they were using these powerful shapings, despite the fact he was drawing through the bondar he'd created, his mother was far more powerful than him. There was nothing he was going to be able to do to overpower her.

He thought about raising the other sword, using that, but even if he did that, he wasn't sure it would be enough.

How else was he going to get power?

What he needed was some greater connection to the elements. But he was at the Academy. How could he not have a greater connection to the elements than he had right here?

The runes provided that connection. That was the purpose of them, the point of their existence, and he could feel that power flowing deep beneath the Academy. Those runes bound the building itself, tying it to the place of Convergence, and Tolan knew he could reach for that power.

The key wasn't attacking his mother with the shaping he was able to draw. The key was changing it in a different way.

Tolan continued to focus on his shaping, continuing to draw power, and he slammed the other sword down into the ground. As he focused on pointing the one sword toward his mother, the other planted into the stone of the building filled with power. Tolan drew up through it, connecting to the greatness of the Academy, to the power existing all around him, using that to help him find even more strength.

It was there. It *had* to be there.

As it filled him, he continued to draw more and more power, letting the strength roll up through him. It was overwhelming, and it came to the point where Tolan had no control over it. It simply exploded through him.

Her eyes darkened, her brow furrowed. She continued to resist, to fight what he was doing. The more he was extending through the Academy, through the runes, connecting to the place of Convergence, the more he knew he'd succeed.

And she knew it, too.

His mother pushed, sending a surge of shaping energy out from her. It exploded, striking everywhere in the room, leading to a burst of darkness.

Tolan tried to push past that darkness, sending fire and spirit exploding out. When it was done, she was gone.

He took a deep breath, holding onto the shaping through the swords, and he glanced over at his father.

"What happened? Where did she go?" his father asked.

"I don't know."

He'd been so focused on his own shaping, on drawing power, that he hadn't paid any attention to the type of shaping she'd used. It was possible she'd used something akin to a warrior shaping, the burst of lightning that would carry her away, but if that was what she'd done, there was no residual energy from it that would tell him that was what it had been.

He had no idea what she'd used.

All he knew was that she was gone.

Tolan had a feeling this wasn't over.

He turned his attention to the Grand Master and pushed out with spirit. Connected as he was the rest of the Academy and to the runes around it, and through them to the place of Convergence, Tolan had considerable power. He pushed out onto the Grand Master and felt a sense of resistance, the strangeness within the Grand

Master, and he pulled, looping around the shaping that confined his mind, sending a burst of each of the elements through him and exploding the connection to chaos.

When he was done, he sent a hint of water shaping, healing the Grand Master.

He sat up, looking at Tolan, and blinked, rubbing his eyes for a moment before glancing at Tolan's father. "Who is this? What are you doing here?"

"We figured out who was responsible for the attacks."

The Grand Master frowned. "Who?"

"Unfortunately, it was my mother. It seems she was once an Inquisitor, and she used her knowledge of spirit shaping to turn my father."

"Why would she have done that?"

"Because my father has knowledge of creating bondars. She wanted to use them to reach for chaos."

The Grand Master's eyes widened. "How is it you know about this?"

"Other than working with Master Minden? I need to help the Grand Inquisitor as well, but I'm not sure where to start."

The Grand Master stood, rubbing his hands together. "Probably in Par. After Irina lost her other daughter, I don't know she would have been able to tolerate losing another."

Daughter? "That's why she went to Par?"

"Emily got involved. I think she wanted to do what she could to save her."

"She has two daughters?"

"She lost one of them in the war with the Draasin Lord."

Tolan turned his attention to his father, frowning. That couldn't be it, could it?

"What was her other daughter's name?"

"It was Felicity."

Tolan shook his head. "No," he whispered.

"Why?"

"I think I know where she went."

"Where?"

"Apparently, I'm the Grand Inquisitor's grandson."

The Grand Master frowned. "What?"

"Felicity is my mother. And she is most certainly not dead. She's the reason you were twisted. Chaos overwhelmed your mind. Had I not intervened, she would have succeeded."

"Succeeded in what?"

Tolan shook his head. "I have no idea what she was trying to do, only that we prevented her from it." He turned to his father. "I need to go. If she's the Grand Inquisitor's daughter, and if Emily is her sister, I know where they are."

And he didn't think he could go by himself. He needed someone who knew the city.

"Where are you going?" the Grand Master asked as Tolan turned away from him.

"I'm going to Par. I'm going to stop my mother and save my grandmother."

He stepped out of the hallway and raced through the building.

As he did, he focused on his shaping, focusing on what he could detect, searching for the signature of Ferrah's shaping.

He didn't detect anything, but he was certain there had to be something.

Master Minden. That was where he needed to go. Hurrying through the Academy, he reached the hall of portraits, and he stood studying them. No answers came to him, though he hadn't really expected them to. The only thing he had hope for was to gain understanding.

As he looked at the portraits, he couldn't help but feel as if there was more than just the one portrait with an image that seemed to be impacted by that strange darkness. He paused at another, this one depicting a castle set on a rocky hillside. The ground had seemingly cracked, and black oozed from within those cracks, pouring out from them. There were other cracks, and he noticed them on the castle itself, almost as if this strange energy was destroying the building.

And yet, that wasn't the main focus of the image. The first time he'd come here, he had seen the portrait of a man with dark hair and deep brown eyes. The artist had him dressed in a black cloak, a sword strapped to his waist reminding Tolan something of one of the soldiers. Power radiated from this shaper—and Tolan suspected it had to be a shaper. That power struck the ground, stretching away from the shaper and toward not only the ground but also toward the building, and at first, Tolan would have suspected the shaping was designed to heal, and yet the more he studied the image, the more he questioned. Maybe it wasn't about healing. Maybe it was more about trying to destroy whatever it was that caused the cracks in the building and the cracks in the ground. Maybe it was more about trying to suppress that chaos.

Master Minden wasn't here. And if not here, then where would she be?

There was only one place he thought she might have gone, and Tolan frowned, wondering if there might be some way to reach it faster.

He focused on the place of Convergence, and as he did, he pulled upon each of the elements, creating a powerful shaping, and exploded downward. When he stepped out of the shaping, he was standing in front of the place of Convergence.

How was that even possible?

Master Minden was there, and though he wasn't surprised by that, he was surprised by the fact he was able to reach this place so easily.

Tolan raced over to her. She was crouched in front of the place of Convergence, her hand making a trail in the liquid, and she glanced up as he approached.

"Shaper Ethar."

"Did you know?"

"Did I know what?"

"About me. About the Grand Inquisitor."

"I thought it might be likely," Master Minden said.

"Then again, I wasn't entirely sure whether it was true or not. It was difficult for me to determine. There seemed to be some connection, but there was something about it that was shifted as well. Now I know about chaos, I wonder if perhaps that had something to do with it."

"My mother faked her death. She was an Inquisitor. She was the Grand Inquisitor's daughter."

"Felicity," she whispered.

Tolan nodded. "Where's Ferrah?"

"Your friend is safe."

"I'm sure she is, but I'm going to need her to stop chaos."

Master Minden shook her head. "Unfortunately, there will be no ending of a conflict with chaos. It is a part of the world, and the key isn't ending it but finding balance within it."

"I don't understand."

"I think that is the part none have ever understood. Including myself. We have always believed the key to stopping chaos was controlling it. But that's not it at all. The key isn't controlling chaos. The key is recognizing it, doing what we can to minimize the damage caused by it, but finding a sense of balance. Think of everything in the world. You have darkness and light, you have left and right. You have order and chaos. One cannot exist without the other. They are connected, bound together, and that is what I think we need to keep in mind. If we can, perhaps we can ensure we can survive."

Tolan didn't know how to do that, but that wasn't the

key right now, was it? The key was finding a way of removing the influence his mother had impressed on others. And for the most part, it involved removing the influence of the Inquisitors.

"I think I know how to do this more quickly," he said.

"I'm not surprised you have uncovered the key," she said.

"Why?"

"You have continued to demonstrate a certain knowledge and resiliency, Shaper Ethar." She cocked her head, frowning as she studied him. "Perhaps I should call you Warrior Ethar."

He felt a flush work through him. "I needed something that could hold bondars of each element. The only thing I could think of that might work would be a sword like the warriors of old had used."

Master Minden smiled at him. "It suits you. You had better be careful, or the Council will try to turn you into a soldier."

"There are two soldiers in the library I incapacitated."

Master Minden huffed. "Unfortunately, they thought they could come to my library and abuse the power we hold. Thankfully they don't have any ability to shape there, so…"

Tolan smiled. "They don't, but I do."

"Which is why you are more like the warriors of old than you even realize."

"I still need to find Ferrah."

The librarian waved her hands behind her, and a

shaping lifted. Tolan hadn't even been aware it was there, but he realized Ferrah had been masked, hidden by the shaping, and as it lifted, he found her resting.

"What happened to her?"

"Nothing happened to her, Shaper Ethar. Nothing more than what had happened to her before."

"She's still out," he said.

The master librarian nodded. "Unfortunately, the nature of the chaos was such that she remains influenced by it. I thought I could bring her here and see if the power of the Convergence might be able to rescue her, but I haven't had the opportunity."

"I need to do what I can to help her."

"I would expect nothing less of you," she said.

What could he do? It wasn't as if he had some additional ability, some power other shapers did not, but he felt as if he needed to do something.

He focused on Ferrah and pulled power through the sword, drawing it all together the same way he had before. This time, he used a hint of power coming off the place of Convergence. As he did, even more flowed through him, and he let it wash over Ferrah. There was no evidence of injury to her, but as his shaping washed over her, she gasped, blinking and sitting up.

She looked over at him. "Tolan?"

Tolan raced over to her, setting the sword down in front of her. "I'm here."

"What happened?"

"More than you can imagine. But for now, you and I need to go to Par."

"Why Par?"

"I can tell you while we're there. I think my mother intends to use the Convergence there to attack my grandmother."

Ferrah blinked. "It really is more than I can imagine, isn't it?"

Tolan chuckled. "It really is. Do you think you can tolerate a shaping?"

"What kind of shaping are we talking about?"

"A new one."

She watched him for a moment before nodding. "I'm ready."

With that, Tolan called for lightning.

21

When the lightning cleared and his vision returned, Tolan looked around. There was energy all around him. It came from the crackling of shaping throughout the city, power that surged and exploded. Tolan searched for anything within that crackling energy that might be familiar.

He held onto Ferrah's hand and continued to look around. She blinked as her eyes tried to adjust.

"You have to keep your eyes closed during the shaping. I should have warned you."

Ferrah glanced over at him. "This is Par."

"It is."

"How did we get here so quickly?" she asked.

"That's the new shaping."

"It's some shaping." She paused. "It feels different. There's something off."

Tolan tested each of the elements. As he did, he could

feel what she detected, the strangeness she was aware of. And she'd simply known something was off.

"You're really well attuned to Par."

She cocked a brow at him. "I grew up here. Shouldn't I be attuned to it?"

"Seeing as how I had to help you in Amitan…"

She squeezed his hand and took in a deep breath. "What now?"

"Now we have to find the Convergence." And the Grand Inquisitor. She was here. Somewhere. Tolan could feel her influence.

Before doing anything else, he should try to find her. She could be of use in the effort to stop whatever his mother planned. He just had to find her.

Standing atop the tower, he focused on the sense of the city, using it the same way he had when he'd come the first time. Not much had changed, nothing more than the persistent sense of energy within the city. It felt natural, as if it were meant to be here, and despite that, he had to wonder if perhaps there wasn't something more than he could tell.

As he stood perched at the edge of the tower, Tolan reached for something that might help him know what would be out there… and found it.

Every so often, there came the steady tapping from a shaping. It was subtle, and yet, the rhythm of it came to him, familiar. He thought he could reach it, but even though he thought he could, there was still another sense mixed within it. It was almost as if there was something trying to block him from accessing it.

That was strange.

Why would anyone try to block him from realizing the Grand Inquisitor was here?

Who would even know?

He continued to hold onto his sense of the shaping and focused on it, keeping it forefront in his mind. Would the warrior shaping work in this case?

He hadn't tried it like this, but if it could help him transport to the sense of that shaping, he could reach the Grand Inquisitor.

"I think I found her," he said.

"Where?"

Tolan pointed. "Out there. I can bring us to her, but…"

"Why do I get the sense I'm not going to like this?"

"It's the new shaping. I don't know how well I can control it."

"The shaping brought us here."

"It did, and I've used it in other ways, but I still don't know if I'm going to be able to use it to bring us everywhere we need to go."

"I trust you, Tolan."

Taking her hand, Tolan focused and sent a surge of each of the elements through himself, twisting them.

When the lightning bolt came, he braced for the return. He surged up, riding the power of the lightning, and waited for the descent.

As they came down, the power roaring through him,

he could feel as the lightning exploded through a building.

And then they landed.

Tolan looked around, pushing out with a shaping of earth and wind, creating a barricade around himself in case there was someone here who might try to harm him.

As his vision began to clear, there was no effort to attack his barrier.

Breathing out, he waited, looking around. There was no one, but that wasn't quite right. There was a sense of shaping. If there was a sense of shaping, there had to be someone nearby.

Ferrah wrapped a quick shaping around herself. It created a barrier, a protection, sealing her off from something that might be nearby.

Tolan pushed out with a sense of spirit. He waited, hoping the Grand Inquisitor would recognize his shaping and would answer. He held onto it, a message mixed within it. A call to her.

It took a moment, but she answered.

There.

She was hidden.

Why would she be hidden?

Better yet, who would hide her?

Someone had done that to her.

Tolan pushed out with earth, disrupting the masking, and realized there was wind mixed in with it. He had done something similar, so he understood the nature of the shaping utilized. As he disrupted it, the Grand Inquisitor came into view.

And so did three black-cloaked Inquisitors.

Glancing over at Ferrah, he hoped she could shield herself.

Tolan hurriedly wrapped his mind, but he'd done so even before leaving Amitan. In doing so, he had sealed off any attempt they might make to reach him. The sense of their shaping struck him, and he realized they were attempting to use spirit on him, but the fact he had already protected his mind held him safe.

"Release her," he said.

At least now he knew why the others in the city had been spirit shaped. And *how* they had been spirit shaped.

"Is this the one?" one of the Inquisitors said, looking at the others. Power radiated from them, an enormous amount of shaping energy, far more than Tolan thought would be normally possible.

Bondars.

There was no explanation other than that.

In order to have bondars, they would have had to have taken them from the Academy—or created them themselves. Tolan had a hard time believing they had somehow created bondars.

"He has the necessary strength, but I don't know if this is the one."

"I'm the one who's going to keep you from harming the Grand Inquisitor."

"This is the one," one of the women said.

Tolan continued to hold onto a shaping, concerned if he let it go and lost control over it, they would use that opportunity to slip in and attack. There was something unsettling about them, and it was possibly related to the fact they simply watched him, as if unconcerned about what he might do. Then again, it might be something more.

Holding onto a shaping, keeping it wrapped around his mind, he doubted they would be able to harm him. To be safe, he carefully dragged his foot across the ground, creating the shape of the spirit rune. He wasn't even certain whether it would work, but he felt as if he had to do something. As he formed the rune, he pushed power into it, sending enough strength and energy through the rune that he thought he might be able to use that strength, that he might be able to force enough of himself out through it in order to create additional power. All he wanted was to draw upon the energy of the rune.

Slowly, there came a sense of strength. It reminded him of what he had felt when he was standing atop the spirit tower. While pushing power out through this rune, drawing upon the spirit marking he'd placed, he was able to use it.

Tolan breathed out. He would hold it and push it out around Ferrah to ensure her safety as well.

That wasn't all he needed to do. Not only did he need to hold it, he needed to use that power and overwhelm the three attackers.

One of them watched him, almost as if aware of what he was doing.

"Grand Inquisitor. Are you—"

The answer came within his mind, a shaping of spirit that sounded so soft and subtle he wasn't even sure if that was what he detected.

"You should go."

"You need my help." Tolan used a shaping spirit to respond, drawing upon the same strength she had, using that same shaping in order to answer her. The more he did it, the easier it became. It began to feel almost natural.

"We can't lose you."

"You're more important than me."

"Not with this."

A powerful shaping began to build from the Grand Inquisitor, pouring off her, and the three Inquisitors turned to her. One of them sent a shaping of spirit roiling toward the Grand Inquisitor. Tolan reacted. He cried out, sending a surge of spirit at the woman who was attacking the Grand Inquisitor.

As he did, it slammed into her and she collapsed.

The Grand Inquisitor looked over at Tolan, her eyes wide.

Something in that expression troubled him. He had done something, and whatever it was troubled her.

Could it be he had used his connection to spirit and his shaping in general in a way of which she didn't approve?

She'd warned him, wanting him to know there were ways of using spirit that were right and ways that were not. In this case, in this way, he wasn't sure he'd used it in a way that was right. How could he when he'd attacked with it?

Now was not the time to question those sorts of things. Now was the time to finish the other two Inquisitors and do whatever it took to ensure the Grand Inquisitor managed to get away. Once he did, then Tolan could focus on the next step.

The other two women turned toward him. Their shaping continued to build, growing with strength, power, and it was almost too much for him. He recognized the strength within it from the bondars.

Then again, *he* had a bondar. He squeezed the ring, grasping it, and pushed out a shaping through the rune he'd formed for spirit, and poured that toward each of them.

The shaping was unfocused. There was no intention behind it, and all he wanted to do was knock them down. He'd seen the way shapings could be used to sedate, and that was what he wanted now.

His spirit shaping struck a resistance, some sort of reflection that came from both of the Inquisitors, but Tolan continued to push, sending more and more strength out, and as he did, he overpowered that resistance.

When it struck again, he continued to push.

Spirit flooded through them. It flooded toward them, overwhelming them.

Tolan continued to push, drawing more spirit than he had any right to. There came a flash of white, and as he pushed, he realized there was something else about them.

The strange darkness he'd found on Ferrah was there.

Tolan pushed. Once they were unconscious, he could

work on removing it. Until then, he wasn't sure it was safe to do.

Tolan took a step toward them.

With a burst, they went down.

He breathed out heavily.

"What did you do?" the Grand Inquisitor asked.

"They've been tainted. Chaos, or whatever the elemental that now impacts them, has influenced their minds."

"What?"

Tolan glanced up at the Grand Inquisitor. He realized her eyes were drawn and there was an edge to her. What had she gone through in the time he had been away?

It was possible she'd been tormented, and it was even possible she'd somehow been influenced by the same sort of shaping. If she were, he'd need to try to remove that same darkness from her mind.

Standing and turning toward her, pulling on his shaping of spirit through the ring, he watched her for a moment. He held out the ring, squeezing it, letting that shaping roll through him. "What did they do to you?"

"They just captured me. I don't know what they were going to do to me, and you interfered before I had the opportunity to find out who they were working for."

"Wait. You *wanted* to get caught?"

"I was never in any danger, Shaper Ethar. And certainly not enough danger for you to have included Shaper Changen."

Ferrah stepped forward, looking around at everything.

"They had bondars," Ferrah said.

"Do you think I came unprepared?" the Grand Inquisitor asked.

She held out her hand, and he realized she had a small length of stone tucked in it. A furios, though a small one, much smaller than any he'd seen before. She held her other hand out, and he realized it held a withering. Fire and wind. She wasn't helpless, not at all. Had he made a mistake by interfering?

"I didn't know," Tolan said.

"Of course, you didn't. You acted impulsively."

Tolan turned his attention back to the two fallen women. The other, the one who had attacked them first, didn't appear to be breathing. It seemed as if his spirit shaping had been too much, and though he knew he should feel more than just a little regret, he had a hard time mustering any emotion. It reminded him of when Aela had attacked him, and how little he'd felt following her death.

"I found Ferrah." He motioned toward her. "She attacked me when I came to the city the first time."

"What do you mean the first time?"

Tolan waved his hand dismissively. "I returned to Amitan with Ferrah, and Master Minden helped me remove the shaping around her mind."

"She did, did she?"

Tolan frowned. Maybe that wasn't quite true. The removal of the shaping had been more him than Master Minden. Master Minden had helped him understand what it was he had done, but she hadn't actually been a part of any shaping removal.

"There is something she called chaos. Some darkness that attacked."

The Grand Inquisitor stared at him. There was something in her gaze, something heavy and unsettling. For a moment, Tolan worried maybe she was a part of it. Would the Grand Inquisitor be involved with what the others had done? He didn't think that was the case, but what did he know—really know—about the Grand Inquisitor?

"She showed me the hall of portraits."

"What did you see?"

Tolan stood, hurriedly drawing upon a shaping, prepared to attack the Grand Inquisitor. If he did, he would at least know she carried two bondars with her, and any attack he might use would have to overpower her. It would be unlikely he'd be able to do so. There was an alternative, but he didn't know if the warrior shaping would work in a confined space like this. It might have brought him here, but would it carry him away if it came down to it?

"Grand Inquisitor?"

"This probably isn't the place to talk about it," the Grand Inquisitor said, looking around, and her gaze settled on the space where he had come through the building, leaving a hole. A shaping spread out from her, wind and fire, and he realized she was drawing upon her bondars. It was focused on the space around the room, sealing them within. It was the same sort of shaping they had used when he was a first-level student, trying to protect himself inside his quarters so that he and Ferrah and Jonas could all talk openly. "Perhaps that's better."

"What are you doing?" Tolan asked.

She sighed, crouching next to one of the Inquisitors. A powerful shaping built from her, sweeping through her mind, and as it did, it reminded Tolan something of the shaping he'd used when he was trying to free Ferrah from the strange dark influence. "You shouldn't be involved in this as only a student." She flicked her gaze up at him, smiling tightly. "However skilled you have proven yourself to be. This is not meant for you. This is meant for others, those with knowledge and experience, and for some reason, Minden decided she would bring you in?"

"I don't know she had much choice," Tolan said. He told her about how he'd pulled free the strange darkness, the chaos, and hoped in doing so, he wasn't revealing anything he shouldn't be.

"I suppose that is reason enough for her to have shared with you." The Grand Inquisitor stood, looking around before nodding to the fallen Inquisitors. "As you've seen, there is a great danger. It's not only the Inquisitors who have betrayed the Academy, though that is a part of it. There is more."

"It's not the Draasin Lord," Tolan said. It was almost a question. He wasn't sure quite what the Grand Inquisitor believed about the Draasin Lord, but the more he understood about the Draasin Lord, the more he recognized whatever was taking place was more than one figurehead.

She shook her head. "The Draasin Lord was a convenient opportunity for us to keep the focus elsewhere. In this case, unfortunately, there is something else. There are only a few who really know about the true threat."

"What true threat is that?"

"I suppose Master Minden sharing with you the nature of chaos is as accurate as I could tell you. We don't really know what it's called, and unfortunately, we have not been able to determine who is responsible for it."

"For what?"

"Over the last few decades, there has been a change. I'm not entirely sure what the change is about, only that it is certain there is something. It is more than just our Inquisitors who have betrayed the Academy."

"Like Master Daniels attacking the Keystone."

"That is another example," she said, nodding. "But there are others. Many others we have encountered over the years. Most are kept hidden, and those who remain in the inner circle are aware of the implications. As much as we have done to suppress it, new attacks continue."

"Why keep it hidden?"

"Because we don't know how to stop it."

Despite the shaping swirling around them, the seal she had placed around the room, the words almost thundered. The fact she was able and willing to admit the fact that she —and he suspected the Grand Master—had no idea how to stop whatever this threat was left him trembling. That was probably the intention, though. How could he do anything other than tremble under the idea there was some great power out there that posed such a threat to them?

"And now that the Inquisitors have revealed themselves?"

"With the Inquisitors having revealed themselves, there was some hope that perhaps we would be able to track what happened. We welcomed them back to the Academy so we could follow them."

"And then I interfered."

"I'm not sure that is necessarily a bad thing," she said, a hint of a smile on her face. "But it would be helpful if you would not be so impulsive."

Tolan looked around. "What now?"

"We have seen attacks in Par as well as Ephra. We can only assume the other cities where the Selections have gone fared the same."

"Master Minden tells me the Council has sent soldiers."

Her brow furrowed. "That is unfortunate."

"Why? They serve Terndahl."

"They do serve Terndahl, but they do so in a way they view as essential, not necessarily in a way we view as essential."

"By *we*, do you mean the Academy or this inner circle you have?"

"We call ourselves the Circle of the Warrior."

The idea he had access to a shaping referred to as a warrior shaping couldn't be a coincidence.

"Why the Circle of the Warrior?"

"Long ago, there were shapers of considerable power. They referred to themselves as warriors, though there was more to it, from what we understand. It was a different time. More brutal. Barbaric in some ways. And yet, they had a different understanding of the nature of shaping than what we have now."

"They were connected to the elementals," Tolan said softly.

"Perhaps."

There was no perhaps about it in his mind. From what he'd seen, the ancient shapers *had* been connected to the elementals, and it was only recently they had begun to separate and force the elementals into the bonds, changing the nature of their shaping. In doing so, it supposedly protected them from the elementals and gave greater power to shapers, giving them the opportunity to draw upon the element bonds in ways they weren't otherwise able to do.

"You think these two—three—were attacked by this chaos?"

"It's difficult for me to know." Once again, she sent a surge of spirit over their minds, and it pressed down.

"Not like that," Tolan said.

The Grand Inquisitor looked up at him.

Tolan felt a flush work through him. "You don't push it down. That seems to change it, and it seems to add more strength to forcing it into their minds."

"Would you have me pull it free?"

"It's more a matter of trying to encircle it." He took a

step forward, crouching next to the woman the Grand Inquisitor had been working on. She had dark hair, dark skin, and lying immobilized as she was, there was something peaceful about her. "Do you mind?"

"Be my guest."

Tolan took a deep breath, focusing on his shaping, sending a surge of spirit not only through the ring but drawing upon the marking he'd made on the ground. It was strange he was still able to use that even though he was not so near it. Using the rune augmented his shaping, giving him the opportunity to draw even more strength. As he did, he sent that power into the woman. He did so in a way that was soft, the touch gentle, and he held it carefully above the surface of her mind.

While doing so, Tolan focused, listening for the possibility there was something here. When it had been on Ferrah, the touch had been vague, hard to identify, but it had definitely been there. In this case, he wasn't sure if it was too late. Not only had the Grand Inquisitor pushed down with a spirit shaping, possibly forcing that strange chaos down into her mind, but he'd attacked all of them with spirit, completely unmindful of what effect it might have on them.

As he held onto spirit, letting it linger, he felt the vague sense. It was there, barely present. The longer he held onto it, the clearer what he detected became.

"Shaper Ethar?"

Tolan ignored her and continued to push more. This time, he started to bend the shaping, swirling it around her mind. At the same time, he tried to trap that strange, almost subtle and impossibly faint sense he detected.

The longer he pushed, the more that strange sense seemed to be aware of what he was doing.

It started to thrash.

Tolan drew upon more spirit, sealing it within the woman's mind, holding it there.

Only then did he pull.

It took effort, but it also took finesse and control, things Tolan still wasn't sure he was able to maintain when it came to his shaping. As he worked, as he took that strange chaotic shaping out of her mind, he held onto it.

That wasn't what he'd done last time, though.

There was something else he'd added, and it had been the key to eliminating the shaping that had touched Ferrah's mind.

Could he do the same thing now?

Tolan sent a surge of each of the elements through his shaping, adding to the spirit, twisting it so he could blast whatever he could at that shaping. Earth and wind, fire and water.

Mixed with spirit, there came a flash of white light. A sense of agony briefly surged within him, and then it was gone.

Tolan leaned back, gasping.

"What did you do?" the Grand Inquisitor asked.

"I…"

The fallen Inquisitor blinked open her eyes. "Mother?"

22

Exhaustion worked through Tolan, and he struggled to stay on his feet. The longer they went, the more tired he became. He needed to rest, but with what they were dealing with, he wasn't sure rest was a possibility.

The first Inquisitor he'd saved sat along the wall, her back pressed up against it, staring blankly out at the room. Other than mentioning her mother, she had said nothing to him.

She and the Grand Inquisitor had been talking quietly, and Tolan had been focused on doing what he could to help the other two. The one he thought he'd killed still lived, though she was weak, and it took a significant shaping of water, along with removing whatever chaotic elemental had influenced her, in order to bring her back.

Then again, the shaping of water had not come from him. That had come from the Grand Inquisitor.

"How are you, Shaper Ethar?" the Grand Inquisitor asked.

Tolan looked up at her. "Tired."

"You have just performed incredibly difficult shapings. Fatigue is to be expected. The nature of the spirit shaping you performed was incredibly complex, and"—She watched him for a moment, her mouth pressing down into a thin line—"I don't know I have the necessary bondar with which to do so."

Ferrah watched him, saying nothing. She'd been silent ever since he'd removed the chaos from the Inquisitors. Really, ever since reaching Par.

Tolan took a deep breath and held out the stone ring. "It's a spirit bondar," he said.

"I surmised that."

"My father made it."

"Your father was able to make bondars? I didn't realize he served the Academy."

Tolan shook his head. "He didn't."

"And yet he made bondars?" The Grand Inquisitor watched him. "It would be impressive for your father—or anyone—to have the ability to make bondars without specific training."

"I knew him as a craftsman. It wasn't until later I began to question whether he was making bondars."

"And now he serves the Draasin Lord."

Tolan took a deep breath before nodding. "The Draasin Lord isn't someone after power," he said carefully. He looked at the other Inquisitors, but they all seemed dazed, no different than the first Inquisitor he'd saved. It was unlikely they were listening, and if they were, it was even more unlikely there was anything they would glean from his conversation. "As far as I know, the Draasin Lord simply wants the elementals freed from the element bonds."

"Such a thing is dangerous."

"I don't know it's any more dangerous than what we've been doing with the elementals. Holding them in the bond changes them. And…" He fell silent, unsure whether he could—or should—go on. When it came to talking about that sort of thing with one of the Inquisitors, he didn't know.

"You can go on, Shaper Ethar."

"I think it's somehow tied to the creation of the waste."

The Grand Inquisitor studied him. "It's possible. After what you described during the attack, I had to question whether or not that was the key. Though I can't say I understand the nature of the runes used, I can say I understand the border of the waste was shifted. Even now, it's different than it was."

"I didn't even notice that," he said.

"I doubt anyone would. Seeing as how I have gone to the edge of the waste hundreds of times, I have a very unique familiarity with it, something not many others would have. In all that time, I have come to recognize the nature of the rock, the changing of the landscape, everything about it there. And the one thing I do notice through all of that is there's always been one aspect of the waste that has been immutable. The border has never shifted. I have been going to the edge of the waste for the better part of twenty years."

"Twenty years?"

The Grand Inquisitor smiled at him. "I am old enough to have made that claim. And old enough not to be ashamed of my age."

"I wasn't trying to—"

The Grand Inquisitor smiled at him. It seemed as if she were more at ease than he'd seen her in quite some time. "I did not think you were, Shaper Ethar. What I'm saying is that I have known the edge of the waste as well as anyone in Terndahl. Because of that, I recognized what should and should not be there. Even now, despite everything that has changed, despite the way you and others claim the border has shifted back into place, I recognize it has not."

"Is it still moving toward Ephra?" Could it be that despite everything he'd done, it might not have made any difference? He remembered all too well how it had seemed as if the waste were encroaching upon Ephra. It terrified him to think what would happen if Ephra were to be consumed by the waste, leaving him to wonder whether there were cities that had been swallowed by it. It was something none of the master shapers had spoken about, though he had to wonder if perhaps that was a secret about the waste, some aspect of it that no one wanted to admit to.

"On the contrary, Shaper Ethar. It has moved inward."

Tolan blinked. "We reclaimed some of the waste?"

She nodded. "Surprisingly, yes."

"How?"

"I don't have the answer, and it's something the Circle would very much like to understand."

There was a silence for a moment, and Tolan debated saying something about the waste, but that wasn't the question he wanted answered. "Is she really your daughter?"

The Grand Inquisitor squeezed her eyes shut. "When Aela took the Inquisitors with her, my daughter Emily was lost."

"Is she..." He wasn't sure how to ask whether there would be any consequences from having her mind influenced by the chaos, by that darkness, and he didn't know whether it even mattered.

"As far as I can tell, she should recover, but I don't know what she might encounter because of what she has gone through. It's possible she will be altered." The Grand Inquisitor took a deep breath. "I thought she was lost. When you returned, I thought there would be no way of saving her. The one thing the Circle has not managed to uncover is the key to helping those who've been influenced by the chaos."

Tolan saw the way the Grand Inquisitor looked at Emily and realized he couldn't say anything about his mother. Not yet.

Looking at the Grand Inquisitor, he said, "There's something I need to do."

"Shaper Ethar?"

"Will you be okay with them?"

"They've been saved. And now I understand the nature of what has influenced them, I think I might be able to prevent others from similar influence."

"We'll return," Tolan said.

He stood, and before the Grand Inquisitor had a chance to stop him and tried asking the question, he drew each of the elements together, adding spirit, and lightning came for him and Ferrah, carrying them back to the top of the tower.

He looked down at the city. He focused on the sense of power down there, the overwhelming sense of shaping energy, and knew there had to be something he could detect. It had to be somewhere out in the city, some way to find where his mother had gone, and some way to find the Grand Inquisitor, but he didn't know what that was.

"In your research, have you ever come across anything that would help you understand where the Convergence would be?"

"No. There's power here, but…"

"Where do you remember learning about the power?"

Ferrah sighed. "That's what I've been trying to study at the library all these years," she said. "As much as I've searched, I haven't come up with anything. I know it's there."

"Where have you looked?"

"There are several possibilities around the city, and I looked at all of them, thinking if I could find something, I might be able to find where it would be, but I haven't come up with anything. Our archives are written in an ancient and lost language. Even they don't really guide us where to find anything here."

Tolan wondered if there was some way to detect that power. He pushed out with a shaping, sending power from each of the elements. As he did, he waited, focusing, searching for anything he could detect, a reverberation, or something that might give him a clue about where the place of Convergence could be located. If there was something here, it had to be masked. If not, it simply wasn't here.

They could be wrong about this.

What if there was no place of Convergence in Par?

"What can you tell me about the city itself?"

"Par is old, Tolan." She reached the edge of the tower, looking out. "You go out into the city, you can see it in some of the buildings. Many of them have runes upon them, the same kind of patterns we find on the bondars. It suggests the people who founded the city ages ago had that knowledge. It seems to hold the city together."

That was similar to Tolan's sense of Par when he'd been wandering through it, and he remembered noticing those shapings, the sense that had seemed to hold the city together. As he had noticed it, he'd felt there was a certain knowledge here, which meant that maybe there was a reason for it.

Why else would they have knowledge of it without having a place of Convergence?

As far as he knew, such places were rare, but they weren't so rare as to be impossible to find.

"Is there anything else you know about it?"

"Other than this tower?" She smiled, sweeping her hand around. "We have stories about the tower. Most of them tell us the tower is as old as the rest of the city. Did you know there are patterns on the side of the tower, much like the patterns found in the Academy?"

Tolan frowned, turning quickly to her. "What do you mean?"

"The patterns. There are markings, runes, as I suppose they're called, and they are found on the inside of the tower. When they open up the tower once a year for the festival of shaping, you can see them. They're old, probably as old as rest of the tower, and for the most part, faded, making them difficult to fully make out. When you see them, you get a sense of the age of this place, and a sense of just how much the people of that time had known."

He frowned. Could it be the same?

Tolan started toward the center of the tower, jabbing the sword down into the stone. He sent a shaping through it, using power from each of the elements.

He wasn't sure what to expect, but as he pushed, he detected something.

There was a reverberation.

It came to him as a sensation similar to what he'd detected when he was in Amitan, and when he'd shaped through the runes at the Academy.

There were runes here, much as she said.

Tolan continued to push, drawing power through him, and felt the ongoing sense, that echoing, and pushed even deeper.

If this was like the Academy, then it was possible there was a reason for it, and if he could uncover what that reason was, if he could find out whether or not these runes were tied to something deep beneath the ground, another place of Convergence, then he might…

There.

He felt it. And it was only because of the bondar sword he'd made that he was able to detect it.

He continued to push, holding onto the sense of it, and power flowed from him. He pushed farther and farther deep beneath the ground, detecting the place of Convergence. Much like in Amitan, the Convergence was hidden.

Lifting the sword, he held that place in his mind. He focused, grabbing Ferrah, and drew upon the warrior shaping.

It carried him down.

There was a blast, a surge of lightning, but it happened even faster than before. He was drawing through the sword, and the shaping was stronger for it. It was sudden, a burst of power, and he exploded, appearing in a vast underground chamber. It was dark, and it took a moment for his eyes to adjust. With a hint of fire, he sent a shaping around, using that to allow him to see what else might be here.

"Where are we?" Ferrah asked.

"Beneath the tower."

He started forward, but he didn't need to go far to see the place of Convergence. He could feel it. It was right in front of him, the same silver liquid as in Amitan. It didn't surprise him they were the same.

Ferrah looked around, her eyes wide and her breathing quick. "Do you know how long I looked for this? You get to hear enough rumors, and the nature of power within Par is such that you begin to think there has to be something, but..."

Tolan looked around. Did the Academy know this place was here?

He doubted it. If they had known, they would have placed more protections around it, and it was possible they would've done more than just place protections—they would have somehow found a way to use it.

Surprisingly—or perhaps not surprisingly—Par was at the edge of Terndahl.

Much like Ephra.

That couldn't be coincidence. The more he thought about it, the more he realized there had to be something tied to it, that the connection between this place and the border of Terndahl had to be tied together.

Tolan continued to pull on a shaping, drawing more and more power, and sent it flowing through the sword.

It couldn't be a coincidence that as far as he knew, Velminth had been untouched. Velminth was more central within Terndahl, which meant it may not have a place of Convergence.

What about other places that had been attacked? Would they all have places of Convergence?

What did his mother hope to accomplish?

Tolan held out his sword, drawing power through it. He made it glow with a shaping of fire, letting that surge out of the tip of the sword. As it did, he continued around the place of Convergence, power flowing from him. The longer he went, the more he began to wonder if perhaps his mother hadn't realized it was here.

He turned back, looking at Ferrah, and his heart nearly stopped.

His mother was there.

"Why am I not surprised you are the one who led me here?" she asked.

She held an item in her hand, and although Tolan couldn't tell what it was, there was power flowing through it. As he looked at it, he could almost feel the dark energy in it.

"I didn't lead you anywhere."

She smiled, looking over at him. "Ah, but you did. I searched for this place, and unfortunately failed. I needed someone who had a different perspective, and that person is you. When you defeated the Inquisitors, I began to wonder if perhaps you might be more than I realized. Then again, I did seek out your father for his connection to the elementals, so perhaps that shouldn't be altogether surprising."

"What do you mean you sought him out?"

"I sought a pairing. I wanted to know whether the two

of us could produce someone who had specific potential. And," she said, grinning at him, "look at you. Look at the potential you have." She took a step toward him, shoving Ferrah in his direction. "While you were given the gifts you were, you would mingle with her? You should use your knowledge, find someone who can help you create even greater offspring, who can help you create even more power. That is the purpose of understanding the nature of our abilities. That is the way the shapers of old did it."

Tolan didn't know what to say. What was there to say at all? He couldn't believe she was trying to convince him he was somehow born as an experiment.

It left him troubled. It left him angry.

"I should thank you for leading me here, but then again, as I knew you would do so, and I planned for this, I don't know that it's so much of thanks as it is an expectation of what would take place."

Tolan stood there, holding onto the sword, but with it, he didn't know if he had any sort of advantage against his mother. If she knew how to overpower him, if she had some way of using chaos through the bondar that she held, there might not be any way of stopping her.

And he suspected she intended to use it on the place of Convergence.

That was what this was all about.

"You aren't able to reach the Convergence at the Academy."

She frowned at him. "They think they can keep it from me, but they won't for long."

"You thought to use the Inquisitors to find the answers, but you also thought the Grand Inquisitor knew."

He was not going to be the reason she found the one at Amitan.

"Why do you need the Convergence?" he asked.

"You can't begin to understand. Perhaps if you will work with me, I can show you, but for now, I'm afraid you must remain ignorant."

"Is it because you're afraid I can stop you?"

She took another step toward him, and he realized she'd used a shaping on Ferrah, though Ferrah still seemed to be unbothered by it, almost as if she'd not been subjected to any type of shaping. At least, not the way she had been before.

How would she somehow be able to ignore that shaping?

Could it be because of what Tolan had done?

Could his shaping somehow protect her?

If so, it meant others who had been subjected to the darkness would also be protected.

"All this time, you needed someone else to show you how to find the place of Convergence. Everything you thought you knew, you still didn't know enough." Tolan watched her, wanting to get her upset. "Why did you even need this?"

"Look at it," she said, pointing toward the place of Convergence, using the bondar. "So pure. A mixture of each of the elements. And people who thought they could access it, the people who thought they understood the nature of that power, have never really grasped just what it could do."

"And what could it do?"

She smiled at him. "It's unfortunate you must come to the end of your training like this, Tolan. But then, if all goes well, I will be the one responsible for continuing it. Once I add a specific influence to this place, you can truly understand what I understood when I took my journey."

"What journey is that?"

She smiled at him. "A journey of understanding. One that few people—including my own mother—thought could be done."

Things the Grand Inquisitor said to him came flashing back to him. Her frequent visits to the edge of the waste. The fact that people had tried to venture across it. The fact the Grand Inquisitor herself had tried to venture across it.

"You went into the waste," he whispered.

His mother glanced up at him. "I went, and I uncovered something incredible. Everyone believes the waste is an absence of shaping, but that's not it at all. It's a place of a different kind of power. It's a place where you can understand others. And I will help bring that understanding to these lands."

Tolan looked at the bondar she held, the darkness swirling from it, and feared if she managed to succeed, if she poured anything into the place of Convergence, Par would become no different than the waste.

He had to stop her.

He began to shape, pulling on each of the elements, drawing power from them, drawing through the Convergence, but even as he did, he realized there wasn't going to be enough. She resisted, using the strange bondar to do so.

It alone had enough power to overwhelm him. As much as he might want to fight, as much as he might want to resist, there didn't seem to be any way for him to do so.

As he pushed, he sent more and more power, drawing from the Convergence, but… It wasn't enough.

He had to get the bondar away from her.

Until he did, she was going to be able to overpower anything he might do.

He wasn't going to be enough.

It might mean he sacrificed something, but if he did, he might find everything. Besides, what did he know about the place of Convergence? He'd seen the way Master Minden had reached into the Convergence, so he knew it wasn't completely dangerous—at least not to her.

Would it be dangerous to him?

He thought about what he'd heard about the Convergence, and about what all of the master shapers had said and thought it might be. Despite everything else, it might be more than he could withstand.

It was a place of all the elements.

It took all of the elements to burn off chaos.

Those two thoughts came together, and he knew what

he had to do. Even if he did this, it might not be something he could survive. It was something he had to be prepared for. Even knowing he might survive, he wasn't sure he was ready.

Maybe he could try something. The only thing he could think to do would be to wrap himself in a shaping, try to find some way of protecting himself, and if he did that, then maybe he'd be able to survive.

"Ferrah?"

She looked over at him.

"I know you can hear me. And I want you to know I care for you."

"Tolan?"

There wasn't any other way of stopping his mother. He wasn't strong enough, even at the place of Convergence. The only way to succeed would be to use the Convergence, to find some way of drawing its power. If he could, then maybe they could overwhelm her.

"I need you to use a shaping of wind and fire angled downward," he said quickly.

Ferrah locked eyes with him and hurriedly formed a shaping. As she did, it created a blast of power surging outward from her, and it slammed into the ground, lifting her into the air. The combination of the shaping was enough that it threw her free of his mother.

Tolan ran forward.

His mother pointed the chaotic bondar toward him but he ignored it, slamming into her, throwing his shoulder against her.

Her shaping struck as he did.

When he crashed into her, he wrapped his arms around her, pulling her in a hug, the kind of hug he once would have given anything to get from her again. This time, they went staggering off to the side, heading toward the Convergence.

A shaping built from his mother, trying to keep them from dropping into the silvery pool.

Tolan pushed and sent a shaping at her arm, sending a blast of fire, earth, wind, and water sweeping at the bondar she clutched. The suddenness of his shaping caused her to drop it, right before they teetered at the edge of the Convergence.

And then fell in.

Tolan wasn't sure what to expect, but when they plunged beneath the surface of the Convergence, it was thick, a strange sensation, and surprisingly warm. It washed over him, filling him with a sense of power.

He struggled, but some distant part of him told him not to do that. It was almost as if it came from one of the elementals, some voice buried within his mind.

He stopped struggling and realized he could feel the bottom of the pool of the strange silvery liquid. The Convergence called to him, drawing him toward it, and he felt that power flowing through him, a reassuring sort of warmth that left him with a sense of surprising safety.

He was in no danger here.

And he held onto the shaping wrapped around

himself. The protection surged, swirling around him so he could be ready for whatever he might face.

Near him, there was a struggling within the Convergence.

It was his mother. She was batting at the liquid, trying to get free. Near her, the liquid had strange bubbles forming, rising up all around it.

Tolan could feel the effect of her resistance, and he could also feel the way the Convergence was working over her, rolling through her, and pushing something against her.

It was the influence of chaos.

Could he help?

As he pushed out through his direct connection to the Convergence, he pressed against his mother's mind. There was nothing he needed to do. The Convergence had taken care of it. It had blasted away the effect of chaos, but it had done more than that.

Her mind was wiped.

The thrashing stopped and she started to sink. Tolan dragged himself toward her, moving across the thick liquid, and when he reached her, he pulled.

She was starting to drop below the surface of the liquid. Tolan grabbed her, pulling her free. Using a shaping of each of the elements, he forced himself clear of the Convergence and over to the edge, where he set his mother down.

She was still breathing, and he checked on Ferrah.

"Tolan?" she said.

He shook his head. "Not yet. There's still something I need to do." He found the bondar his mother had used—or intended to use—on him.

He drew from the Convergence, sending power out, and wrapped it around the bondar. He used each of the elements, drawing not only from the Convergence, but also from himself, and sent it flowing into the bondar, much the same way as he had with the ring. It took incredible power—far more than he would've been able to draw anyplace else—and then the rod cracked. The darkness started to seep out. Tolan shifted the focus of his shaping, wrapping around it, and shaped each of the elements into it. With a burst, even that disappeared.

He sagged to his knees.

Ferrah was there, slipping her arm around him. "Tolan?" she said again.

He nodded. "I think it's done."

"What's done?"

"Whatever was influencing my mother." Then again, whatever had influenced her had come from someplace within her as well. It wasn't just chaos. She had welcomed that. "And her bondar. I think… I think we can figure out a way of removing the influence from others."

It would take time, and it would take considerable strength, but they would need to do so. Now he knew what to look for—and now he knew what to do—he thought they would be able to do it.

First, he wanted to find the Grand Inquisitor.

That wasn't what he wanted to do first. Instead, he

wrapped his arms around Ferrah, and then kissed her gently on the lips.

"What happened to your clothes?"

"My clothes?" Tolan glanced down and realized he was completely naked. Then he realized his mother was completely naked, too. There was something about the Convergence that burned off their clothing, removing it entirely.

Were he around anyone else, he might have been embarrassed, but this was Ferrah.

"I need to find the Grand Inquisitor," he said. Not just the Grand Inquisitor, but perhaps his grandmother. Through everything, she'd been faithful to the Academy.

"We need to get you some clothes. Then we can worry about the Grand Inquisitor."

Tolan smiled, tipping his head toward his mother. "We need to bring her, too."

He grabbed Ferrah by the hand and grabbed his mother with the other one, pulling on the warrior shaping.

It carried him back to the rooftop at the Academy, somehow streaking beyond the place of Convergence, carrying him beyond Par and back to a familiar location.

And he glanced over, realizing this wasn't where he needed to be. Not yet, at least. Drawing on another warrior shaping, he used it to carry himself into the small room where he had awoken after the attack by Tanner.

He set his mother on the bed, grabbed a poorly fitting robe off a hook nearby, and headed out into the hallway, closing the door and sealing it with a shaping of each of the elements. It might not be enough, but there would have to be someone else who could place the shaping, or perhaps even separate his mother from her ability to shape. It was something he was going to have to ask the Grand Master—and even Master Minden—about.

"What now that you found the one responsible?"

Tolan breathed out. "That's just it. I don't know that I found the one responsible."

"I thought from what you told me—"

"There are others involved. It's not just her." Glancing back at the door, he shook his head. "She mentioned it, but it's also more than that. It was also the fact that when I was coming back from Ephra and I was attacked—I have to tell you about that—my attacker told me there was someone there who was responsible but wouldn't reveal his name."

As much as he wanted it to be over, it didn't seem like it was. They still had much to deal with. More than that, his mother had revealed something that had told them part of the secret, though to pursue it meant a dangerous venture. It was the kind of dangerous venture he wasn't sure he wanted to make, but someone had to. It would mean traveling to the waste, and then beyond the waste, to find where the tainted place of Convergence was, and discovering if there was some way to remove it.

Ferrah wrapped her arms around him. "I think you need to rest."

"Without any clothes?"

"It wouldn't be the worst way to spend our time."

"Maybe once we move into the third-level rooms," he said.

There came a surge of shaping power, and Tolan looked up to see Master Minden appear. As she did, she frowned at him. "Shaper Ethar?"

"Sorry, Master Minden. There's someone here that I need your help with."

"I take it you submerged yourself in the Convergence."

Tolan glanced down. "I did."

"I was there."

"There is another place of Convergence. Probably many. Including one already tainted by chaos."

Her breath caught and she frowned at him. "How?"

"As far as I can tell, it's somewhere across the waste. And I don't think my mother was acting alone."

"Then we must be prepared."

"How would we prepare?"

She glanced from Tolan to Ferrah. "I think it is time for the two of you to join the Circle."

Grab the next book in Elemental Academy: The Chaos Rises

The Draasin Lord is captures but a greater threat remains.

Now that Tolan knows the secret of the Draasin Lord, he recognizes more needs to be done. As a student, he's not in a position to be able to do more, but as a master shaper, he'd be free to travel as he feels necessary.

When another attack targets the academy, Tolan knows his unique abilities might make him the only shaper able to respond.

He must survive crossing the waste, but even if he does, how can he stop the chaos where none can shape the elements and where no elementals can survive?

ALSO BY D.K. HOLMBERG

Elemental Academy

The Fire Within

The Earth Awakens

The Water Ruptures

The Wind Rages

The Spirit Binds

The Chaos Rises

The Cloud Warrior Saga

Chased by Fire

Bound by Fire

Changed by Fire

Fortress of Fire

Forged in Fire

Serpent of Fire

Servant of Fire

Born of Fire

Broken of Fire

Light of Fire

Cycle of Fire

The Endless War

Journey of Fire and Night

Darkness Rising

Endless Night

Summoner's Bond

Seal of Light

The Elder Stones Saga

The Darkest Revenge

Shadows Within the Flame

Remnants of the Lost

The Coming Chaos

The Shadow Accords

Shadow Blessed

Shadow Cursed

Shadow Born

Shadow Lost

Shadow Cross

Shadow Found

The Collector Chronicles

Shadow Hunted

Shadow Games

Shadow Trapped

The Dark Ability

The Dark Ability

The Heartstone Blade

The Tower of Venass

Blood of the Watcher

The Shadowsteel Forge

The Guild Secret

Rise of the Elder

The Sighted Assassin

The Binders Game

The Forgotten

Assassin's End

The Dragonwalker

Dragon Bones

Dragon Blessed

Dragon Rise

Dragon Bond

Dragon Storm

Dragon Rider

Dragon Sight

The Teralin Sword

Soldier Son

Soldier Sword

Soldier Sworn

Soldier Saved

Soldier Scarred

The Lost Prophecy

The Threat of Madness

The Warrior Mage

Tower of the Gods

Twist of the Fibers

The Lost City

The Last Conclave

The Gift of Madness

The Great Betrayal

The Book of Maladies

Wasting

Broken

Poisoned

Tormina

Comatose

Amnesia

Exsanguinated

Printed in Dunstable, United Kingdom